# shades of

# noir

book one

# archon gaming inc.

Cover by Tom Simonton
Frontispiece by Howard Chaykin
Interior illustrations by Steve Carr, Matt Haley, Ang Lee, and Dan
Lawlis.
Shades of Noir, book one is an original publication of Archon
Gaming, Inc. This work has never before appeared in printed form.

Archon Gaming, Inc.
6 Headwater Cove
Barrington, IL 60010
Archongame@aol.com
AGICAST@aol.com
AGICAST@archongaming.com
Visit our web page at www.archongaming.com

ISBN: 1-889864-01-3
First Printing: December 1996
Printed in the U.S.A.

10  9  8  7  6  5  4  3  2  1

this book is dedicated to
the most fatale femme i've
ever known in my life,
my mother,
geri knippen,
with all my love.

# acknowledgments

special thanks to
arcadia design group, creative
interests agency, steve
donnelly, valarie jones,
geri knippen, waylon manns,
nicholas manns, mcnaughton and
gunn, meroni & meroni, harris
miller, mickey o'donnell,
brian s. roe, dakota schiller
and all the fine artists and
writers who have shared their
stories.

# table of contents

# blues dressed in red
## by gina mcintyre

It's surrounded by haze of too much gin and restlessness. Isolated moments are still clear, though I'll be damned if I can get any of them out of my head, maybe then I could fall asleep. Instead, I toss and turn over his gestures, his scars, savoring and embellishing them like the romantic I will never admit I am.

I do realize I should let it go–he certainly has. But I swear I thought this time was different. I guess it was just the alcohol and the heat, but the way he touched me radiated sincerity, filled me with awareness, a physical rhapsody, made me hum with intensity the same way I do when I sing. The times it's just me and the music and the words pour out like a sermon about purity and deceit. Purity and deceit? Jesus, I'm starting to sound like a piano player.

Then again, maybe I'd be better off if I did play the piano. Abe doesn't have these bouts of melodrama. It's easier when you can sit down and play the blues on a familiar set of keys and being alone doesn't matter. You don't need anybody else the way I do. Besides, you get more respect when you're a musician. Singers are just a dime a dozen, especially ones with bad habits like too many Tangueray and tonics and one night stands with men who never stop by on their way to the club. I thought he'd at least pay another 2 a.m. visit sometime, but I guess it's easy for him to forget the whole thing. Every time I look at the parlor floor, though, I've gotten a friendly reminder about who I can be when my judgment is clouded and my stockings are straight.

Times like these, I lie awake in the rumpled sheets I need to wash, taking twisted pleasure in my insomnia, remembering the way my body quivered with exhaustion as I watched his back descend the staircase, knowing we'd never speak again despite the pleasantries we exchanged. I still hear the sound of the motor as he drove away, except now it merges with the sound of his breathing and his murmurs. He has a gravity of character, and a distinct lack of integrity, but he's what I needed then, and now - an escape from this drudgery manifest in the physical. He was my accomplice in what I knew was wrong, but I needed to be touched, and at least he was honest about his intentions. I admired that about him.

1

Even after that, though, I thought I could belt my way into lights, freedom and fame, if I had the right piano player and a string of lucky breaks. Abe came along just then, but the rest never did. Just a seemingly endless train of the wrong men waiting to take money, sex, love, whatever they could get their hands on, just like in all those songs I love to sing.

Abe, he's another story. Sometimes I wonder what it would be like to settle down with him in one of those big houses on the other side of town, where the drunks don't cry outside your door. Maybe Abe and I could get together and grow up and grow old together in a place like that. I have to admit, it's a tempting thought, but it would be just a matter of time before our crowd would show up at the wrought iron gate, bringing their parties and their noise and squalor with them. I'd hate to have to see those well educated members of the upper crust muster up enough bravado to ask us, in their most polite and clipped tones, to leave and take the parties, noise and squalor back to where it came from; back to where we belong. Not to mention, respectable women don't drink gin and succumb to their improper desires.

Besides, Abe isn't the kind to have a rendezvous on the parlor floor, and I could never let him see me be that brazen. He thinks to highly of me. I see the way he watches me at night, especially when I wear the red satin dress. He always tells me he loves to hear me sing the blues dressed in red, right before he sets down a fresh gin and tonic for me on the piano. I notice the glass sometimes leaves a ring of condensation on the grainy surface of the wood, but Abe never seems to mind. He just watches me as I close my eyes and sip from the glass, listening as my voice quivers, sometimes hovering too long over a single note.

Abe has this amazing talent of knowing when to leave. He'll stick around till the end of a set or a bottle, which ever comes first. Then he'll say, "Lizzy you deserve better than this," before he fumbles with his fedora and heads out the door. Every now and again, he'll stay at the club and tell me about the day when we'll strike it rich and stop playing dives, and we'll start drinking champagne from glasses with thin fragile stems with thin and fragile people. Critics will praise us and we'll be whisked away in one of big shiny cars. He still believes it will happen, and I don't want to disappoint him, though I know things won't ever change. When his maudlin mood hits, I just nod, smile, slide him a wink or my hand along the sleeve of his shirt before he stumbles

2

home. He means well. He's honest in his own way. For him these aren't lies, they are the images that sing to him in his whiskey lullabies.

Maybe I'll call him in the morning, it's just a few hours away now. Abe's always willing to buy me a black coffee for breakfast and compliment my dress. I think he needs to find himself the right kind of girl, one who can mend the tattered cuffs of his shirts and doesn't drink gin. And I think I need to find a way to get back to sleep and stop listening to temptation.

# introduction

Welcome to *Shades of Noir*, the first anthology for both Archon Gaming Inc. and *Noir, the Film Noir Role-Playing Game*. Being people who don't like long introductions, we're hoping to keep this one from devolving into a long rambling monologue. No promises, of course, but we will attempt to do our best.

So what is *Shades of Noir*? Well, that's an excellent question to which we hopefully have an equally excellent answer.

First and foremost, *Shades of Noir* is an experiment. It is a study of what happens when a group of people get together to create and populate a world with people and places that have never before existed outside their own minds. It is about what happens when a small group of writers, taking a lot of ideas and a fair amount of source material, try not only to form a world of their own, but also a world that others can enjoy and add to. In fact calling this book an anthology seems a bit inaccurate. *Shades of Noir* is not simply a collection of short stories that share a similar theme, but a shared world created and brought to life by several people (some of whose works appear in this book). Admittedly, *Shades of Noir* is not the first time something like this had been done. Everything from the Cthulhu Mythos of H.P. Lovecraft to the works of just about any comic company have employed this idea of "shared worlds". The real originality in this book comes from the fact that this is the start of a new world. The talented and exciting group of writers who have contributed to our exercise honor us and our world with their words and ideas.

Of course to call the alternate world where the stories in this book take place wholly new would neither be true nor fair. No, the backdrop for these stories should look familiar to most readers because it pays tribute to some of the most influential entertainment of our culture.

Rather unsurprisingly, we're talking about the films of the film *noir* genre. For those of you not familiar with this term, film *noir* was originally coined to refer to many of the films of the 1930s, 40s, and 50s that used techniques typically involving strong lights and shadows, creating an existential view opposed to the bright and shiny look of most studio films of the era. These films typically also had morally "grey" themes and tended to focus around crime, betrayal, love, and the darkness of the human spirit. This was a backlash begun in the depression, feeding off the work of the pulp writers of the time and the desperation of the people. Later, the trend was furthered by pre and post World War II despression and fatalism. *The Third Man, Murder, My Sweet,* and *The Maltese Falcon* are good examples of this sort of film. Some, like *Gun Crazy,* shocked and disturbed. Others, like *Double Indemnity,* simply surprised with their twists and double back turns.

However, these films are not the only place where this book draws inspiration. Novels, comic books, and more modern films that share similar elements also were great sources of inspiration. Howard Chaykin's *The Shadow* and upcoming *Cyberella,* Mickey Spillane's *Mike Danger,* with Max Allan Collins, the Coen brothers film *Blood Simple,* David Lapham's *Stray Bullets, Chinatown*...everything from Frank Miller's *Sin City* to Ridley Scott's *Blade Runner* lent inspiration.

The result is the world of *Noir.* A world of smoldering cigarettes and smoking guns, of hot cash and cold stares. It is a world that takes the mood and attitude of all the elements of our past, combines them together with a slightly more modified worldview wherein there are not such clear divisions between race and sex, and uses them to form the shadows of a hazy metropolis we like to just call the City.

The City is the essence of this world of *Noir.* It is the place where all things, good and bad, happen. It has no time or place as we would understand it. It is set in the minds of the writers and readers of its stories. Some of us may decide it is 1932, others may see it as a view of 1955. Any and all opinions can be right about the City, since it is wholly a creation of the mind.

Hopefully this little essay has informed more than it has obscured. Either way, we thank you for bearing with us. Now, let's take a look at this world of *Noir.* Let's look at this imaginary urban landscape known only as the City and see what life is like for some of its inhabitants. We know we really enjoyed these stories and their tough guys and femme fatales.

Now it's your turn. Enjoy.

*Lisa Manns*
*Jack Norris*
*1996*

Art by Matt Haley

# the hour of lead

## by eric luke

*This is the Hour of Lead—*
*Remembered, if outlived,*
*As Freezing persons, recollect the Snow—*
*First—Chill—then Stupor—then the letting go—.*
Emily Dickinson (1830–86)

*I'll drill ya full of lead, ya lousy bastids!*
Jimmy Cagney as Johnny Ghiloni in "Steel's Island" (Warner Brothers, 1948)

It was a plain brown envelope. Pretty normal as these things go. It was placed in my hand by a man with a sick grin. Looking back, the grin was there for a reason.

Plain brown seems to be the color of choice for death messages.

You know me.

You've seen me a couple dozen times. I'm the guy standing over Cagney's right shoulder when he barges into a room and makes demands. There are three or four other guys who look a lot like me and we just stand there in back of Cagney with our hands in our pockets, staring down some poor sap. You never look right at me because you're always looking at Cagney, but next time you're up late and find me on the classic channel, take a look at my face. Look at my eyes. My attention will be somewhere off camera, on the sap, but you'll see it.

I'm blank.

That's my look. It makes people nervous and like it. I cultivate it. I look like I'm thinking about something else, which makes me even scarier, like I don't care whether I kill something or not.

Then Cagney turns to me, leans close, murmurs, and I leave the room.

This is about what happens after I leave the room.

This isn't the movies. I don't work for Cagney. I don't work for Ghiloni or Dewey or Friedman. I don't work for anybody. I'm a Courier.

Whenever there's something that's too hot or messy or evil to be whispered over the phone or dropped off on a doorstep, they call for a Courier. They used to send their own men, but they kept getting shot in the leg and tortured for information about their bosses, so that stopped being a good idea. They needed independents who didn't know what they were carrying. They needed Couriers.

This doesn't mean there aren't third parties who won't kill the Courier to get the message. It becomes the Courier's job to make the delivery alive.

What keeps me alive? Two things.

The first is honor. The Courier's code is never to know anything. The minute you do, you're dead. And everyone has to know that you don't know anything, so it won't be worth their while to shoot you in the leg and torture you. Honor is a powerful thing when everybody's depending on it to make things work.

The second thing that keeps me alive is the City. I know every back street and alley and alternate route from Central to the Docks and back again. My personal record is Greek Town to New Harlem in fourteen minutes and twenty five seconds last summer in 102 degree rush hour, with a bum carburetor and a dumb kid trying to make a name for himself by actually trying to tail me. Me! I ask you. And if the car catches a bullet, I make it a point to be good on foot too. I know every Chinatown kitchen with a wok full of hot oil waiting to be dumped behind you if some punk turns out to be faster than you.

I needed both of these things more than I ever have when what I'm about to tell you went down.

It was a Saturday night in February. I love the City on Saturday nights in February. You can stand at the end of one of the docks out by Westburg and face North and close your eyes and feel like you're right on the edge of something. On one side you've got the cold salt wind coming off the ocean carrying the clanging from the buoys out by Steel's Island, and a few lone gulls, and nothing else but the giant darkness, which to me is very much like a feeling of death. On the other side is the City: a huge, living monster, full of the smells of sourdough bread and crab from dockside restaurants, and the hum of traffic and a million voices all talking at once, and the warm glow of life you can see even through your closed eyelids.

Standing on the edge of life and death, waiting for the pick-up. This is where I see myself in the last moments before everything went to hell.

The man who brought me the envelope had curly red hair and sunken eyes, and was one of those guys who thinks everything is a joke. Every word sounded like he found a black humor in back of things that was about to make him snicker.

"Herald?" he walked up to me at the railing. It's part of the Code to choose a name with a Courier meaning, so that's me: Herald. I carry the messages.

"You're new," I said. I don't like surprises, but this wasn't so far out of the ordinary as to set off alarms. My usual contact with the Ghiloni's was a handsome blond kid from northern Italy named Manfredi who the waitresses used to drool over in the dive where we met for deliveries and pick-ups. You hated him for his good looks but couldn't help liking him at the same time. He'd been dropping off messages for the Ghiloni's for two years and now he was either promoted or dead. A surprising little pain hit me in the chest and I reminded myself for the millionth time that nothing ever stays the same. Sometimes you get attached to people without realizing it.

"You're old," he shot back, his grin making him squint until his eyes disappeared in shadow. I realize now that he stuck out the envelope when he said it, which should have been a clue, but I wasn't thinking. I'm pretty good with strategy and such, but not so good with people. I don't pick up things I should from looks, from inflections. I can maneuver down a crowded street by knowing which way someone's going to turn three blocks ahead, but sometimes I have trouble navigating from one end of a conversation to the other. Jill thinks it's weird that I can handle a whole city full of people, but when it comes down to just one on one, I get stuck.

"Where's Manfredi?" I usually don't ask any questions, but something about this guy made me want to push him a little. I wanted to watch him hold out the envelope a little longer.

"Just do your job"

He must have been ten years younger than me. I wanted more than anything to walk away, to let him know he depended on me to take his stupid little message. But I didn't. I held out my hand for it, a few inches away. I made him give it to me. It took him five seconds to do it, like he had to redefine for himself that he wasn't losing anything. Punks on their way to the top are always the most fragile.

"It's for Dewey. He'll be at Callahan's in half an hour. You know it?" He was trying to be insulting in the worst way. You never ask a Courier if they know a place.

I threw one of his sick grins back at him and walked away. I didn't wait to see his expression. Maybe I should have. Though in the end it wouldn't have made any difference.

So I stood at the edge of darkness and the city. I took the message

9

from the grinning man.

And I walked toward life.

I don't drive a power car. I drive an old Renault. It can accelerate over short distances, but its main talent is that it slides through traffic like a hot knife through margarine. You don't need speed in the city. You need what Jill calls the Zen approach to the road. You feel the flow. You sense every mind on the street and instinct tells you which way they're going to move. You approach traffic as if it were one big animal. Jill says she can't believe I never hit anybody because it doesn't look as if I'm seeing the road. She calls it my thirty yard stare. It's a lot like the look I cultivate to make people think I'm a killer. I just use it on the road instead.

Some Couriers carry guns. I don't. It interferes with the driving. If you let yourself feel just one heartbeat of the confidence that wearing a gun gives you, you lose the road trance. If you don't carry a gun, you work with everything. The city becomes your weapon, and if you know how to use it, it's a thousand times more dangerous than a bullet.

I stayed on Grand south of Westburg and took it through the old financial district. At night the buildings are like giant tombstones. With the wind off the ocean whistling between them, it's even too cold for the bums. It feels emptier than any other part of the city. This is architecture that bankers jumped off in 1929. I'm not especially morbid; there's just a kind of grandeur down there at night.

Grand cuts north of Chinatown, which is a good place to stay out of. They have their own system and the less I know about it the better. I had a friend from school named Tony Leung who went to work for the Tongs around the time I apprenticed to become a Courier. We stayed pretty close over the years. In fact, he was the one that introduced me to Jill. When we were young enough to still trust each other, we used to compare notes, even share Courier secrets. The only difference we could see that was that the Tongs give you more chances when a delivery doesn't make it. Couriers get a bullet in the head. Tong messengers start to lose body parts. I stay out of Chinatown.

I had just crossed the tracks and was skirting the railroad yards when the I heard something that sounded like a hummingbird cut through the wind on the passenger side. I always drive with the window down, and let the wind blow in my face. Jill says it's like I'm driving by sense of smell, but you'd be surprised how much you can tell from listening. You get used to the current, so when there's a change you can feel it with your whole head. That's how I knew it was a bullet.

This meant one of two things. Either somebody was stupid enough

10

to try and take a message meant for Dewey, or worse, somebody didn't want the message delivered at all. Either way, they knew my route, which meant they'd been watching me for a while, and I hadn't spotted them. I felt stupid. Couriers are supposed to know what's going on way before the bullet ever gets fired. I'd screwed up big time.

I gunned the engine and pulled my first trick. There's a dirt road that runs along the train tracks just west of shanty town. You can take it at full speed because the bums are all warming themselves by sterno cans between the lean-tos away from the tracks. I turned off my lights and went into the trance.

There was nobody in the rear view mirror, but that didn't mean anything. If they were smart they'd have somebody waiting up the line. I started deliberately breaking a few driving patterns, plotting alternate routes. This wasn't going to be a snipe hunt. It was going to be a chess game. It also meant they were watching. I gave the Renault more gas and kicked up a dust cloud, just in case.

The next attempt came in the industrial section of Meridian right where it gets dangerous. It's a deserted area, and they've been talking about putting an elevated freeway over it for years, but it never happens. The empty factories divide downtown from Westburg like a wasteland. Pools of light from the security lamps over the gates make the streets look even longer.

A plain brown Seville came out of a dark cul-de-sac and pulled up alongside, matching my speed. Though I couldn't see him, I had to admire the way the driver understood the road. What I did see was the back window rolling down and the barrel of the gun catch the light for a second. The first instinct in these cases is to hit the brakes and shy away, but one secret to staying alive is doing the exact opposite of what they're expecting. Killers have their own little rituals, and if something goes wrong they get thrown.

I cranked the wheel left and slammed into the side of the Seville, accelerating as I went. I felt the metal buckle on my door and press against my thigh, but that was nothing compared to what the Seville was doing. If you hit a car, even a big one, hard enough on the front right corner, it will go into a spin. The back wheels are still powering it forward, but with the front re-directed sideways, the whole thing becomes a pinwheel. I saw the gunman's surprised face whip away from me as the car went into a skid.

The guy was blond, and handsome, and I recognized him. It pulled me right out of my Zen driving trance. It was Manfredi.

I pulled my mind back into the zone and sped away from the

Seville as it hit the center divider, the occupants slamming against their shoulder belts, their heads whipping forward and then hanging loose. Things were getting interesting. Why would the Ghiloni's give me a message and then send one of their own to stop it? A change of heart? They could have just flagged me down. Were there two factions in the Ghiloni family now, one playing against the other? Even the closest family has its squabbles, but Papa Ghiloni wouldn't let it come to this. Unless he was losing control. Or dead.

It wasn't my concern. I'd been given a delivery. The question "Why?" is not in the Courier vocabulary.

I'd turned off Meridian onto one of the streets that cut down through the new financial district to Irish Town when the next hit came. A bullet spanged through the roof of the car and kicked a chunk of stuffing out of the back seat. I knew then that this was big time. They had a sharpshooter up somewhere high, probably on top of the Goldman Building. It's centrally located, one of those new pyramid-type buildings that would have a great view of any street I'd take south of Meridian.

A second thought turned me cold. This wouldn't be Ghiloni business anymore, not with access to one of these buildings. Ghiloni is old money, with plenty of resources in Westburg and Little Italy, but the family hasn't made inroads into the new business district that centers around the intersection of Axis and Meridian, other than supplying the cement for the buildings. So was it Friedman, whose purview was usually Oldentowne, but had owned some of the real estate these skyscrapers were being built on? Or even worse, was it somebody new? Rumors had the Yakuza lurking in the shadows of some of the corporations that had their names in giant letters all over the new buildings.

For the first time since I was a kid, I felt scared. A Courier makes his living by knowing the rules, and I didn't even know what game we were playing.

The sniper was easy enough. I chose a route that kept any tall buildings between me and the top of the Goldman Building. I make it a habit to know everything about the city, including how many floors in each major skyscraper. Some of the other Couriers make fun of me when I rattle off facts and figures, but it sure came in handy now. No more bullets through the roof.

I made it to Callahan's. It was the most vivid fifteen minutes of my life. I can tell you how many seconds it took every traffic light to

12

change, and the make and year of every car to the front, back and either side of me on the way there, but I made it. I took a service alley in case there was anybody waiting out front. The alley was dark, the only sounds the distant hum of the city, and music out of the back of a few bars: The Chieftains, or The Cranberries in the more upscale ones. I left the Renault running.

The envelope felt dry, which irritated me. I hate it when my palms sweat. It feels weak. I lose the distant look in my eyes. I took a deep breath, focused on the delivery, and stepped over the garbage spilling out of the dumpster by the back door.

The kitchen at Callahan's is a boxcar where everybody has to squeeze past each other: the cook, the waitresses, the dishwashers. The shape of the room saved my life. I was half way through it when a tall, redheaded waitress ahead of me went out the swinging doors into the restaurant. She didn't slam into them like they usually do. She was being careful about something on the other side.

I turned, dumped a pot of boiling water into the fryer, and ran. Two torpedoes waiting in the restaurant stepped in and pulled guns out of their coats. The steam from the fryer had rolled over the tiny room, and their shots impacted against the door frame over my head as I dove out the door.

I kept the dumpster between me and the back door as I ran to the car. Dealing with bullets is a geometry problem. Everything becomes abstract shapes that you juggle to cut off lines of sight. Once they're able to draw a bead, it's usually over. It's the strategy leading up to the shot that counts. After that it's all luck. I don't trust in luck.

I've timed myself getting into the car and releasing the parking brake, but I keep trying to shave seconds off. That night I set a personal record. I had two options, one of which was throwing the car into reverse and trying to back out of the alley, which basically meant presenting them with a receding target. I went for the other option.

I rammed the Renault into the dumpster, driving it back into the restaurant door, effectively sealing it off. The torpedoes may have been between the dumpster and the wall, I don't know. It gave me time to back up and make it out of the alley. The front end of the Renault was a wreck, but all I needed were a few more minutes to make it out of the area. My main problem was that in the instant I'd seen the torpedoes come through the kitchen door, I'd recognized them.

I ran a few lights going south on Axis, which is the fastest way out of the city, before it hit me. They worked for Dewey.

Fifteen minutes later I hung a right into a residential section, took a

13

few turns until I was hidden on a quiet little suburban street, and parked in the shadow under an elm. I sat in the dark.

Then I broke the cardinal rule of the Courier. I opened the envelope.

It was a blank, white piece of paper. No writing, no watermark, nothing. I turned it over a few times, then just sat and looked at it.

I'd been retired.

A time comes in every Courier's life when he knows too much. If you hang around a war long enough, you get splattered. It's little things at first, if only by osmosis: where people eat, what clothes they wear, the kind of cigars they smoke. Your mind starts to put pieces of information together until all of a sudden, without wanting to, you know secrets. You can't help it. Everyone realizes you're not an impartial observer anymore. Your usefulness is over. You're obsolete.

The problem is, Couriers are hard to kill. They don't have friends, so you can't pay anyone off to get close to them. They have no personal lives, because it's a weakness they can't afford. Even the killers get to have wives and families. The Couriers get nothing. As a result, they're not easy to catch. Everyone has to go out hunting, all at once, like they did tonight.

But if the hunt fails, then they've got a problem. I'm out here. I know secrets about everyone.

I'm not a Courier anymore. They retired me. Now I'm a player. And since I don't have a personal life, there's no way to get to me.

Now all I've got in the world is the city. The city, and Jill.

You're wondering about Jill. If I've got no personal life, where does she fit in? Well, I'll tell you, Jill's a trooper. It's been rough for her. After tonight she'll never be the same. But we'll make it through. Just the two of us.

See, Jill's my car.

# once upon a
# midnight dreary

## by carmen fisher

*Once upon a midnight dreary*
*As I pondered weak and weary*
*Over many a quaint and curious*
*Volume of forgotten lore*
"The Raven" by Edgar Allen Poe

Will Cooper was a man worn down in life not by tragedy, sorrow, and woe, but by a lack of it. If some hoodlum had offed his entire family and gotten away with it, well that would mean that he had a family to love and grieve for, and an intense hatred to cling to. He'd even try to catch the guy himself, and that'd give him a goal. Or if he'd caught a future bride with his best pal; same sort of thing. And those were just a few of the nasty things that *could* have happened for him to give a damn. Surly something good enough to make him care about the world *could* have happened too. But none of those things *had* ever happened, and he was as apathetic as he could be about his fellow man. He didn't bear them any ill-will, he just figured the world had thrown him just about as much good as bad in his time, so they were even, and–

"...that's just fine with me," Will mused, finishing the usual trail of thought he took when he started contemplating his views on life, which generally wasn't often. He turned his cab down a street in one of the City's semi-ritzy areas and looked for potential fares outside the clubs. The few people who knew Will often wondered why he drove a cab for his living. Their suggestions ran anywhere from opening a detective agency to giving a it go at professional boxing. They didn't seem to understand that no one cares about a cabby, and that was just his style. It paid his rent, bought food, and put a new book in his hands every few days that he read sitting in the threadbare chair under one of the three lights in his apartment. He rented the cab so he didn't have to deal with a boss. He didn't have to stay out cruising around wasting his time if it was hopeless. He set his own hours. In fact, he was considering giving it up for the night just as it started to rain. The brilliant veins of light that stretched across the sky, followed by the rumble of thunder, daunted many people's spirits in the City that night, but not Will Cooper's. In fact it was one of the few things that could just about cheer him up for the evening. People who ordinarily didn't mind a bit of a walk ran scurrying for cabs with newspapers over their heads during storms like this, and since he had nothing better to do than cart around sissies afraid of the rain, he had no problem with making the money.

He knew who would be hailing him as soon as he saw the looks on their faces when they stepped out of the buildings, and more often than not what they thought about having to take a cab. First, it was a young couple leaving a restaurant. There's the girl who was absolutely aghast at the thought of the water or mud spoiling her favorite dress, not to mention the hair and makeup. And her beau, who probably shaved for the first time tonight (whether he needed to or not) wondering if he has the dough on him for cab fare *and* the movie. So Will charged him about half what he normally would when he drops them off, and gets a kick out of the relieved look on the young guy's face. Then he started to look for someone to make up the difference on the next fare.

He didn't know where she came from, but there she was. A woman with the blackest hair and palest skin he had ever seen. If she was being followed by seven short guys he would have sworn she was Snow White, but the brothers Grimm never imagined a dress like that. Made of tight black satin it revealed curves more dangerous than any he'd ever encountered on the road. Standing there in the rain, with a cigarette dangling from those full crimson lips, she looked like an angel, but not one God cares to associate with any longer. Sure, he didn't really care about people, but a dame like this would still turn his eye. And he wanted to hear her voice, even if it was just for her tell him where she lived with her rich important husband.

He pulled up to the curb, hopped out and opened the door for her. This wasn't usually his style, but this broad had enough class that he did it before he'd realized he was doing it. Then he tried to regain his aloofness. Will Cooper saw no use for women, and certainly wasn't going to go out of his way to try to impress one, no matter how beguiling she was. So his voice was cool as December when he asked her, "Where to, ma'am?"

"1307 Winston Avenue," she replied. Unexpectedly, it was her voice that quivered.

"Right-o," he answered, to his chagrin. Right-o?!? With tripe like that he'd never provoke a reply from that voice; it stood out more than the lightning, but rolled with the soft intensity of the thunder. To his relief, she spoke again anyway.

"What's your name, Mister?"

16

"William Cooper, but I usually go by Will. Is it important?"

"Oh, in a sentimental kind of way..." She sighed.

Having no instincts as to how to reply to this oddly romantic and ominous, if overdramatized, statement he resorted to, "And you are?"

"Raven Malone...I suppose it might help later if you remember it," she responded in a resigned tone.

"No need to worry about that," he muttered under his breath. He almost thought she smiled slightly after that, but her entire figure gave such an overwhelming picture of sadness and resignation that he knew he was imagining things. He searched for something more to say, but communication was one skill that did not come naturally to him. So he just drove, wondering what could affect such a beautiful creature this way, and wishing he knew how to question her without offending her. Then he remembered that he didn't mind offending people and asked "So...something got you down tonight?"

"Oh, I've found a way to deal with it..."

"Nothing too drastic I hope!" trying to sound flippant but meaning it to some extent.

Her brief "When did this become your concern?" ended the conversation until they reached the address she had specified.

"That'll be–" was all he got out before she dropped enough money over the seat to cover three times the distance. He watched her walk away, presumably toward the only nearby building, a large house he could barely make out from the road. When she was out of sight, he began to back away slowly, until his headlights caught the black purse laying in the gravel. He tried to ignore it, but how often does the perfect excuse get ignored?

Pretending that this was his first and only good deed of the day, he picked up the purse and began walking toward the house. He rang the bell, and when confronted by the imposing butler, asked impressively for Ms. Malone, only to be told that no one by that name lived there, nor had anyone arrived in the past fifteen minutes. After what seemed to be a month, but in reality was a moment, Will took off in the night toward Winston Bridge, the existence of which he had only just remembered.

He reached it, and saw what he feared more than he thought possible. Raven was sitting on one of the rails, staring at the rocks below, poising her body to move forward into the fall.

At this point a decision had to be made. He wanted to run toward her and grab her before she could jump, but he was afraid that the sudden action might frighten her into jumping, or worse, he might knock her over himself. So as quickly and quietly as he could, he snuck up behind her. Fortunately, her mind was completely wrapped up in her worries

17

and she didn't notice him. He grabbed her around the waist and yanked her down. She screamed in surprise, and began to fight him. He easily blocked her attempt at a slap and restrained her wrists to keep her from hurting herself. It didn't occur to him to get out of the mud as he attempted to catch his breath, slow his heartbeat, keep a grip on the slippery satin, and think of something to say all at the same time. Finally he decided to keep it simple.

"Lady, you dropped your purse."

For some reason that completely broke her down. She burst into sobs and threw herself against him. There were few moment's in Will's life when he had absolutely no idea how to respond, and this was one of them. He tried to concentrate on understanding what she was saying, hoping it would explain her suicide attempt.

"But...he...he...he'll kill me if I stay with him, an...and he'll kill me if I leave him, and I can't win unless I just do it myself! I can't go back again, I can't! I know he's been drinking and..." she broke off into uncontrolled whimpers.

For whatever reasons, Will did have a very strict code of ethics, and rule number one on his list was "Don't beat women, children, or dogs." For the first time he noticed the bruise on Raven's cheek that had been carefully concealed with make-up and resolved to do something about it. He didn't know what, but he decided to start by getting her out of the rain.

"Come on" he said gently as he pulled her to her feet. Still clinging to him she began to protest.

"But I don't have anywhere to go but home...don't make me go there!"

"Well, how 'bout if I take you to a hotel?"

"He didn't give me any money this week, he says I don't have enough of a head on my shoulders to be carrying cash around."

"A friend?"

"The few he lets me see are too frightened of him not to give me away."

"Then for tonight you're coming to my place, because you can't stay outside and you're not jumping off that bridge!"

She looked at him with a mix of gratitude and apprehension. "But, that isn't right, a woman coming and spending the night at a strange man's house."

"Well, this isn't right either," he almost whispered, holding his fingers over the bruise on her cheek. She hadn't realized that he'd noticed the purple splotch, and turned, as if she were ashamed.

"No," he turned her face toward him, "You shouldn't be the one who has to hide."

When they arrived at his apartment, he made her as comfortable as he could. Having no care for his own comfort he didn't have much around, but he made her some coffee, threw together a stack of books that he thought might relax her, and told her to take full run of the apartment.

"Where do you and your husband live?" he asked her, trying not to sound too gruff.

"The penthouse of Stanton Arms, why?"

"I'm going to go talk to him, to tell him you're leaving him and he damn well better make sure you're supported. If he threatens you at all, I'm going to the cops. You just stay here for the night, okay? I'll get back whenever I can and sleep on the couch."

"That's too dangerous, Will! I couldn't ask anyone to do that for me and you don't even know me! I'll find a way to deal with it on my own, really I will!" She clutched at his arm as her eyes pleaded with him not to go. Her dark eyes behind long lashes made him want to just sit down beside her and comfort her throughout the night, but she was too appealing. He was afraid she was the only woman in the City who could ensnare him, change him, when he liked his life the way it was. He gently removed his arm from her grasp and noticed her wedding band shining on her left hand. It was beautiful, and expensive, Will was sure of it, though his knowledge of gems and jewelry was next to none. He slipped it off her finger and into his pocket.

"You won't be needing this anymore. I'll keep it for now and you can figure out what to do with it later. As for your husband, you have found a way to deal with him, and that way is me."

"Well, at least take this," she implored him, pulling a .25 automatic out of the purse he'd retrieved for her. "For my peace of mind, I don't know what he'll do when you show up!"

He hesitated for a moment, then took the gun. After all, he could always leave it in the cab. The pistol was obviously a weapon designed to catch a lady's eye. It was small enough to hold and carry easily, and the pearl handle and delicate detailing made it seem almost nice, although the bullets fired from it could be just as deadly as those from a cold, plain, grey piece. He tucked it into his waistband for the time being.

"I'll be fine," he reiterated, and walked back out into the storm.

Stanton Arms, was one of the fanciest places to live in the heart of the City, and Will knew exactly where it was. He'd dropped off a lot of rich broad at this place, her arms loaded with packages from a long day of shopping, which the doormen took from them immediately. And at night, sober friends of rich, drunk businessmen sent him there with their buddies, who could barely find their cars, much less drive home. This was the first time he'd been there for a personal reason. As he drove, his movements became more and more determined, such that when he got out of the car, he forgot to leave the gun. He didn't have much trouble sneaking past the security guard into the stairwell, and made his way up to the top floor. He didn't know what he expected to see when the door opened, but he knew what he got wasn't it.

An obvious businessman stood before him, still in his suit, tie and all. Sure, he'd been drinking, probably way too much, but he didn't look nearly like most of the wife beating trash Will had ever seen in his life. But Will knew better than anyone that you can't judge a book by its cover.

"Mr. Malone, I've been speaking with your wife this evening and..."

"Mr. *Malone*? My *wife*? Fella, the name's Eric Stanton, and I don't have a wife. Now I have a toy named Malone, Raven Malone, and if you know where she is tonight, you better start talking. She was supposed to be in an hour ago! My *wife* . . . if I ever married her she'd be the death of me for sure. Is the only reason you're here to spurt misinformation about my life?" The contempt in Stanton's voice was obvious, for Will as well as for Raven.

It took Will a second to regain his bearings, but even if he'd misunderstood the situation, this man was obviously a tyrant and Will felt committed to doing something to get him out of Raven's life.

"Maybe I do know where she is tonight, and I also know where she's never coming back here. I'm here to inform you that Raven is leaving you, and you'll have to find someone who can put up more of a fight to practice your boxing on!" It didn't come out quite as intimidating as he'd hoped, and was rather clinched, but he thought he got his point across.

"Oh, like you?" Stanton replied calmly, as with equal composure he drew a .38 from the holster beneath his suit jacket and turned it toward Will.

It was a mistake. Will's reflexes had always been quick, and his reflex when a gun was pulled on him was to draw the one Raven had given him and shoot. He fired twice at Stanton's chest as the thunder roared its loudest, and it was over. He stood for a moment, waiting for the yelling and footsteps, the people shouting, the cops asking questions he knew must inevitably follow what he'd just done. What the hell had he been thinking? When he realized that no one was coming, that the

20

thunder must have covered up the shot, he barely hesitated before he shut the door with his elbow and snuck out of the building the same way he had snuck in.  Based on what he knew about Eric Stanton III, he knew he'd shot an important man.  He'd read his name in the papers many times, not to mention his father before him.  Some small time cabby's word wasn't going to mean much to the police.  The Stantons had been pillars of the City's community for generations.  They had a hand in half of the businesses and gave money to practically all the charities.  Only in recent years had the Stanton name been associated with criminal activities.

Will drove by the River and threw the gun in where he knew it would sink down into the mud.  Then he drove back to his apartment, not knowing what to tell the mistress?  Fiancee?  Whatever she had been to Stanton, telling her about his death, his accidental death...oh, hell, his murder was going to be hard.  She was the only one who could point the finger at him, but he had freed *her,* hadn't he?  But when he arrived back at his apartment, she was gone.  This worried him, but there didn't seem to be anything he could do about it.  After reading for a while to calm himself down, he managed to fall asleep for a few hours.

Loud, harsh knocking on his door woke him up in the morning, and he'd read enough detective stories to know what to do.  Grabbing a few things, he made his way out the fire escape.  He started toward his cab, but the boys in blue seemed to be helping themselves to a bit of an inspection.  He needed to talk to Joe, and do something he hadn't paused for since seeing Raven in the rain–think.  Without his cab, he'd have to take a careful walk across town, but he didn't have any other options at that point.  He pulled his cap down over his eyes and started off.  The cops didn't notice, but rather better trained driver of the car that followed him *did.*

In a straight line, the coffee shop where Joe usually spent his mornings was only about three miles away.  Trying to be quick and cautious at the same time, it took Will about an hour to get there.  He might have made the sleek black car that was following him if his attention hadn't been concentrated on looking for men in uniforms and replaying the events of the previous evening.  He was trying to figure out how he'd gotten himself into this, and how he was going to get back out of it.  It's hard to prove yourself innocent of a crime you committed, and it's hard to claim self-defense when you were in a building you had no legitimate reason to be in, and carrying a gun you had no reason to carry.  Luckily, he arrived at the coffee shop before that thought had time to drive him crazy.

21

He stood outside the window coughing into his hand to prevent most of the regulars from spotting him. When Joe finally looked up it was obvious he had some information about what was going on, with the subtlest of nods he indicated that Will should meet him at his apartment, instead of waving for Will to join him as he usually would have. Will took a zigzagging route to the old apartment building and arrived just after the older man. It was only a stroke of luck that the one-way streets in the area made Will's shadow lose track of him in the crowd and miss seeing what building he entered.

"All right, Will, what's happened?" Joe asked, the concern evident in his voice.

"That's an interesting question, and I was hoping you'd help me figure out the answer. Why don't you tell me what you've heard from your cop buddies and I'll fill in the pieces from there."

"Well, it seems like Eric Stanton, businessman, philanthropist, and dirtiest rich bastard in the City was shot last night in his apartment. You're the prime suspect based on a report from someone who saw you park your cab in front of his building last night and enter in a hurry. That in itself wouldn't have been so suspicious if the front desk had any record of you coming in. Then there was an anonymous tip saying you were with Stanton's lady friend last night. Pretty girl, lots of charisma. They say she won't wear anything but black. What's she call herself? Raven somethin'."

"Malone, Raven Malone. Yeah, I picked the broad up in my cab last night. Women...I should've known when I saw her she was trouble. You ever hear of this Stanton guy hitting her?"

"Stanton? Nah. I mean, you can never tell, but it sounds to me like Stanton was a coward at heart, the type of guy who could've been tough if he had a gun pointed at someone, or if he had them surrounded by a bunch of his thugs. A guy like that might have beaten an ordinary woman, but from what I've heard this Malone broad is no ordinary woman.

As good a shot as most men I worked with on the force, she's just as likely to slug a fella twice her size for not doing what she wants as to charm him. A chick like that could have taken care of herself with someone like Stanton. I'm sure she let the guy think he was in control, but I'd bet she called the shots in that relationship.

Wait a sec, I think I'm starting to get it. She conned you, didn't she, boy? Fed you some line about this abusive boyfriend she couldn't get away from and counted on your male ego and pride to send you running into a kill or be killed situation. Damn, she must be good to get you of all people to fall for that kind of line." Joe shook his head with a slight

22

smile, as if the incongruity of Will getting taken in by a woman's charms was keeping him from understanding the seriousness of the situation. Only his troubled eyes betrayed the true depths of his concern.

"Yeah, she was good, and I was stupid. I haven't pulled my face out of my books long enough to learn the first thing about people or I would have spotted it a mile away. God dammit, if I'd been thinking!" With this Will slammed his fist into one of the harder walls in the apartment, the pain serving to begin clearing the anger from his mind so he could start planning his next move.

"That bloody hand going to help you out of this, Will?" Joe asked patiently.

"I don't know what is, at this point," he replied.

"Maybe this will," Joe answered, directing Will's attention to a stack of bills on the table. "I've got more than enough pension to live on, and this has just sort of been building itself over the years. It's not much, but it should get you out of town quietly. You would have ended up with it someday anyway, and I think you need it 'bout as much now as you ever will. But you better take it now and go, before someone down at the station remembers that their prime suspect is Joe Cooper's son."

Will looked at the money, then at his father. "Dad, I–"

"It's nothing my father wouldn't have done for me, Will." He slipped the money into a green canvas pouch and held it out to Will.

They looked at each other for one moment, with understanding that only comes in a crisis, after which Will grabbed the money and left, with a hasty, "Thanks, Pop, I won't forget this."

Will took off down the street, pondering exactly how he wanted to try to leave the City. He played with the pouch in his hand and tried to remember when he'd seen it before. Something in the smell brought back memories. He was startled out of his train of thought by a sharp jab in his finger.

"What the?" He opened the bag and sifted past the bills to find the offending sharp. It turned out to be an old fishing lure and hook of his dad's, and suddenly he remembered the fishing trips he and his dad took when he was small. That was before his dad got promoted and started spending more time at the station, when he still thought of his father as "Daddy" instead of "Joe." They used to go to a cabin on land that belonged to Joe's family in the north part of the state. It was run down, but it was quiet, a place where a man and his son could get away and be by themselves for a while without distractions–or a man who needed to not be seen for a while. That's what his dad was trying to tell him with the old pouch he used to keep his favorite lures in–go to the cabin, a place he'd always been safe. A few hours ride would bring him close enough to hike the rest of the way. He could stay in a hotel tonight and in the morning make it up to the cabin in time to catch himself lunch in the lake. He started to make his way toward the bus station, wishing he'd been able to retrieve the book he'd been reading from his cab.

Joe watched the door close behind his son and in moments was gathering clothes, canned goods and every warm blanket and camping supply he still had left in his apartment. The cabin wasn't kept as well supplied these days and it was cold outside. He planned to go visit his hometown and have a cousin deliver the supplies to Will. As much as he wanted to go back up there himself, he was simply getting too old. Besides, his license plate could already lead anyone interested a little too close to Will's location with his plan to go home. But what good would it serve to send the boy off to beat a murder rap only to let him freeze to death? He'd prepared several good-sized bundles when the sound of his front door being kicked in stopped him in his tracks.

Three imposing men with guns prominent, but not poised for action strolled into the room. They were followed by a woman Joe knew could only be Raven Malone. He didn't bother to speak, but stood preparing to answer the questions he knew would inevitably come.

"Hello, Mr. Cooper, so sorry about your door," she apologized, making it clear with the chill in her voice that she never regretted anything. "Did we interrupt you, you seem to be packing for something? Blankets ...a lantern...food...looks like a camping trip to me. Going alone?"

"I don't think I feel like being toyed with today, Miss, so why don't you ask your questions straight out, I'll refuse to answer them the same way, and we'll see what happens from there."

"Mr. Cooper, why do you think I'm looking for Will? Obviously you can figure out that's why I'm here, but you don't seem to understand or you'd be more cooperative. I want to thank him, and help him with that mess with the police. I've talked to them myself already, and I'm sure if Will would just come down to the station with me and explain things to them, everything would be fine. I've even arranged for him to have use of my attorneys when he talks to the officers, and I assure you, they are the best available. So if you could please tell me how to get in touch with him, it would save so much trouble for everyone involved."

"Miss, you may not realize it, but your considerable charm works much better on those with young fools' blood like my son. It boils better and keeps a man from thinking straight. And besides you haven't even bothered to ask me if Will told me where he was going, which he didn't, so I couldn't tell you even if I wanted to, which I don't. Now can't you just leave an old man a—"

24

His sentence got cut off as another burly man hurried into the room, stomping over the broken door with a clatter. "What are you doing here?" Raven seethed, "Aren't you supposed to be looking for someone?"

"I found him," the new arrival puffed as he tried to catch his breath, "he went to the bus station, but I missed what bus he got on."

"You absolute blithering idiot! We almost missed out on this lead because of you, and that cop on the payroll saved you by filling in the gap you left. Was your boss's life so cheap to you that you twice, not once, but twice in a day lose the man who killed him?" She grabbed a revolver from one of her other men and leveled it between the eyes of the ill-fated hireling. The gun was heavy and cruel looking, designed to inspire fear, to inflict pain and to kill. In an ordinary woman's hand the weight of the weapon would have caused her whole arm to shake, as the eyes of the man it was pointed at shook behind his tough guy composure, which was quickly melting into a sweating mask of fear. Raven's expression was also changing. The anger which had been evident on her face a moment before gave way to a look of satisfaction at the terror she was causing, and at the idea of firing. The power of having a man's life at her fingertips turned her on. A malicious smile crept up her face as her finger tightened on the trigger. The no-longer-so-tough guy swallowed hard and closed his eyes, as if not staring down the pistol's barrel would make it go away. As a result, he didn't see Raven suddenly bring the revolver back and smack him across the face with it. He opened his eyes slowly, still not sure if he had received a temporary reprieve of pain, or if he would live to serve his new boss better another day. When he saw that Raven had handed the gun back to its owner he silently vowed never to let her down again. He wiped the blood from his face with the lacy black handkerchief Raven handed him as she turned around and addressed her troops with perfect calm.

"Looks like Mr. Cooper here is our only lead in catching our murderer, boys. Bring him along."

Will arrived at his hometown and checked into a motel for the night. The town had grown in the years he'd been gone, and he chose a place that had been built since his time, hoping that he wouldn't be recognized. He had enough money left to buy some supplies the next day, then he would make the walk to the cabin. But tonight he just wanted to do two things: call Joe, and get a good night's sleep. Neither one turned out to be possible.

He dialed the number intending to hang up when he heard Joe's voice. Joe could easily figure out what he was trying to say. Will tensed as the phone rang four, five times. Finally there was an answer. The voice sounded odd, a combination of sadness and detachment, tired, but with a resolve that almost covered up all of the other feelings. "Cooper residence, this is Vargas."

Will was silent. He hadn't thought about the possibility of anyone but Joe answering the phone. And although the name "Vargas" was familiar, he didn't think it was one of his father's poker buddies, and certainly not one close enough to answer the phone.

Agitated now, the voice on the phone demanded, "This is Detective Tony Vargas, who is this?"

Detective Vargas. An image flashed across Will's mind of an FOP picnic he'd attended with his father as a teenager. He could see Vargas, a young cop bragging about his new homicide career. Homicide.

The cold earpiece dropped back into its cradle as if of its own accord.

Will knew it was true. He didn't know how, but he knew it. He didn't for a second let his mind distract him with the possibility that this was a different Vargas, or that Vargas had switched departments. She had killed Joe, and now, tenfold more than before, Will was determined to make her answer for what she had done. She would pay, and she would suffer. He didn't care if took days or decades, he wanted her to lie in bed at night wondering if he would choose that night, or the next day, or the next to put a bullet between those gorgeous, wicked eyes. He would haunt her like a ghost, terrify her, enrage her, frustrate her. And when he felt she'd suffered enough, she would die.

Raven sipped a glass of sherry in her private sitting room. While there were guards at the door outside, her most trusted men had the job of disposing the body in such a way that the police would discover it quickly, without them getting caught. She'd decided when the smoke had cleared that if the old man couldn't be used for information, he could still send a message to his devoted son. If she was going to establish herself on two solid feet, Will Cooper had to take the fall for the murder. It was the only way, and she was determined that it would be so.

Sam cut in on her thoughts from his seat in the corner where he had maintained silence for an admirable 12 minutes and 36 seconds. "You're handling this really well Raven, the way you interrogated that old guy, I was absolutely riveted, and dumping him . . . "

"I did what I had to if I'm . . . if we're going to run this establishment as we've planned." Her "slip" was intentional. They both knew that she wanted his name, Samuel Stanton, alone to help her with her plans, and she could substitute another if she absolutely had to. But

Sam was willing to go along with her, since it meant he would finally have access to the Stanton empire to which he felt he had always been entitled. But deep down he knew he didn't have the brains to run it on his own, or else he might have been stupid enough to try to take control from Raven.

"Man, when that guy was talking, I got chills. But you, you just stood there like a statue, you didn't move anything but your trigger finger. Those were some beautiful last words though, weren't they? How did they go again?"

Raven didn't bother answering out loud, but played the scene in her head perfectly from memory. By that time, Joe Cooper should have looked tired, older, worn-down, defeated. He'd been tied to the chair for hours, with Raven hoping that hunger and discomfort would defeat his pride and conscience. Instead he sat there calmly, his look saying that he would wait silently until she chose to shoot him, or let him go. It didn't seem to matter to him either way.

Finally, in desperation her men didn't pick up on, she questioned him about that. "Aren't you afraid of death, Mr. Cooper? Aren't you afraid that I'll leave you tied to this chair and stick you in a little dark room and just let you die on your own from thirst, soiling yourself, the smell, the pain in your hands, your throat too dry and hoarse for you to cry out for me to come listen to you tell me where Will is, even just for the pleasure of having me shoot you and get it over with?"

"Miss, you don't know what death is like when it's bad. I had a six-year-old girl die in my arms one time. She didn't go easy either. Her little blue eyes were filled with pain, as her young body tried to live another moment, then another, but she didn't make it. All because some fool couldn't drive any better than to run her down while she was playing in front of her house. In the War, fields of guys, some with families, some not, were slaughtered. Away from home, from everything they ever knew, they died, because somebody decided they needed to fight. I had a good friend, a young guy with kids, who got gunned down in an alley because his partner turned coward and ran. And you think an old man like me, who's had a good life already and out lived his wife and all his friends, is going to be afraid to die for his son? Raven Malone, you don't know nothing about death."

Then he closed his eyes, as if he died peacefully before the slugs from Raven's gun exploded through his chest a moment later.

The next day, Will was back to the City, with the beginnings of a plan in mind. He only hoped he had the daring--and the luck--to pull it off.

His first step was to buy a newspaper to see in black and white that

Joe really was dead. It was all there, the story, the obituary, hailing Joe as a fallen saint, as he deserved. Will allowed a single tear drop on the page, smudging the symbol of a badge next to the obituary which designated Joe as having been a police officer, then silently renewed his vow for revenge. The story about the murder said that while the police had suspects, they had all provided alibis and there was no physical evidence linking any of them to the crime. No arrests had been made, and police were not hopeful in attaining a conviction.

He gathered himself, then turned to the now third-page story about Stanton's death. It told him that police still considered him to be the main suspect, but that they assumed him to have skipped town. Instinct and knowledge about how the police worked told him that unless he practically walked into the station and confessed, they would no longer put enough manpower into the case to catch him. With this possibility of hope he turned toward his apartment.

Lieutenant Vince Vincent arrived at the junior Cooper's apartment to check up on the young cop who had been assigned to watch it. O'Malley was on guard, the look on his face one of the inexperienced cop who dreamed of more exiting police work and considered this assignment to be only a small step above desk work. "It'll come in time, son," Vince thought silently, "and there'll be plenty of days you miss this kind of work."

"How's it going O'Malley? I thought Neeson was supposed to be here by now." Vince greeted him in his friendly way that was familiar to all the young cops he dealt with.

"Not much happening here, sir, and I've been stuck here alone since seven this morning. Neeson called in sick today and there was no one else to take over."

"Haven't you had the chance to get any lunch yet?"

"No sir, I couldn't leave the scene unguarded!" O'Malley was thrilled at the chance to express his dedication to his favorite superior officer.

"All right, I'll look after things here and radio to see if I can get someone to come take over. In the meantime, you go get yourself a meal and a cup of coffee on me." And he handed the younger officer a few bills from his wallet.

"Thank you, sir, I'll get back as soon as I can!"

"No rush, O'Malley, you're keeping me from some paper work at the station that can wait 'till I'm retired as far as I'm concerned!"

Vince followed O'Malley out of the apartment and locked it behind him. He preferred to do his watching outside, as he had no taste for sitting in a man's home without his permission, even if he was a criminal suspect. He had too much respect for a man's space. He sat on the building's steps and watched O'Malley turn the corner out of sight. He sat back to spend some time thinking on the Stanton case. Something about it smelled wrong to him, but he couldn't do anything about it. By no account he had heard was Will the type of man to go shooting at people unless he had a damn good reason. But the evidence was clearer than in most murder cases. He shook his head and reminded himself, as he usually did several times a day, that if he'd really wanted things to be black and white, he'd be giving out traffic tickets.

His intuition told him that the movement near the cab was wrong before his eyes figured out who it was. He moved his hand to his .357 Magnum and took it out, then he called to the crouched figure "Will!"

Will froze defeated and came out. He knew that if the cops had him, his chance of making Raven pay for Joe's death was gone. The thought of jail time, or even execution, was insignificant except for that fact. He slowly moved from behind the cab, barely looking at the officer who had accosted him.

Vince looked at Will and sized him up. He could tell Will had a plan, and it wasn't just to get out of town or he would have done it by now. And it must involve the cab or Will wouldn't have come back for it. And it wouldn't take Vince three guesses to figure out who Will was plotting against. Sometimes justice is not the law's jurisdiction, he thought, and put the gun away.

"You're slouching, Will. You and your father always had that slouch," Vince commented, as he fumbled for his cigars and matches.

"Mr. Vincent? Vince Vincent?" Will asked, hoarsely, more frightened than ever now that he knew who his captor was. An inexperienced rookie he might have gotten away from, but not the near legend that confronted him now.

Vince tried to light the cigar, only to have the match blown out–despite the windless day. He cursed to himself, and turned his back on Will to make another attempt. He expected to hear footsteps and a car door anytime.

Will stood there confused, and still frozen.

Vince paused briefly to ask, "What are you waiting for?" wondering if he was going to have to hold Will's hand and start the car for him.

That was enough. Will was in the car and down the street in a moment, hoping that Vince wasn't the only one watching the apartment.

Max couldn't believe his luck when he saw Will drive away. He didn't know how the little rat had gotten away from the cop, but he didn't plan on being that incompetent--not again, anyway. His jaw was still a little bruised from when Raven had hit him with the pistol and he wanted to get back into her good graces. He followed Will to a gas station and watched him go into the men's room. He stared at the door, wanting to make sure he didn't blink and lose his man. After 15 minutes his eyes were starting to get sore, and he wondered if he might have been given the slip again. To check he went up to the restroom door and pounded on it. It swung open slowly. He stepped in and began to curse at the small empty room just as the tire iron connected with the back of his head.

Will wrapped the big gangster's arm around his shoulder and guided him to the cab, as if he were a drunken fare he was trying to take care of. No one cared, or noticed. Once he was in the back seat, Will took Max's gun, keys, and identification. The gun went in his waistband, the i.d. in a garbage truck that was filling up, and the keys were thrown into the front seat of Max's car which was in full view of some teenagers who were standing around looking like exactly the kind of trouble Will needed to get rid of the car. Then Will topped off his tank for the short trip his car was about to make.

First he drove by Joe's apartment hoping that if he cruised slowly enough he wouldn't have to drive by again. One sharp eyed cop on the scene actually spotted the cab and identified the driver, and the chase was on. A few low-key black sedans holding Raven's men followed the cop cars that followed Will, as he raced through the City streets, seemingly erratically, but knowing exactly where he was going. As he drove, he took his wallet out of his pocket and tossed it in the back seat, glad for the high quality leather that would protect its contents in the worst of circumstances. It had Will Cooper's drivers licences, Will Cooper's social security card, and a few of Will Cooper's other things in it. Will Cooper would soon be dead.

The cab roared over the roads that led out of the city, then through a road block that stood warning drivers that the road ended in a large ravine. Boards scattered everywhere, as the police cars, and the dark cars driven by less lawful men, slowed as they continued pursuit. They pulled up short and saw the cab slow drastically, but plunge into the chasm anyway. A dozen men got out to survey the wreckage. One of them listened briefly to the cops around him talk then went to call his boss.

"We don't have to worry about Stanton's killer no more, he's dead. Car wreck in the ravine while he was trying to leave town again. Cops are planning on wrapping up the Stanton investigation as soon as they get back to the station. I'll make sure everything's kosher here and report back later. Oh, and, by the way, I haven't heard from Max all day. You think he skipped town like you thought he might?"

Raven hung up her end of the line with a catlike satisfied smile. Her new career had begun.

Vince Vincent arrived on the scene and surveyed the damage. As a matter of course he viewed the nearby crowd for potential witnesses. One man in particular caught his eye walking away from the gorge. By that time a team had gone down to the burning wreck and checked it out, along with the fire department who quickly put down the flames. "Definitely him, sir, even though the body is beyond recognition. His cab, and his I.D. was in back. Terrible way to go, the impact threw him all the way into the back seat," the young detective reported proudly, holding out Will's wallet in a plastic evidence bag.

"Well, if you're sure it's him, so am I. I guess the case is closed. Let's get the coroner in here and go home." Vince lit a cigar and prepared to leave as he watched the slouching figure who had caught his eye when he arrived walk down the edge of the canyon with the purposeful steps of a man who knows his goals, who can and will achieve them.

Art by Steve Carr

# firetruck no. 5

## by nancy collins

Simon Alexander eased his wheezing Oldsmobile up the drive that lead to a four-story mansion set atop a low hill. He didn't need to check the address against the letterhead to know he was in the right place. The giant "B" on the wrought iron gates blocking the way told him that. The neighborhood was one of the ritziest in the city, and a far cry from Alexander's usual stomping grounds. But then, multi-millionaire industrialists like Rayford Blackman usually didn't hang out in Chinatown or the Bowery.

Following the instruction in the letter he'd received that afternoon, Alexander leaned out of the driver's window to press the button on a call-box set near the gate. After a long moment the gate made a buzzing noise and slowly swung inward. Alexander gunned the motor, heading for the house on the hill. He could see the gates swinging shut behind him in the rear view mirror.

Alexander had no idea what a high-roller like Blackman could want with a penny-ante gumshoe like himself, but he wasn't going to question his good fortune. Blackman had made reference to something "of the utmost sensitivity and importance", and nothing else. Not that his curiosity needed satisfying. The fifty dollar bill tucked inside the letter he'd received was incentive enough to drag him halfway across town in the middle of the night. Work had been slow the last few weeks–slow enough to make the idea of re-enlisting with Uncle Sam look almost tempting.

He parked in the turn-around in front of the house, next to a working fountain with a cement replica of some ancient water god spurting away in the center. The entrance to the house was as big as a two-car garage, with a smaller version of the driveway's iron gate in front–making it look more like a factory–or a prison–than a home. A man in his early thirties, dressed in the formal livery of a butler, was standing just inside the entrance way.

"Mr. Blackman has been awaiting your arrival, Mr. Alexander," the butler announced stiffly as he opened the gate.

"I'm sorry if I kept your boss-man cooling his heels, Jeeves, but I got a little lost on the way over. This isn't exactly my neighborhood."

"Indeed," sniffed the butler. "And the name is Williamson , not

33

`Jeeves'. Sir."

As they entered the grand foyer, Alexander had to fight to keep from whistling in amazement. The place could have passed for Grand Central Station, except for the wood paneling. The floor looked to be a solid chunk of unbroken Italian marble, burnished to a high polish, with a handful of Persian carpets tossed down for good measure. A double staircase curled up and back, leading to the house's east and west wings. Set at the center of the arched roof was a stained glass window that was a replica of the ones in Notre Dame. He recognized it because he'd seen the original back when his battalion liberated Paris, a few years back.

Alexander grinned and gestured with his hat. "Some digs, Jeeves— I mean, Williamson."

"Mr. Blackman is in the study," the butler sniffed, moving to open a door off the grand foyer.

The study was as big as his three floor walk-up, not including the toilet at the end of the hall. The walls were paneled in oak and the maroon carpet was thicker than most people's mattresses. The heads of animals unlucky enough to have crossed Rayford Blackman's path in the past hung on the wall, looking either surprised or pissed-off. Seated behind a huge mahogany desk, puffing on a hand-rolled Cuban cigar, was none other than the lord of the manor himself, watching Alexander much the same way he imagined he'd looked at the animals on the wall when they came down to the water hole.

Blackman was an older man in his early sixties, but he was far from elderly in appearance. At six foot two, with shoulders wide enough to put Knute Rockne to shame, he looked little different from the virile young man who single-handedly put Amalcor at the top of the New York Stock Exchange.

"Mr. Alexander, I presume?"

"Um, yes. You're Mr. Blackman—?"

"Who the hell else would you expect sitting here, Gary Cooper?" snarled Blackman, tapping the end of his cigar into a large glass ashtray. "I don't like being kept waiting, Alexander."

"Uh–sorry. Like I told your man, I don't get up to this neck of the woods that often…"

"I can believe that," Blackman grunted, eyeing the private investigators ragged cuffs and rumpled rain coat. "Take a seat."

Alexander eased himself into a high-backed leather chair that faced the desk. Blackman stood up and fetched a cut-crystal decanter from the sideboard. He poured himself a drink then turned to his guest.

"Scotch?"

"Yes, thank you."

"On the rocks?"

"Neat."

Blackman poured the whiskey into a highball glass and handed it to the detective. "You might not be punctual, but you know how to appreciate good scotch. I admire that in a man."

"Thank you. I think. Look, Mr.Blackman–it's not that I think I'm a putz, but one thing's been bothering me since I got your letter. What the hell does a guy like you want with a guy like me?"

Blackman sighed and perched on the corner of the desk, staring down at the highball glass he held in his hand. He seemed to age right before Alexander's eyes, his face collapsing into worry-lines and crows-feet. "What do most men want with a guy like you, Mr. Alexander?"

"You think your wife's foolin' around on you?"

Blackman nodded wordlessly and drained his scotch in a single gulp. When he lowered his glass, the weariness he'd displayed a moment before was gone, replaced by a steely resolve. "Two years or so ago you did some work for an old acquaintance of mine, Hank Shearer, concerning a young lady who accused him of fathering her baby."

"Yeah, I remember." Actually Shearer had been as far from a paternity suit as Porky Pig was from Kosher. The "young lady" was actually a young man who liked to wear high heels and panties and take incriminating photographs of his older admirers in similar attire. If Shearer wanted to tell his friends otherwise, that was his prerogative. Alexander certainly wasn't going to contradict Blackman, whatever the case.

"Hank said you were reliable and discreet. I appreciate discreet, Mr. Alexander. You see, I'm sixty-four. My wife is twenty-nine. Lately I've felt a certain…coolness on her behalf. You see, Mr. Alexander, although there is thirty-five years between my wife and I, up until recently we'd enjoyed a vigorous lovelife. Probably better than most couples, regardless of their age. For her to suddenly have become so unresponsive–I'm not a fool, and I refuse to be played for one, Mr. Alexander. If my wife is seeing another man, I want to know about it."

"Do you want a divorce?"

"That's my business, Mr. Alexander, not yours."

"Certainly, sir. Nothing personal. It's just that, well–if you're planning to divorce her, I have to gather certain kinds of evidence that'll hold up in court. You know–photos, copies of motel ledgers, that sort of thing."

"Yes, I understand. It's just that I'm not a hundred percent certain she is having an affair, mind you."

"So, let me get this straight–you want me to shadow her for a couple of weeks to see if she's meeting someone. Then I can leave it up to you as to what you'd like done. Do you have a photograph of you wife, Mr. Blackman? It would make it easier for me when I follow her."

Blackman handed a 5x4 picture frame resting on his desk to Alexander. " Here. This was taken at the reception. We were married in Mexico. I have a villa down there. It was a spur of the moment thing. I chartered a plane and invited a dozen or so friends to come along. It was a wild weekend."

The picture was black and white and looked like the kind of souvenir snapshot made by nightclub photographers, only blown up and cropped so only two people were visible. One was Blackman, dressed in a tuxedo with a white carnation in the buttonhole, wearing an oversized sombrero and grinning like a drunken idiot. Beside him, her slender arm looped through his, was a woman half his age, the right side of her face obscured by a fall of blonde hair. She was wearing a white satin strapless gown that looked like it'd been painted on her and a strange half-smile that seemed out of place on the face of a new bride. There was something familiar about the woman, and it took him a few seconds to place where he'd seen her before.

Alexander blinked at the photograph, then looked back up at Blackman. "You're married to Celine Marchand?"

"Blackman. Her name's Celine Blackman now. So–you recognize her?"

"Recognize her? Hell, half my battalion had her picture up on the walls of the barracks!"

"I beg your pardon?"

"She did this USO show in London, and half the U.S. forces stationed in England turned out to see her! She sang that song of hers— you know the one?"

"Firetruck Number Five."

"Yeah, that one. Afterwards, she signed autographed pictures of herself. I didn't get one, but a few of my buddies did. That's how I recognized her. She has a wonderful voice."

"Yes. She did."


Shadowing Celine Marchand was hardly the toughest assignment he'd ever pulled. The biggest problem he had was trying to blend into the background at the posh restaurants and shops she frequented. He was hardly the Daddy Warbucks type, after all.

The retired chanteuse usually didn't get out of bed until well after ten, and it was a rare day when she left the house before two in the afternoon. Sometimes Williamson drove her around town in a black Bentley that gleamed like the shell of a scarab. However, she often left the house on her own behind the wheel of a Dusenberg.

Outside of her choice of automobile, her routine away from the house seldom varied. Mondays she went to the country club, where she played tennis–doubles, usually with the wives of other club members. Then she'd go shopping at Bloomingdale's. On Tuesdays she had lunch at the Egret Club, a pricey downtown eatery that attracted show biz types and where she had her own table. Then she'd go shopping at Macy's. On Wednesdays she went to the beauty parlor–if you could call a spa that specialized in mud baths, seaweed facials and Swedish massage a "beauty parlor". Then she'd go shopping at Tiffany's. On Thursdays she went to the movies. Alone. Depending on whether the bill was a double or triple feature, she'd then go shopping for shoes. On Fridays she met her husband for lunch at the Crimean Tea Room, a toney uptown joint known for its samovars and Cossack waiters.

As far as Alexander could see, Celine was keeping her nose clean. Her weekly routine of luxury and excess didn't give him much in the way of dirt, but it did give him a chance to look at her up close, if not exactly personal. Blackman was one lucky old man, that much was for sure. Celine was one of the most luscious babes he'd ever laid eyes on, and that included some mighty fine lookers in Paris and Rome.

She was a statuesque blonde, with the right kind of curves in the right kind of places, with skin as pale and unblemished as a magnolia blossom. Her eyes were big and expressive, and her lips shaped for kissing. In fact, her lips were the first thing you noticed when you looked at her—they were always painted bright red, as if she wetted her mouth with fresh blood instead of lipstick. Whenever she moved it was with the fluid grace of a big cat. Even the smallest gesture on her part seemed fraught with erotic undercurrents. No wonder the old man was worried about keeping her down on the farm. But if Celine Blackman was stepping out, he couldn't find any evidence of it. As far as he was concerned, the lady had a clean bill of health and nothing to worry about—if you didn't count a jealous older husband.

It was his last night of surveillance, and he was parked in his usual spot, just outside the mouth of the cul-de-sac, which gave him a view of the front of the Blackman estate, when he saw headlights curling down the hill in the direction of the entrance gate. He checked his watch. Eight o'clock. Normally the Blackmans went nightclubbing on Saturday nights. It was Saturday night, all right, but if he wasn't mistaken, Mr. B was off at a shareholder meeting in Chicago. Maybe there was something to the old man's paranoia, after all.

He slumped down behind the steering wheel, narrowly dodging the lights of the Dusenberg as the beams swept across the windshield. He then popped back up and put the car into gear, following the Dusenberg as it left the ultra-ritzy suburbs and sped towards the freeway. Alexander did his best to follow her without getting so close she'd grow suspicious, or lag behind so far he lost her in traffic. It soon was obvious that wherever she was going, it wasn't anywhere in the city.

After a half hour's drive, the Dusenberg pulled off the highway and parked in the crowded gravel parking lot belonging to a roadhouse that claimed to be, in pink neon atop its gabled roof, The Hideaway. Celine quickly hopped out of her car and hurried to the door. He could see she was wearing a cobalt blue satin Dior gown with matching shoes and clutch purse. Pretty fancy get-up to go grab a burger and some suds. Alexander drummed his fingers against the wheel for a few seconds, deliberating on whether or not he should follow her inside. Judging from the number of cars in The Hideaway's lot, there was a good chance he could mingle with the regulars and not draw any undue attention to himself. Besides, it was Saturday night, and he could use a couple of drinks. After all, Blackman was buying.

After straightening his tie and running a quick comb through his hair, Alexander strolled across the gravel parking lot and entered The Hideaway. As he opened the door, he wondered how it was he'd never heard of the place before. Normally he prided himself on knowing every jumping joint in the tri-county area.

Then he got a good look at the clientele and realized why he'd never heard of the roadhouse.

The interior was no different from any other, except for the dance floor, which was jam packed and jelly-tight with men–dancing with other men. Most of the revelers wore evening suits, but there were several dressed in drag as well. Alexander stared in amazement as a man he recognized as the District Attorney tangoed with a heavy-set drag queen sporting a Carole Lombard wig and a too-tight red taffeta gown. He was suddenly aware of several sets of eyes on him, and he hurried over to the bar.

The bartender, dressed in a starched white jacket and neat black bow-tie, was shaking up a daiquiri. He gave Alexander the once-over but said nothing except; "What can I getcha, pal?"

"Scotch. Neat."

The bartender nodded and poured the daiquiri he'd been shaking into a glass and garnished it with a little paper umbrella and a maraschino cherry. A waiter appeared out of nowhere and snatched the drink up on a tray and disappeared into the crowd.

Alexander cleared his throat as the bartender set his scotch in front of him. "I wonder if you might be able to help me."

"Depends."

"I'm, uh, looking for a friend—'

"Ain't we all, pal."

Alexander's face purpled. "That's not what I mean! I'm looking for a woman! Her name's Celine."

The bartender raised an eyebrow. "You a friend of hers?"

Alexander smiled nervously. "Well, not exactly. More a fan, really. I heard that sometimes she comes here."

The bartender was really giving him the fisheye now. "Really? Who told you that?"

He had to think fast on this one. Alexander scanned the crowded dance floor for a second then turned back to face the bartender. "Hank Shearer."

The bartender's face relaxed from tight suspicion into an open smile. "You know Hank?"

"Yeah. Used to work for him a while back. Swell guy."

"Any friend of Hank's is okay with me!" He leaned forward and stage whispered into Alexander's ear. "You're in luck tonight, pal! Celine's about to go on stage! We never know when she'll show up, but whenever she does the boys in the band are ready for her!"

Just then the house lights went down and the six piece band on the stage stopped in mid-note. The Hideaway's patrons halted whatever they were doing and turned to face the darkened stage. A baby blue spot sprang into life, illuminating a tall, willowy man dressed in a floor-length silver lame ball gown, white opera gloves and a hat that would have done Hedda Hopper proud.

"Ladies and gentlemen," the Mistress of Ceremonies announced in the dulcet tones of a familiar radio actor. "The Hideaway is proud to present–Celine Marchand!"

The crowd applauded enthusiastically as Celine swirled onto the stage in a flash of blue satin and ruby red lipstick. Her previous languor was nowhere to be seen. The woman on the stage crackled with enough energy to run a dynamo. She shot a sly glance in the direction of the bandleader, who nodded and took up his baton again. The band swung into *That Old Black Magic*, and Celine began to sing.

Alexander had only heard her live once before, near the back of an auditorium full of anxious, horny servicemen, singing through an army-issue public address system, but even then he'd recognized her voice as beautiful. Now he realized it was awesome. She sang with the skill and range of a whiskey-drinking angel, going from pure as a bell one moment to bluesy and heart-felt the next, as she made her way through

*Don't Get Around Much Anymore, You'll Never Walk Alone, Baby It's Cold Outside,* and *Lavender Blue.* The audience ate it up, applauding and whistling after every song with genuine pleasure. After she finished *I'm Gonna Wash That Man Right Out of My Hair*, the spotlight went from blue to red, and for one disorienting moment it looked as if she was standing in a pool of blood. Then she launched into her signature piece; *"Firetruck Number Five".*

It was a jazzy little swing number–a strangely upbeat song about a woman setting fire to all number of things, finally her own house, so the fireman she has a crush on would come rescue her because he's too shy to ask her for a date. It was a nutty little novelty song that hit a chord with wartime audiences, and for several months she was all over the celebrity magazines, posing in fireman's hats and riding on the back of a hook and ladder with captions like "torch singer hits big with hot song about lovestruck pyromaniac." But hearing her sing it live, Alexander was struck by the undercurrent of longing in her voice. And for the first time he realized the song was about a woman willing to destroy everything around her–including herself–in the name of love.

After she finished the last song the audience broke out in a final, thunderous round of applause, and the Mistress of Ceremonies came back on stage to hand Celine a bouquet of red roses. Alexander decided now was a good time to make his exit, and hurried out the door.

He slipped back behind the wheel of his car and fished his notebook and a pencil stub out of his breast pocket. So this was what the missus was up to when the old man was out of town. Blackman had nothing to worry about from his wife's admirers, but something told Alexander that the industrialist would not be pleased to find his wife pursuing her career on the QT.

Suddenly the passenger side door was yanked open and the odor of White Shoulders filled the car's interior. Alexander gawked as Celine Marchand slid in beside him. She was still wearing her Dior gown and clutching her purse to her like a shield. Her lips seemed to shimmer in the dim light from the roadhouse, as did her eyes.

"You're him. The man my husband hired to follow me." Her voice was soft and far from accusatory.

"Ma'am, I don't know what you're talking about…"

"Please don't play games with me," her voice hardened, as did her eyes. "You've been following me for the last two weeks. Your name is Alexander. Williamson told me."

Alexander grinned crookedly. "I though Williamson was your husband's man."

"Williamson has been with me since '46. I married Ray in '47. My husband thinks he owns a lot of things that aren't his," Celine replied acidly, fishing a cigarette out of her purse.

"Like your voice?" She glanced up from her purse, and Alexander found himself looking directly into her eyes. They were the same color blue as her dress. He'd never been close enough to her to notice that before.

"You're an astute man, Mr. Alexander." She opened a platinum cigarette case and lifted a Kool to her glossy, blood-red lips. "Light me," she said. It wasn't a request.

Alexander thumbed his Zippo and she leaned forward to catch the flame, her eyes never leaving him the whole time. "It's my job to notice things, Mrs. Blackman."

"Celine. Call me Celine."

"I'd rather not, Mrs. Blackman."

She studied him for a long moment, then blew out a streamer of smoke with an exasperated sigh. "I'm not cheating on my husband, Mr. Alexander."

"I know."

Celine looked at the glowing end of her cigarette then back at him. "Don't tell him what you saw tonight. Please."

"Mrs. Blackman, your husband hired me to do a job–I'm just doing what I'm being paid to do."

"You don't understand, Mr. Alexander! As far as my husband is concerned, what I do here is as bad, if not worse, that sleeping with another man! He's insanely jealous, not just of who I might give my favors to, but of every aspect of my life! I've been a virtual prisoner since we married two years ago."

"I've seen your jail. It's pretty swank for Alcatraz, sister," Alexander replied, popping a Lucky Strike into his mouth..

"Don't be fooled, Mr. Alexander. It might have gold bars–but it's still a cage."

"So why don't you leave the old bastard?"

"Because I'm afraid. Ray's a ruthless man. Far more than you realize. Once be buys something, it's supposed to stay bought. Unless he gets mad and breaks it–then he has to get a new one."

"What do you mean?"

"I'm not the first Mrs. Blackman, or didn't he tell you? His first wife broke her neck falling down the stairs. She had all kinds of bruises on her."

"What are you saying, Mrs. Blackman?"

"I'm saying my husband is a brute, Mr. Alexander." She stabbed out her cigarette and reached for the door handle. "I really must go now.

41

Ray will be calling the house soon. He likes to call the house in the middle of the night to make sure I'm there alone."

As she got out of the car, Alexander caught a glimpse of her calf. She was wearing blue hose, but even the dark stockings could not camouflage the large bruise discoloring the back of her leg. Alexander winced. The last time he'd seen a bruise like that it was on the leg of a Bowery hooker whose pimp had gone after her with a belt.

He tried not to think of her as he lay on his bed, staring at the cracks in the plaster with a half-empty whiskey bottle clutched in one fist. He lay there fully dressed except for his tie and his shoes, alternating hits of his Luckies and the bottle. The stuttering neon from the all-night beanery across the street flashed on and off, bathing the room first in shadow, then pink, then shadow again. The more he tried not to think of her, the more her voice echoed in her head.

He knew he was falling. Falling big. And for a dame who belonged to one of the most powerful—and dangerous—men in the city. Hell, in the country. It had been a long time since anyone had gotten to him the way Celine had. When he closed his eyes he could see her face hovering above him, with its flawless white skin, piercing blue eyes and red as blood lips. Then he thought about the bruise on her leg and he knew what he had to do.

Blackman studied the typed report, peering over the tops of his reading glasses every now and again at the detective. "Is this all there is?" he asked.

"Absolutely, Mr. B. You're wife's got a clean bill of health."

Blackman grunted and leaned back in his chair, rubbing his chin. "I'm greatly relieved to hear that, Mr. Alexander. But I'm still bothered by Celine's change towards me..."

Alexander shrugged. "Maybe she's got the blues. Women are like that, you know. Maybe she misses show business. You know what they say about old race horses and the track."

"I seriously doubt that, Mr. Alexander," Blackman responded tartly. "Celine has no interest in the stage anymore."

Alexander shrugged. "If you say so, sir. Now, about my fee—"

"Ah, yes. I believe we agreed on twenty dollars a day—"

"Plus expenses."

"Ah, yes. Which would come out to—?"

"Three hundred dollars."

Blackman pushed himself away from his desk and went to a small oil landscape, which hid a wall-safe behind its canvas. After spinning the lock for a few seconds, Blackman opened the safe and retrieved a thick sheaf of twenty dollar bills. He peeled off fifteen and returned the remainder to the safe, then turned to Alexander.

"Here you are, Mr. Alexander. Would you like to count it?" Alexander palmed the bills as neatly as magician. "No need. I trust you, Mr. B."

"You're the only one I've met lately!" Blackman laughed humorlessly. "Are you sure Celine never caught on? I'd hate to have her find out I was having her followed."

"I swear on my mother's grave, Mr. B—she never knew I was there. Not once." Alexander wondered if Blackman would be able to tell he was lying. Then again, Blackman had no way of knowing Ma Alexander was still alive and kicking, either.

"Good. I'd hate to have her think I didn't trust her. I'll have Williamson show you the way out—"

"No need. I can find my way," he said, heading for the door. "It was a pleasure doing business with you, Mr. B."

He waited for Blackman to say "likewise," but the industrialist was already preoccupied with some paperwork on his desk. Alexander shrugged and left the room.

His footsteps echoed in the grand foyer as if he was walking through a church. Halfway across the cavernous hall, he got the distinct feeling he was being watched. He turned and looked towards the twin staircases .

She was standing on the landing that lead to the east wing, dressed in a red silk kimono, her hair pulled to one side so that it spilled over her right shoulder. Alexander touched the brim of his hat. Celine dipped her chin in acknowledgment, then turned and disappeared into the shadows at the top of the stairs.

It was pouring down rain when he got the call.

Three days had passed since he'd last seen her. And, to be honest, he thought he never would again—except in his dreams. Then the phone rang at eight o'clock. Normally he was out of the office by that time of night, but he'd been held up by some paperwork that evening. The "paperwork" consisted of clippings he'd gotten from a source at the daily paper concerning the death of the first Mrs. Blackman, who died from injuries sustained in a fall back in `43.

He picked up the phone on the third ring. There was a lot of static on the line, and at first he didn't recognize the voice.

"—come right away."

"What? Who is this?"

"The Blackman estate. It's urgent." He recognized the butler, Williamson's voice just before the line went dead.

Alexander shrugged into his raincoat and put on his hat. As an after-thought, he took the Smith & Wesson from his desk drawer and put it in his coat pocket. He wondered what the old buzzard wanted with him on such a crappy night, but he assumed there would be money in it for him. There damn well better be, if the bastard insisted on dragging him out in such weather.

The storm was going full force by the time he reached the gates lead-ing to Blackman's place. Judging by the winds and the lightning, there had to be a tornado somewhere in the county. No doubt the tornado sirens were going full blast in the city proper—not that you could hear them out in the suburbs.

Just as his eggbeater coasted to a stop in the turn around, there was an eye-searing sheet of lightning, followed immediately by a massive, ear-splitting crash of thunder, and all the lights in the Blackman man-sion winked out.

Alexander turned up his collar and dashed for the front door. He could hear his knocks echo inside the house. He shouted Williamson's name, but there was no response. After a few seconds of repeated pounding on the door, he tried the handle. To his surprise, it was unlocked.

He stepped into the foyer, rainwater pouring off his sodden coat and hat. The interior of the house seemed, if possible, even bigger in the dark.

"Hello? Williamson? Mr.Blackman—? Anyone?"

Another crash of lightning flash-lit the foyer, making the stained glass eye glow for a brief heartbeat. Alexander cautiously made his way across the hall in the direction of the study. Halfway there his attention was snared by a glimpse of white at the head of the stairs.

"Mr. Blackman? I came as soon as I could—"

Lightning filled the hall with its blue-white glare, as if the world's largest flash-bulb had just been triggered. Standing at the head of the stairs, dressed in a floor-length ermine coat, was Celine Marchand.

"My husband's not here, Mr. Alexander. I'm the one who told Williamson to call you."

Before he could ask her what she wanted with him, she smiled and opened her coat. Underneath the white fur she was completely naked. Then the darkness returned, plunging everything into shadow. Still, her pale flesh seemed to glow, like a beacon drawing a lost ship home-ward—or to destruction on clashing rocks.

He was moving up the stairs as if in a dream, and even though he

44

knew that what he was doing was incredibly dangerous, there was no turning back, no breaking away. The smell of her perfume filled his senses, erasing everything except his need for her.

She lead him to the east wing. It was too dark to see anything, but he could tell the sheets on the bed were satin. When she came to him, it was like being wrapped in the heart of a flower. She tasted of honey and ginger and her kisses tingled against his flesh as if electric. He was drunk with her, his head swimming as if he'd just taken a hit off an opium pipe. It was good. No. It was better than good. It was real.

Dawn found the storm long past and Alexander alone amongst the satin sheets. The first thing he noticed upon opening his eyes were that the sheets were bright red, as was the carpeting. Disoriented, he sat up, rubbing the sleep from his eyes.

Celine turned from where she was standing in the window, looking out past the crimson drapes to the yard beyond. She was wearing the red silk kimono he'd seen her in a few nights before. "You're awake."

"Good morning to you, too," he smiled, stretching.

She returned his smile and nodded in the direction of the window. "The storm played hell with the grounds. There are tree limbs everywhere."

"Is the electricity back on?"

"I suspect power lines are down all over the county. But that doesn't really matter. There's a generator out in the shed. Williamson's seeing to it."

As if on cue, there a sudden hum and all the lights in the room surged back to life. Celine turned from the window and moved back to the bed. Alexander reached for her, but she slipped out of his grasp.

"Do you trust Williamson not to blab to your old man?"

"I trust him implicitly. We have history." She frowned and pulled away as he tried to embrace her again. "You better leave now. Ray will be back tonight. I don't want him to smell you on me. Or my sheets."

"Where is your hubby, by the by?"

"He had to leave town to talk to some very important people. He's trying to arrange a deal."

"What kind of deal?"

"He's trying to keep from going to jail."

Alexander raised an eyebrow. "For what? Wife-beating?"

Celine smiled humorlessly. "He received word a few days ago that he's being brought before a senate hearing committee."

"What—? Is he a red?"

"Be serious, Simon!" Celine muttered. She leaned across Alexander

45

and took a cigarette from a cut crystal canister on the nightstand.. "One of the senators received documents proving Amalcor knowingly sold substandard machine parts and other materials to the Defense Department during the war, defective ammunition in particular. An entire battalion was wiped out by the Nazis in `44 because of faulty ammo. Some of the soldiers were killed when their own guns exploded in their hands."

"Jesus!" Alexander grimaced. "Is that true?"

Celine lit her cigarette and exhaled, watching the smoke rise for a moment before speaking. "Of course it's true! Who do you think sent the senator those documents? My brother was one of those soldiers. His head was nearly ripped off his shoulders when his gun blew up! Johnny was only twenty-two when he died."

Alexander stared at her for a long moment. In the cold light of morning Celine was still beautiful, but now he could see the pain and the anger in those electric blue eyes of hers. "Did—did you know that when you married him?"

"No. No, I didn't. It wasn't until a month ago I found out the truth."

"That's when you started giving lover boy the cold shoulder."

She nodded and stubbed out her cigarette. "When I saw those papers, something inside me died. To think I'd been sharing a bed all this time with the man responsible for my kid brother's death! The very thought of him touching me was enough to make me sick!"

"Does he suspect you're the one who fed the senate committee the evidence?"

"No. He was more worried I was fooling around. Ray doesn't think I can do anything except spend money and screw. Besides, he doesn't know about my brother. If he suspected me of being involved in this, I'd be dead even faster than if I was cheating on him."

"How is he planning to keep out of jail?"

"He's gotten to a couple of the members of the committee. That's where he was this weekend—meeting with them to work out a deal. They want one hundred and fifty thou apiece to clear his name. I'm sure he agreed. Ray's very good at keeping himself out of real trouble."

"Like avoiding being charged with murder?"

Celine suddenly got up and went and sat at her make-up table. Although her back was to him, he could see her face in the vanity mirror. There was genuine concern in her eyes as she nervously sorted through the collection of cosmetics in front of her. "I shouldn't have told you that! If he ever finds out you know about his first wife—"

"But he won't find out, will he?" Alexander replied, sliding out of bed. "You're not going to tell him, are you? And I'm sure as hell not going to—so what are you worried about?"

Celine picked up a tube of lipstick and began to outline her lips, her hands as steady as a heart surgeon's. "Ray has his ways of finding things out, Simon. He's a ruthless son of a bitch—and he's not afraid to hurt people. Even the ones he loves." She set aside the lipstick tube and pulled a sheet of tissue paper out of a nearby caddie to blot her lips. "So imagine what he'll do to someone like you!"

Alexander shrugged his shoulders, trying not to look intimidated. "I used to know a girl who always wore this shade of lipstick," he commented as he picked up the lipstick, idly turning it over in his hands.

Celine raised a perfectly sculpted eyebrow "Really? Was she your girlfriend?"

"Kinda. It was a long time ago—before the war."

"Was she pretty?" Celine was staring at his reflection in the mirror. There was a strange intensity in those blue eyes of hers that made him not want to meet her gaze, even indirectly.

He shrugged and tossed the lipstick back onto the vanity. "I guess so. She was just a kid, really. She died back in `40. I signed up with the Army the day after she croaked. I was drunk as a skunk, but that didn't keep Uncle Sam from taking me. But you've got nothing to worry about—she was nothin' like you, babe!"

"I wouldn't be so sure."

"Huh?"

"We both fancied you, didn't we?" she smiled, her eyes twinkling.

Alexander leaned forward, wrapping his arms around her as he nuzzled her neck. "You really are something, Celine! I don't know if I could ever get enough of you!"

She returned his kisses then pulled away. "You better go. Like I said, Ray is due back today. I can't run the risk of him finding out about us—'

"When I think of him touching you—hurting you—it makes my stomach clench like a fist," he whispered, running his fingers through her silky hair. "It's not right, Celine. It's just not right."

The look on her face was so cold and far away it made the hairs on the back of his neck prickle. "I learned early in life that there's a lot that's not right in the world. My old man was a no-good drunken bum who used to treat my mom and me and my kid brother and sister like we were his private punching bags. Mom died when I was ten. I spent most of my childhood looking after the others and trying to keep dad away from spending what money we had on booze. He died five years later of cirrhosis, leaving us kids to shift for ourselves. That was fourteen years ago. And now I'm the only one left."

"I-I'm sorry, Celine."

The smile on her face was the same one she'd worn in the wedding photo sitting on her husband's desk. "Yeah—aren't we all?"

He couldn't get her out of his head. No matter how hard he tried, every time he looked inside himself, there she was. He never thought about a broad for more than a day or two, tops. But here it was a going on a week and she was still lodged in his brain like a catchy melody that won't let you alone. He found himself brooding over how Blackman treated her like she was some kind of wind-up music box, like the kid's story about the emperor and the nightingale. That the old bastard thought he had her voices under lock and key bothered him the more he thought about it. And he thought about it a lot, as he lay in his unmade bed, staring up at the ceiling instead of sleeping.

On the rare occasions he would drift into sleep, he'd start awake, convinced he had caught a whiff of White Shoulders or felt the caress of satin sheets. He'd frantically look around the room, but all he saw were piles of dirty laundry and ashtrays full of cigarette butts.

It was after midnight when the phone pulled him out of a drunken slumber. He clawed the receiver off the hook and mumbled something into the mouthpiece that might have been "hello", might have been "who the hell is it?"—he couldn't be sure.

The sound of her voice, distorted by sobs and hysteria, was enough to snap him into full wakefulness.

"Simon, you've got to help me, Simon! He's out of his mind! He found out! God help me, he found out! He started hitting me and hitting me! Williamson tried to make him stop, b-but Rayford turned on him instead! Oh God, I think he killed him, Simon! I think Rayford killed Williamson! I was able to get away and locked myself in the study—that's where I'm calling you from, but I don't think I can—" There was a splintering crash in the background and Celine screamed once, then the line went dead.

Alexander leapt out of bed and grabbed his gun and his shoes. He drove to Blackman's estate in record time, all the while trying to force the visions of Celine's battered body being hurled down the stairs out of his head. He wasn't going to let the bastard kill her like he had his first wife.

The gates to the mansion were standing wide open, but he was too concerned for Celine's welfare to notice. He was halfway out of the car before it came to a halt in the drive, yelling out her name as he dashed for the front entrance. The huge oaken door was unlocked and the grand foyer as dark as it was the night of the storm, the only illumination coming through the stained glass skylight. And there, in a multi-colored pool of moonlight, lay a ominously still figure.

"Celine!"

Alexander rushed forward to where the prone figure lay sprawled. His heart was hammering so fast it felt as if it had stopped beating altogether. He had felt such panic only twice before: the day his buddy, Carlo, caught a sniper's bullet at Anzio, and the night Lilly died. As he knelt beside the body, he was relieved to discover it was that of the butler, Williamson. Blood still leaked from the corner of his mouth onto the marble floor. The poor bastard had apparently given his life for his mistress—but where was Celine? And, more importantly, what had Blackman done to her?

He got his answer in the form of a scream from Blackman's study. The door was hanging off its hinges, the lock splintered, as if someone had used a battering ram against it. Alexander leapt to his feet, pulling his .38 from its holster, and ran in the direction of Celine's voice. He prayed he wasn't too late. If that murdering rat bastard had hurt her, he'd pay with his miserable life!

The interior of the study was in shambles. The only light was from the desk lamp, which lay on its side on the carpet. Papers were scattered all over the desk and floor, books tipped out of their cases, and the wall safe was sitting wide open. Celine was in the far corner of the room, dressed in her blue Dior gown, pressed against the bookshelf and the wall, one hand raised as if trying to shield herself from a blow. Her hair was tangled and there were bruises on her lovely face. Alexander's brain was filled with a rage as red as the blood smearing her perfect lips. She had yet to notice him, her fear-glazed eyes focused on something Alexander could not see.

"Celine," Blackman said, his voice strangely calm for a man who'd just killed his butler and beaten his wife. He stepped out of the shadows, looming before his terrified wife like one of the beasts whose heads decorated the walls. He was wearing red silk pajama bottoms and holding a gun in one hand. He took a step toward Celine, his tone still eerily calm. "Don't be afraid, sweetie. I'm not going to hurt you—"

"Blackman!"

The older man spun on his heel, bringing the muzzle of the .45 up faster than Alexander thought possible. There was the sound of thunder and the stink of cordite and he was slammed against the expensive wood paneling. As he slipped to the floor, all he could think was how it felt as if someone had put out a cigar on his shoulder and hit him in with a sledge hammer at the same time.

Everything went gray around the edges for a moment, then he was revived by the fragrance of White Shoulders.

"C-Celine?"

She was hovering over him, her face filling his vision like the moon. He was slumped against the wall, his right shoulder a throbbing mess of pain. His collarbone was shattered, but otherwise nothing vital had been hurt.

"You're alive," she said. She sounded surprised, but far from relieved.

"Like they say in the movies, sugar; it's just a flesh wound," he groaned. "Blackman? Is he—?"

Celine went over to where her husband's body lay sprawled in a pool of red. She knelt beside him, picking up his gun.

"He's dead. You got him right through the heart."

"Lucky me." He struggled to stand, but fell back dizzy. The pain in his shoulder was making his mouth dry and his head swim. "Honey, could you phone for an ambulance? I need some medical attention…"

Instead of going to the phone, Celine drew back her foot and kicked Alexander squarely in the balls with her high-heel shoes. Alexander cried out in pain as he clutched himself. Celine quickly snatched up his dropped gun and moved back out of arm's reach.

"You crazy bitch! What the hell did you do that for--?" he choked out.

"I did it for Lilly."

Alexander stopped rocking back and forth, the agony in his shoulder and crotch telescoping down to nothing. He looked up at Celine, who stood holding Blackman's gun pointed at him.

"W-what did you say?"

"You heard me, Simon. I did it for my baby sister."

"I-I don't understand—"

"I told you there were three kids in my family. I was the oldest. My brother Johnny was two years younger than me; my sister, Lilly, was four. I believe you knew Lilly, Simon—quite well, actually."

"Lilly—Lilly was your sister? But your name isn't—"

"Marsh?" Celine finished for him, sneering in contempt. "You're a private detective, Alexander—haven't you heard of aliases—or stage names? When I started working nightclubs in `39 I changed my name to Celine Marchand. Sounds a lot classier than Selma Marsh, don't you think?"

"Oh, god—"

"Lilly was only sixteen when she met you, Alexander. She was working as a waitress at some greasy spoon, trying to save up enough money so she could go to night school. But you know that already, don't you? What I bet you don't know is that she wrote me about you. You weren't a detective back then, were you? You were just a lousy truck driver. But you were older than her. You were twenty-two—I know that doesn't seem like much now, but to her you were King Solomon and Clark Gable rolled into one! You were her world, damn you!"

"Celine—I'm sorry—It was an accident! I swear to god, I never wanted to hurt Lilly—"

"*What* was an accident? Her getting pregnant? I don't blame you for that—those things happen. But what about later? It was your idea to take her to that butcher, wasn't it? Answer me! Wasn't it?"

"Y-yes."

"Even that I can forgive. But not what came later. What happened, Alexander? Did she start to hemorrhage before or after the doctor left the hotel room you rented for the job? Was she dead when you left her? Or was she still alive?"

"Celine—You don't understand--"

The tip of her shoe caught him in the ribs, knocking him onto the floor. "What I understand, you miserable son of a bitch, is that you left a sixteen-year-old girl to bleed to death alone!" As he rolled onto his back, she brought her high heel down on his wounded shoulder, grinding the point into the bullet hole. Alexander screamed until the thought his lungs would burst. Celine stepped back, the gun remaining level with his head. "Is that how she sounded, Simon? Is that how my sister screamed when that quack perforated her uterus?"

"Celine—"

"Shut up! I don't want to hear your pathetic excuses! They're nine years too late, anyway. God, it was so long ago and it seems like yesterday! I still remember how the cops smirked when Johnny and I came to identify the body. Like it was her fault she was dead. One of them even asked me if she was a prostitute or just a whore! They wanted to know the boyfriend's name, but I didn't give it to them, even though I knew it was you. Johnny and I were going to take care of you ourselves. But when we stopped by your place, the landlady said you had left with no forwarding address.

"We had to get on with our lives after that, Johnny and me. But just when things finally started to look good for us, Johnny's number came up. The next thing I know it's `44 and I get this telegram from the War Department telling me that Johnny's been killed. A couple of years later I find out about Blackman's dirty little secret. That's when I began working on my little scheme.

"You weren't supposed to live, you know. The plan was for you and Blackman to blow each other away. I guess the old fool's age was creeping up on him, after all. That was the beauty of it all—that the two men I hated most of all would conveniently kill one another, each of them thinking they were defending me!"

"What?" Alexander rasped, blinking in confusion.

"You know, the funny thing is—Ray actually was a good husband," she said with a smirk. "He doted on me, waited on me hand and foot."

"But—the bruises—? What about his first wife?"

"Appearances can be deceiving, Simon." Celine grinned, pulling a hanky from her cleavage and wiping the bruises off her face. "Geraldine did die from falling down the stairs—but it was because she was a souse! Ray covered it up because him having a dipso wife would look bad in the papers. And as for the bruises—well, he never raised a hand against me—unless I wanted it that way."

Alexander closed his eyes, more to try and deny the horrible reality of what was being said than to block out the pain. Celine only laughed and kept on talking.

"I got Hank Shearer to introduce me to Blackman at a party back in `46. Getting him to marry me was a piece of cake. Getting you involved was a little tricky, though. It was important to make it seem as if I had no connection to you whatsoever. I didn't want Ray to get suspicious—at least not for the wrong reasons. Then, when Hank had his problem with that blackmailing little nellie, I recommended that he go to you, knowing he would drop your name with Ray when the time came. It's pitifully easy to manipulate men—even homosexual ones.

"Men accuse women of being controlled by their emotions, all the while being lead around by their egos and lust! You know something, Simon—? I can understand how Lilly fell for you. You're good-looking, a smooth talker, and not bad between the sheets. But I'm not an innocent, lovestruck sixteen-year-old kid."

"If you hate me so much, why did you seduce me?"

"Isn't it obvious? I needed you to kill Ray! And you can't set a trap without laying down some bait. Once you had calmed my husband's fears and assured him I was a good little wife, I set about arranging this little scenario. Ray always goes to bed early on the week nights. That's why we had separate bedrooms. He was sound asleep when I called you. He didn't even wake up when I wrecked the study to make it look like it was ransacked by burglars! I waited until I saw your lights coming up the dive—only then did I scream loud enough to wake him. I knew he kept a gun in his night-table. He came running to my rescue, just as you were pulling up in the drive."

"And Williamson?"

She shrugged. "Window dressing, really. I needed both of you to think I was in genuine danger, whether it was from blood-thirsty intruders or a jealous husband."

"You're crazy—if you think you can get away—with this—" he gritted through his teeth. "How do you expect to explain all this to the cops?"

"Maybe I will. Maybe I won't. And I'm not planning on explaining anything. I left in my car for a two week stay at a health farm in New Mexico a few hours ago. At least that's my story. They can check with the spa—I booked myself a room over a month ago. Maybe someone will find Ray before I get back, maybe not. I know how cops like their cases handed to them on a silver platter. If it looks like Rayford Blackman died protecting his home from a burglar, then that's what they'll write in their reports. You're a shady customer, Simon. Everybody knows that." She walked over to where Blackman's body lay, looking down at his dead face as if studying a mildly interesting sculpture. "My husband hired you for a little detective work. You saw where he kept his money and got the bright idea of helping yourself. The rest is simple enough for the stupidest flat-foot to piece together."

"Except you forgot one thing—" Alexander grunted, as he staggered to his feet. "I'm not dead."

"Oh, yes, you are, Simon." she smiled, turning back to face him, aiming Blackman's gun at his chest. "Didn't you know? You've been dead since 1940."

Once the gunsmoke cleared, Celine carefully wiped her fingerprints from both her husband and Alexander's guns, and placed them in the dead men's hands, making sure their cooling fingers were wrapped about the triggers. She then went to the safe and took out a fistful of money and some jewelry—she decided the blue diamond necklace Ray had given her for their second anniversary would do nicely—and shoved them inside Alexander's raincoat pocket.

The rest of the three hundred thousand Blackman had set aside for buying off the senators she scooped into a satchel. There was no record of the money, and normally Blackman never kept more than a ten thousand cash in the safe at any time. Still, for a gumshoe like Alexander, ten grand would be seem a big score. One worth some risks. At least that's what the cops would think. If they bothered to think at all.

She stepped over Alexander's body, careful not to track his blood out of the room. She made a mental note to ditch the Dior and matching shoes before crossing into New Mexico. She could always get new

53

ones later. Her high heels tapped against the marble floor as she strode across the empty foyer. As she opened the heavy front door, she noticed the lock had been expertly jimmied. She smiled to her self and hurried to where the Dusenberg waited, its engine idling.

"Is it done?" Williamson asked from behind the wheel.

"Would I be here if it weren't?" she laughed, tossing the satchel full of money into the back seat. "There was a little trouble, but I cleared it up. You did a good job on the door—what about the front gate?"

"I didn't have to do much. Most of the relays were fried during the storm and hadn't been fixed yet."

"Good. That'll make it easier for the cops to figure out how he got in. I don't want any clever dick puzzling things out for himself."

A grim satisfaction crossed the butler's face. "They can rest easy now. Johnny, your sister, my buddies—they're at peace. I can feel it. When I came to your dressing room back in`46, all I was looking for was someone to hear me out—to listen to what I had to say about what happened that day we went up against the Krauts and not tell me I was lying or crazy. And when you told me your plan to get back at Blackman, I never dreamed you'd be able to pull it off. But I should never have doubted Johnny. He said you had the smarts and the guts to get whatever you wanted, and he was right."

Celine smiled and touched his face. "I couldn't have done it without you, Jim. We make a great team, don't you think?" Her brow suddenly creased and she pulled the hanky from her cleavage and daubed at a red stain at the corner of his mouth. "Hold still. You've still got some raspberry topping on you."

"I was pretty convincing, huh? Think I have a future on the stage?"

Celine laughed and tucked the soiled hanky back between her breasts. "I think you better put this chariot in gear! Remember, I have a reservation at a health spa to make!"

As Williamson eased up on the clutch he shook his head and shot her a look of pure admiration. "You're a good sister, Selma."

"Believe me, honey," she sighed, "goodness had nothing to do with it."

# the bookkeeper
## by dan shanley

I went up to the bar, ordered a scotch on the rocks and looked around the room. It was a dive, full of a bunch of losers and drunks. Smoke was all the air there was and the floor hadn't been swept since before the place was built. The table next to the wall near the stage, the meeting place, was still empty. I looked at my watch and it agreed with me–he was late. I took my drink and went to the table to wait. I had a feeling he wouldn't show. He'd stiffed me twice that week already. Extenuating circumstances, he said.

I didn't want to look like a cop, so I had dressed down–just like drinking when I was on duty. I had to blend in. I had also picked a bar out of my jurisdiction. I've busted too many to go undetected on my side of town. Of course, not knowing the area too well, not to mention this particular spot, I felt like a fish in the wrong pond, and I didn't know which sharks to keep an eye on, or where the riptides were. But going so far from where our action was was the only way I could get him to show up.

The lights dimmed and the stage lit up. I checked my watch again. The curtains opened to reveal a sultry dame in a sparkling red dress. Every man in the place went nuts, and I hooted like one of the boys. She started into a song, a real slow one, with a voice that slid through the smoke in the air and the din in your ears. She was just a kid, but she'd been doing this enough to know what she was doing.

Right behind her at the piano was this short, shrewd, mousy twerp in a monkey suit. He played like he was one up on every guy in the room, like he knew everything about her and more. But looking at him, I knew she was smarter than that. I looked at him too long, and his eyes looked up and found mine. I realized I was just in reach of the stage lights. I stared him down, and he looked away. Twerp.

I actually started paying attention to the songbird, the way she seemed to be looking at every joe there like it was just him and her in a private room. The way she swayed her hips and shoulders made me regret my late nights and my empty apartment.

"Enjoying the show, Lieutenant Parsons?" I shot a look to my left and saw him sitting where there was an empty chair before. "And drinking while on duty? Tsk, tsk..."

He was looking toward the stage, but his mind was elsewhere. Last time I saw him, he had on a pair of reading glasses and a tiny little mustache. That was all gone and replaced by a clean-shaven man in a big hat and a high-collar coat. Sure, the last time I saw him was through a pair of binoculars at a guy huddled over a ledgerbook, but just like me, he didn't want his friends and enemies coming up to him and saying hello. He had a little smile on him that was supposed to make him look confident, but he wasn't fooling anyone but himself, and maybe not even him.

"Where the hell did you come from, Webster?"

"I've just been sitting here quietly, watching you admire the young lady."

I ignored his comment. I didn't even see him sitting three feet from me. I didn't think my detective work was that rusty.

"I should think you understand, Lieutenant, that I can't afford to make too big an entrance. Did you think I would have the bouncer announce my arrival?"

Cocky bastard. I looked back at the stage while the band was setting up for the next number, but I kept talking to my guest.

"Still, you're late. I was startin' to wonder if you were gonna show up at all."

"Patience, Lieutenant, patience. As important as our business together may be, I hardly think it should be subjected to too rigid a schedule."

"Damn right it's important. We're not exactly picking out curtains here. You just make me nervous, that's all."

"In that case, perhaps we should get down to business. Who knows when they'll check in to see if I'm gone."

"OK. Where's that book of yours?"

"It's tucked away in a very safe place. They won't know it's gone until noon tomorrow."

"Fine. What time would you like to go downtown an' see the DA with me? I can make an appointment."

"A bit public, don't you think? I was hoping to avoid that."

"It's either that or a subpoena."

He chuckled and shook his head. "That won't do either of us any good. They'll find out and I'll ... Let's just say I can't accept an invitation that is quite so forward."

"Then an appointment it is. When's good for you? My afternoons are booked, but I can squeeze you in before my morning coffee. "

I turned my head to see what he was staring at, and found myself staring down the piano player again, sitting still with the commotion of the band around him. The twerp looked away again. I looked back to Webster. For the first time, Webster looked away from the stage, around the room. We were lost in a crowd of strangers. "Couldn't we just set up a series of meetings like this one? Overall, I think I would be worth more to you that way."

"I don't think I need that much information over a long period of time. All I need is that book and you to describe the transactions line by line. One appointment, and we're done with you. After that, you can take our protection or you're on your own, I don't care. Just tell me what I want to know now, or tomorrow morning in the DA's office."

"So I can—oh what do you call it—'sing,' right? Like a canary?"

This guy was getting on my nerves. "Yeah, that's right."

"It's so easy for you, Lieutenant. When all this comes out, they're not going to come looking for you."

"That's why, it seems to me, you should want to get.out all at once, and not be around when they do come looking for you."

He started looking around again. He still hadn't looked at me.

"Is there somewhere we could speak more privately?"

"What for?"

"Being seen in public together is hardly good for your image or mine. Or ours."

I didn't understand. I figured the whole reason he agreed to meet me here was to keep himself safe. No one was going to hit him in a crowded room. But I was tired of playing games with this chump. I threw two bucks on the table and looked around for the songbird, but of course she wasn't there. I led Webster outside and down one door, up two flights of stairs to a cheap hotel room right over the bar. I had reserved it so that I could meet my partner later, and in case we needed to protect our canary as soon as tonight.

I kept my eyes peeled around every corner, with every step. I examined every creaky door we passed, and on the old and smelly carpet at every flake of paint that looked like it had been on the wall the last time I was there. I knew I shoulda had my partner here already. I was nervous as hell, and so it only bothered me more that Webster was so calm and cool. But he was walking slowly, like he just happened to be wandering the same place I was going. When I got a chance to look him in the eye, he didn't seem to care. He was somewhere else.

I had already seen the room, but it still struck me as a dump, even compared to my office downtown. A single light bulb hanging from the ceiling lit the room as much as it could. A broken mattress with a thin sheet sat in the corner on a rickety frame, and a table and chair sat in the other corner. I had moved both the bed and the table away from the window so my new friend couldn't be too easy a shot. There was a door in the far wall leading to the can, but from the smell I was too scared to go in, even with my gun. I hadn't seen or heard any rats, but I knew they were there.

I went to the phone on the bedstand and called my partner. I told him to come on over, and to bring a couple plainclothes cops for backup. I hung up and found Webster sitting in a chair, staring across the room at the wall.

"That was my partner," I told him. "He's coming over with some added protection. He's also making that appointment, but we can always reschedule if you're a late sleeper."

"That won't be necessary. All you need to know is in the ledger book. There are no code names or secret notation, it's rather straight forward. You won't need any assistance from me."

"You're not backing out on me, are you Webster?"

"No, I'm merely proposing a trade. A different transaction."

"I'm not here for just the book. We still need you. It's that little problem of making evidence stick. That book's just a dime store novel to any judge without your testimony."

"But I'm a security risk. You can hide and transport that book a lot easier than you can me. Besides, they won't come looking for the book after you have it. Records are easily forged and changed." He looked at me for the first time. "I, however, am not as easily rewritten. And they won't stop looking for me."

"Hey, wait a minute. If you just wanted to hand over the book, why did you come at all? And you don't think they're gonna let you live if you're around and the book isn't? Just what are you trying to cook up?"

"If you would like, I could ask around a few of my colleagues. I'm not the only one acquainted with the books, and perhaps someone else would be more willing."

"Cold feet? Or just a change of heart?"

"Perhaps I simply feel that I am not the man for this job. Perhaps I don't feel that I can—"

"What, rat on the boys?"

He looked me straight in the eye. "They've done a great deal for me, Lieutenant Parsons. They look out for me and take care of me."

"That doesn't change the fact that they're crooks. Pimps. Killers."

"I didn't say that I was proud of the work of my associates. That's why I suggested perhaps getting in touch with someone else. That way you can still do your job without me being involved."

"Hell, Webster, you'll still be involved, all right! If someone else sings for us, you'll wind up in the pen with the rest of your bodyguard hoods!"

"I can live with that!"

"Can ya? Goin' to jail's better than bein' the rat, huh?"

"Would you ever take a bullet for one of your fellow officers, Lieutenant Parsons?"

"I have, Webster. What of it?"

"I've met my share of law enforcement, and I can safely say that they haven't all been model citizens. Everyone has their secrets, don't they Lieutenant? Everyone has a weak spot. I'm sure there are plenty of police officers who drink too much, lie to the boss, conveniently forget the rights of someone in handcuffs and deliver an extra kick...perhaps beat their wife now and then?"

"Yeah, you get a few of those. We're just ordinary people. So?"

"You would take a bullet for the average man that just happens to be a police officer?"

"You're defendin' the worst crooks in the city because they look out for you?!"

"Just because they don't hide their secrets, their weak spots, as well as your colleagues, they're not worth defending?"

"You got a sick sense o' loyalty!"

"Can you blame me, Lieutenant? They treat me better than you do."

"You'll never be wondering when I'm gonna blow your brains out! Can you say that about them?"

But he'd clammed up again, just looked back at the wall. I shook my head and headed for the can. I couldn't look at that guy anymore, and there comes a time when nature's call inspires great courage, enough even to go into a bathroom like that. I turned on the light and looked in the mirror. From where I stood, I could still see Webster sitting in the corner. What the hell was I going to do with this mug? I decided to wait for my partner to show up with a new perspective.

There was a knock on the door, but it wasn't the right knock. Webster called "Yes?" It took me just a second to pull my gun, but it turned out to be one second too many. I heard the door as it was broken open, and I saw Webster stand up and face the door. Two shots from a .45, and Webster flew back into the corner. I looked at his body, again for one second too many. With gun in hand, I rushed out into the hall, to find no one there. Just peeling paint and weak light bulbs.

I went back into the room and looked at Webster again. That superior yet nervous smile that had driven me crazy was unrecognizable. I went to the window and saw my partner's car rounding the corner. I looked down at the front door of the hotel under me and saw a hood in an overcoat come out and holster his gun. I fired without aiming, as did my partner from his car. The hood ducked into the bar. I ran down the back stairs into the bar to meet the hood and met my partner instead. We searched the building, but I already knew he was gone.

My partner looked at me, and I knew the look on my face told him everything. I scanned the room, hoping to find anything, but all I saw was a bunch of stupid looking losers and an empty piano bench, and next to it a dame in a sparkling red dress, leaning on the piano, not a bit surprised.

No book. No bookkeeper. No case. And a bar I could never go back to again. I left the backup to clean up the mess and got into my partner's car to go back downtown.

# to serve and protect
## by jack norris

It was Myerson's voice that brought Vince out of his absent-minded state of cigar-puffing and watching the slouching young man with the ragged clothes disappear into the fast approaching night.

"Okay, Lieutenant, the M.E.'s on his way and we've got the evidence tagged and ready to go." The young officer was still beaming about his discovery of the wallet that closed the case. The way he saw it, he just saved the taxpayers thousands in court costs and the police an extended manhunt for a man who was already dead.

Vince turned to face the self-confident young detective with a look of annoyance only time could cultivate.

Myerson's grin faded.

"What's wrong, sir? We got him and the case's closed." The young man still thought he was right, but Vince was his superior and if he didn't look happy then something told the detective he shouldn't be either.

"Don't be so happy about an ending like this. That Cooper kid may have been bad, but his old man was one of the finest cops I'd ever seen. He deserved better than what he got and until the gavel falls and the jury cries guilty, you have to remember that maybe his boy did too." Vince's words cut sharp into the young man before him, each one blasting away at Myerson's five long months of experience, and leaving him a fresh-faced rookie cop again.

Vince turned away in disgust. Damn rookies thinking they can shove the world into little plastic bags and find the meaning of life at the end of their Academy textbooks. They should all...

*No. Let's be honest, shall we, Vince?* The voice in the back of his head put an end to his self-righteous tirade almost as quickly as he had started it. *You're no more mad at Myerson than you are at Cooper, or anybody else. You're mad at yourself.*

Vince smiled slightly to himself and sighed. Yeah, okay. He was mad at himself. He couldn't be mad at Myerson. It was the rookie's lack of experience and gung-ho attitude that had made Vince choose him to head up the investigation of the scene. He had wanted the kid to screw up and jump to unfounded conclusions. If he got a bit too happy about it, it should have come as no surprise. It wasn't Myerson at all. It was him.

He made a decision today. A decision that no law, rules, or conventional moral code will accept or validate. He chose to let a wanted man escape the law. Not because he had a gun in his face or because there were hostages at risk. No, he let him go because of the look in the man's eye and the feeling in his own gut had told him to. He had thrown the system by the wayside to satisfy a hunch, and now he was going to do it again so that a young man could ruin his life on revenge.

Of course even that was just another hunch. In fact, there was only one thing that he was certain would come of this entire mess, and that was that people would die. It may be Joe Cooper's kid or the rat-bastards that killed his dad. It may even be a cop or some innocent bystander. Whoever it was, when the blood began to flow some of it would fall on Vince's hands, and all he could do about it was hope he was right. Right about the old cop's death, right about the look on the kid's face when he let him go, and right about the feeling in his gut that told him the blood that he would one day have to wash away was the type that would come off with a little soap and water.

"Lieutenant? You okay?" Myerson looked like a scared puppy now, the kind that's too dumb to know why he got scolded but is still afraid of accidentally repeating his offense.

Vince stuffed the cigar back into his mouth and drew himself upright as if shrugging a large weight of his shoulders.

"Sure, kid," he grabbed the car keys out of his coat pocket and tossed them to the rookie. "Here, you drive." He smiled slightly as they bounced off the young cop's chest and dropped to the ground. He left Myerson groping at the earth for his keys as he opened the door to his sedan and slid into the passenger's seat.

"Christ," he muttered to himself. Rookie cops who can't smell a set-up, vigilante cab drivers out for justice, good cops six feet under with slugs in their chests and a river of blood on the horizon so close he could almost see it as clearing as the red clouds that lingered after the fading sunset.

"I fear for the future." He rasped from beneath a stream of smoke.

"What's that, sir?" Myerson had found the keys and was peering in through the open driver's side window.

"Nothing, kid. Nothing, just get in and drive."

In a week Myerson was dead.

The rookie had gone into investigate reports of a homicide near the shipyards of North Marine and had come away with two bullets in his chest. The perp had been a sailor, just another kid who had a little leave time and too much rotgut to be trusted with the pistol he'd been carrying. He'd picked up a girl and tried to have his fun before his ship sailed again. As luck would have it, when his companion's husband came home and started threatening certain parts of his anatomy with a cleaver, the kid did the predictably stupid thing and emptied six slugs from a cheap thirty-eight into him. By the time Myerson burst in with his badge in one hand and high ideals in the other, the sailor was completely out of his mind with paranoia about imprisonment and death. Unfortunately for Myerson, the one thing he wasn't out of was ammunition.

The coroner had said it was quick. He didn't say instantaneous or painless, just quick. "Instantaneous" or "painless" meant that it hit you so fast you didn't have time to do anything but fall to the ground and die. It had been that way for the poor broad's husband, but not for the young detective. No, it was only "quick". "Quick" was different; it meant that you had enough time for it to hurt more than anything you've ever felt, curl yourself up around the wounds that have insulted your otherwise healthy young body, and mutter at least a short prayer for an end to the pain. For the sailor it wasn't even "quick," but that's the end a cop-killer can expect in this town. Enough years on the force will teach you things like that. Vince had enough years on the force to know these things, and enough extra to know that none of it did a damn bit of good to anybody. It was all death, and that never helped anybody but the undertakers.

It rained on the day of the funeral, but the crowd was still big enough for passersby to look across the gravestones at the ceremony and wonder who important died. That was one of the main perks of being a cop in the City. Even if no one knew you in life, you could count on a fair number of your brother officers to join you in death. To most, this was only a tradition, but others saw it as a form of insurance. Vince could see both these feelings in the looks of the many officers who gazed on the casket from a sea of blue uniforms and polished badges. Some were those of regret and sorrow, but just as many were the looks of those who hoped that their presence somehow guaranteed an equally respectable turnout when it was their turn to be the mourned instead of the mourner.

Vince hadn't bothered to wear his dress blues for the ceremony. Sure, Myerson had been one of his men and he'd spent more time with the kid than just about anybody else on that muddy field, but when it came right down to it he was a plainclothes cop, just like the kid, and it seemed a bit dishonest to get all dolled up just to make a show of something he shouldn't have lived to see.

Myerson's family gathered near the flag-covered box that held their son, nephew, or whatever. They looked as sad as anyone who lost a boy to an end like that would, but the rain and the warm summer mists mixed with their tears, diluting them and making the whole affair somehow less than heart-wrenching. There was too much water to tell the teardrops from the raindrops, and Vince saw that even his own kin couldn't help trying to speed through the affair to get on with their grief in a much more pleasant and drier locale.

After the minister had said his words, Vince saw his own brother Harry walk forward and say a few words over the departed. He, at least Vince knew, was sincere in his sorrow. Harry had never known Myerson before today. He probably hadn't even seen the boy while he was alive, except perhaps in a crowd of young faces at the academy graduation ceremonies. Still, Harry was the Chief, and he took every man and woman in his command to heart. Vince always thought this was to make up for all the young men he lost during the War, but there as some things even a brother never can say for sure. Still he could say to anyone who would have asked that the crack in Harry Vincent's voice and the pained look in his eyes as he spoke of death, duty, and sacrifice were as real as the body in the casket, the rain on the field, and the sounds of the gunshots that echoed off the stone after the speeches were done.

After the service ended, the crowd quickly dispersed to more pleasant places. Places where they could shake off the wet of the rain and the gloom of a young man's funeral. Vince had been invited to the family's wake, but he had dodged this responsibility just as he had the request to say "a few words" at the service. He had attended enough wakes and said enough words after his stint as a sergeant in the War and in his years since returning that he didn't even need to take part to know how such things would be handled.

He was good man. It's always a shame to lose one so young as Myerson. No, that's not right...Doug, that had been the boy's name. Man, Vince you'd think you'd never buried anybody before...

*No, that's okay, Mrs. Myerson, I've got enough coffee. How well did I know your son? Well, other than the harsh criticisms that most rookies get from us veterans, and giving him that advice that he threw out the window right before he got plugged, I must confess I don't know much about the boy. And of course there was that phony case I threw him because I knew he'd close it up without any messy questions. Top of his class in high school? Really, that just makes it all the more tragic doesn't it?*

"Oh shut up." Vince muttered aloud to those dark voices that gnawed at his brain. He didn't want to turn this tragedy into a farce, not even if it would make him feel better.

64

"Well, that's a fine way to talk to your own flesh and blood!" The clear strong voice brought Vince out of himself and back to the muddy fields and gravestones.

"Hello, Harry."

The Chief of Police stood before his brother in his medal laden uniform. His clear blue eyes looked wearily at his younger sibling, but there was no hint of weakness in his stance or his voice as he addressed the only man on the force who he regularly let call him by his given name.

"Hello, Vince." He stepped forward and to the side to let the shelter of his umbrella loom over both of them. Vince smiled slightly at this.

"Forever the big brother. Afraid I'll catch cold?" Vince quipped, though he did not scoff so much as to pass up the dry moment to light a fresh cigar.

Harry grunted as he had since as longer than he had been a cop. His grunts were the only thing about him older than his uniform, his medals, or the piece of enemy lead in his shoulder that still made him wince a bit as he gestured back to the hole in the ground that had swallowed Myerson's casket minutes before.

"Nasty business, that." Vince nodded as he inhaled deeply and blew a plume of smoke out from underneath the umbrella.

"Was the boy married? I didn't hear any mention of a wife, but the young lady with his family..."

"That was his sister. They were supposedly pretty close." Harry's nod showed a deep understanding. Of all the people at the ceremony, the Vincents understood family bonds. Family bonds and grief.

"So, what's going on, big brother?"

Harry turned his gaze to meet his sibling's. He stared at the premature grey hair and the lines that etched Vince's face at a picture of hardship and strain. This was hardly a surprise. Vince was several years younger and respected as a great cop, but when it came right down to it, so many people still saw him as the burnt-out younger brother of the most successful policeman in the city's history. For a moment, Vince even thought he saw a bit of pity before the Chief opened his mouth to speak.

"I was going to meet Connie for lunch, but something's come up." He looked at Vince expectantly; waiting for him to voice the offer he knew was coming. The fact that anybody knew him so well was irritating, even coming from his own brother.

"Sure, I've got an hour or so, and it'd be nice to see the kid again." He drew again off his cigar and blew a plume of smoke around his head as he looked around, expecting to see the young woman materialize at the mention of her name.

Harry picked up on Vince's inquisitive gesture and replied, "She's gone to pay her respects at the wake. I was supposed to meet her there."

When Vince turned back to looked at his brother his gaze had gone cold. Harry had figured out that he'd no intention of going to the boy's wake and had figured out a way to make him show up anyway. Harry was his brother and he loved him dearly, but he could still really piss him off with his "big brother knows best" bullshit.

That's the problem with family, Vince. They know you too well for you to really like them.

"Couldn't you just order me to go? It'd be much easier to complain about then." Vince paused to stamp out his cigar in mock disgust. After all, if he was really so angry, he'd have just walked.

"Come on, Vince. He was one of yours. It's only proper that you at least..."

"Do what? Cry over the corpse? Send flowers? The boy's dead, Harry. Nothing's gonna change that, no matter how many wakes I go to." He really thought he'd been doing well until Harry had taken that parental tone he usually reserved for young officers and children.

"Vince..."

"Look, big brother." Vince was in his face now, stabbing his finger into Harry's chest to punctuate every phrase only stopping to point to himself whenever he mentioned his own actions.

"I trained the kid, I told him what to do, and he didn't do it! He screwed up and got himself killed. And I did the right thing. I smoothed over the report so it looked like he followed procedure. I even took out his gun and put it in his hand so he didn't have to go into the ground as an unprepared, overconfident screw-up. He messed up, got himself killed, and I made it look like a run of terminally bad luck. I made him into a hero because he was too much of a fool to be alive. If I have to go to his home and sit there with his family having tea, I might mess that all up. If that sister of his asks me with tears in her eyes to really tell her how he died, I might not be able to lie to her no matter how many feelings it'd save. Do you really want that? Just bury it and leave me alone!"

By the time Vince had finished his outburst Harry's eyes were glassy with rage. He shrugged his shoulder and stretched his neck to one side in a vain attempt to relieve tension and then came back with a gaze that was even more colored with visible anger than before, his mouth opening to hurl a hail of machine-gunned words at his brother.

Then he stepped back, not in retreat, but to allow the shelter of his umbrella to fall away from Vince's head. As the cold rain ran down his neck and his eyes flashed defiantly at his superior officer and elder brother, Vince saw his brother do something he would have never expected.

He shut his mouth. Harry Vincent, the most decorated and respected policeman ever to serve any department anywhere closed his mouth and didn't say a word. He looked at Vince for another long moment and then turned and walked away.

"Well, I'll be damned." Vince whispered, shaking his head in disbelief. As he did water tricked from his wet hair into his ears and he almost didn't hear his brother's parting words.

"I'll tell her to meet you outside."

Connie Vincent was standing outside the Myersons' home when Vince pulled his car up to the curb. He couldn't help thinking that she looked strangely awkward holding an umbrella over her finely pressed police uniform. Somehow the two images just didn't mesh. Of course, the image of her in police blues still really didn't fit; Vince still remembered her as gangly young kid playing football with the neighborhood boys in his brother Frank's back yard. She smiled widely when she saw him pull up and made a quick dash for the car. She quickly covered the thirty feet between the Myersons' front porch and Vince's grey sedan and pulled open the passenger door half a second after he had reached over to unlock it. She slipped inside the car, pausing only to close her umbrella and drop it onto the floorboard.

Vince was already pulling away from the curb as she reached out and swung the door shut. Connie mused to herself that he looked almost consumed with his desire to put as much distance between himself and the mourners inside the deceased family's home as possible. After a handful of seconds and a few blocks she spoke up.

"So, not in the mood for funerals today?" She was careful to sound just playful enough to avoid igniting the famous Vincent temper in him.

"I never am." Vince still snapped his reply a bit tersely, but after a moment his mood softened. He wasn't one to stay upset for too long after he'd had a chance to vent his grievances. And if there was one thing his conversation with Harry had accomplished, it had given him a great opportunity to discharge his hostility, and his voice was void of venom when he spoke again.

"You look good. The uniform suits you." He wasn't just making small talk, it wasn't one of his talents, she really did look as if she was made to be a cop. Not that that was surprising, the Vincent family had been police officers since before their ancestors had come to America.

Vince remembered when Connie had first told him she wanted to a be a cop.  It was after Harry and he had had to tell her that her father, Frank Vincent, wasn't coming home from the War.  She had looked up at him, a young girl with her face still wet with tears and said she want-ed to a be a policeman just like her daddy.  Frank had been Vince's old-est brother and though he had a partial exemption from the draft because he was a cop, he had been the first of the Vincent brothers to enlist.  He had died towards the end of the war on a blood-soaked beach in France, and his bones were still buried six feet under a foreign countryside.  Vince had not wanted her to follow in the family "business" back then, but as time passed he came to realize that she was serious in her goal and instead of discouraging her, he had driven her to the academy to start her training.

"Uncle Vince, are you okay?"  Connie's voice brought him out of his introspection.

He forced himself back to the present and replied, "Yeah, just remembering."

"Oh,"  If Connie had caught on to what her uncle had been thinking she decided to let it go.  "Can you drop me by my place before we go to lunch?  I'd like to change."

"Sure."  He took a left and began to drive towards Connie's apart-ment as the little voice in his head piped up.

*Wouldn't we all?*

It had taken Connie less than five minutes to shed her damp police uniform, change clothes, and rejoin Vince, who was waiting in his car outside her apartment.  It had been barely enough time for Vince to start on a new cigar and make an attempt to stop dwelling on the past.

"Okay, let's go."  Connie said as she slid into the car again.  She was wearing a man's suit tailored to fit her and her light brown hair was tied back.  Practical and tough, Vince noted.  Connie had always been a tomboy and when you combined that being a cop, tight dresses and high heels just weren't useful or practical attire.

Connie coughed slightly she pulled the door shut.  Vince cracked the window as pulled away.  Raindrops sneaked through the space between the door's frame and window to pepper his left shoulder with moisture, but at least it diffused the cigar smoke enough to allow Connie to breathe.

"You know, If you're not careful, those things will kill you."  She said, jokingly.

"So will being a cop."  He mumbled from around the cigar still clenched in his teeth.  As soon as the words were spoken, he had to sigh in exasperation.  So much for not dwelling on the past, you lasted almost ten minutes.

"It's okay." Connie said, with a voice filled with forced cheer. "You were just at a funeral; it's hard not to think about what happened."

He nodded and took the cigar from his mouth. He stubbed it out in the car's ashtray and forced another smile.

"Yeah, I guess it is. So, did you know Myerson?" If he couldn't stop thinking about the ghosts of his past, at least he could turn the most recent into a conversation piece.

"Sort of. We were at the academy together, but I never really knew him. We kept in touch a bit, but we never really spent too much time talking. The last time I had seen him was when he called me to tell me he made detective. He'd said he wanted to tell me he'd be working with you and wanted to know if there was anything that would help him get along with you."

"So what did you tell him?" He thought it was kind of funny that Myerson had called Connie to find out how to deal with him. Still, cops had their gossip and politicking just like another profession, so it really didn't come as a surprise. What was surprising, however, was that Myerson had never dropped Connie's name around him. He had other rookies drop names of old friends and relatives to try to get special treatment, but Myerson never had. He may not have been smart enough to keep himself from getting killed, but at least the boy had character.

"I told him that, aside from Uncle Harry, you were the toughest, hardest, and best cop on the force." She paused and continued with a more mischievous tone. "I also told him that if he tried to kiss up to you, you'd throw him out a window."

Vince looked at her with both surprise and amusement. Okay, so maybe Myerson had gotten some help avoiding rampant brown-nosing.

Connie smiled wider at seeing something resembling good humor pass over her uncle's face and then corrected herself "I said a low window. No more than three stories...definitely no higher than five."

He didn't laugh, his mood was still too sour for that. However, Vince did chuckle a bit and manage a smile that was genuine. It had been his first since the Cooper case, and he hoped it would be the start of a new trend. He was still smiling as they rounded the corner and parked outside a small restaurant with Japanese kanji painted on the large glass windows.

Kyoto Joe's was an exercise in impossibilities. After the War, no one would have predicted that any restaurant run by an Oriental would survive anywhere outside Chinatown. However, Joseph Yamaguchi hadn't taken that attitude. He knew that a Japanese man trying to make a business work would have the same problems in Chinatown as anywhere else in town. So when he had managed to get a good deal on a storefront near the center of Westburg, he ignored the many people who had told him he should give up and made Kyoto Joe's into one of the best family restaurants in town.

Vince's good mood persisted as Connie and he walked into the restaurant. He had known Joe since just after the War and he was a good friend of the family. Yamaguchi's brother, Ben, had served with Vince's brother Harry's battalion. Ben Yamaguchi had been the man who was responsible for Harry coming back with a slug in the shoulder instead of a bayonet in the heart. Unfortunately, Ben fell to an enemy artillery barrage just before Harry had been shipped Stateside. It had fallen upon him to deliver Ben's medal for valor to a nineteen-year-old Joe, who promptly walked away from a promising academic career and enlisted in the Army. Joe only saw three months of combat before the hostilities ended, but he too returned home with a medal and, unlike his brother, his life.

Kyoto Joe's was a lot like the man who owned it, a strange mixture of East and West. The decor was predominantly classical Japanese, with beautiful paintings and sculptures that had been in his family of generations decorated the room in places of honor. However, the occasional autographed photo or signed athletic jersey that hung framed upon the walls disrupted any illusion of strict tradition. Joe had a signed portrait of heavyweight champ Goliath Murphy hanging Joe's family mon, or crest. This marked the boxer as the most recent person to join his long line of esteemed customers. Vince and Harry's pictures hung upon the walls as well, though they had been moved long ago to make room for new arrivals. The furniture was standard for any restaurant, chairs, tables, and a small counter with a cash register near the door. One would find it hard to accuse Joe of being anything but American, but it would be just as difficult to say that he was a man who didn't remember where his roots are.

"Vince!" Joe cried, working his way from the kitchen, through the dining area, to the door. He clasped Vince's hand enthusiastically and smiled even more so. Joe was a hair over five-feet six and slender but in better shape than most athletes well-over his height and girth. He was wearing a spotless apron over his clothing, a fact that never ceased to amaze Vince. Joe was a hellion in the kitchen, and how he always managed to keep himself so clean was a mystery to him.

"And who is this lovely young lady?" Joe looked at Connie out of the corner of his eye grinning with impish glee. "She kind of looks like a little girl who used to play catch with me in the park, but she's much to grown."

"Hello, Joe." Connie sighed and Vince chuckled in amusement. It was a little game the two played whenever Connie came to the restaurant. Joe would remark how old she looked and compare her to the young girl she once was, Connie would pretend to act annoyed, and then...

"Come here, lotus blossom." Joe stepped forward and hugged Connie warmly. The two laughed at their old joke and then Joe turned back to Vince.

"My table still ready?" Vince asked.

"Always, my friend." Joe beckoned for them to follow him back to the rear of the restaurant. He led them to a large table separated from the rest of the dining room from a rice paper screen. Vince noticed as he passed that even though it was after the lunch rush the place still had a good twenty to thirty people enjoying the cuisine. When they had taken their seats, Joe pulled out a pad of paper and a pen from his back pocket.

"So, what will you have?" Joe asked. This was his and Vince's little joke. Five years and Vince had always ordered the same thing.

"Tempura and tea."

Joe nodded and feigned surprise before taking Connie's order. Then he walked back into the dining room. He would cook their meals himself. Even though he had some of the best chefs around, Joe always insisted on cooking his friends' meals.

Vince reached into his pocket and took out a pack of cigarettes. Joe wasn't too fond of cigars and Vince found that they never went well with tea anyway. As he lighted a smoke he noticed Connie reaching over to drag another from the pack.

"Since when do you smoke?" Vince asked, hoping he didn't sound too much like a concerned uncle.

"I don't." She answered, defying reality as she raised the cigarette to her lips. She looked at her uncle expectantly. "Light?"

Vince was about to say something, but thought the better of it. One cigarette was no reason to ruin a good mood, so he simply passed Connie his lighter. She popped it open and lit her smoke, exhaling an elegant plume into the air.

Vince stopped staring as soon as he realized he was doing it and spoke up.

"So how are things down at the twelfth?"

Connie shrugged. "About the same as everywhere else I guess. More boring if anything. We don't get much action. Most of the crime around there is restricted to jaywalking and parking violations."

71

"You should be glad things are so calm."

"I would be if they were that way all over."

Vince nodded. Connie's precinct covered some of the richer northern neighborhoods. It was a great assignment for old cops who wanted to count the days until their pension, but it wasn't much of a job for anyone else. As much as Vince loved his niece and wanted to protect her, he also understood that she wanted to make a difference, and she couldn't do that at the twelfth. He understood that just as much as he understood he could never tell her that Harry had gotten her that assignment to make sure she would be safe. Connie had defied his attempts to get her a plainclothes job, but she hadn't been able to affect which beat he had her walk. Now she was beginning to feel trapped in a job where nothing ever happened that was bad enough for her to feel as if she was making a difference. Vince had known when she got her assignment that it was only a matter of time. In a way, he was surprised it had taken her so long to get restless.

"Well, there is an opening at the thirty-second. It's homicide, so you'd have to give up the blue suit for a detective shield..." He didn't like offering Myerson's job to his own niece so soon after the guy's funeral, but his department was too short-handed to consider such niceties.

"Uncle Vince," her tone was almost scolding. "I appreciate the offer, but I want to make it on my own." She finished her cigarette and stubbed it out in the dragon-shaped ashtray on the table. Vince took one final drag and followed suit.

"I wouldn't offer if I didn't think you could do the job."

"I know, but I want to be a beat cop." The twinge of sadness in her eyes completed the sentence in Vince's mind, like my father.

Vince raised his hands in surrender. "Okay, subject dropped."

Just then a round face poked around the corner of the screen. The face was quickly followed by a small Japanese boy carrying a tray almost as big as he was. He set the tray on the table and began to unload two small handless cups and a teapot.

"Which one's this little rascal?" Connie teased. The boy blushed slightly as Vince reached over to tussle his hair.

"Why, this is Jimmy. I'm surprised you don't remember, but then he's gotten so big. Pretty soon he'll be bigger than me."

Jimmy Yamaguchi smiled. The youngest and hence the smallest of Joe's children, he liked being compared to the big man sitting at the table. Vince was the kind of guy Jimmy wanted to be. He was big, tough, and didn't let anybody push him around. He knew nobody made Vince Vincent go to bed or finish his meals. Of course, if he wanted to

72

be as big as Vince, he also knew he'd have to get his rest and eat more than candy bars. It was the type of quandary only a five-year-old could understand.

"Howdy, Vince!" Jimmy moved his hand to his forehead and acted like he was tipping an imaginary hat. That, combined with the mimicked western twang in his voice when he spoke informed Vince that Jimmy had seen more than his fair share of cowboy films lately.

Jimmy finished setting up the tea, pointed to Connie, and said "Who's the pretty lady?" His feigned accent made it sound as if he said "purdy" and Connie couldn't help giggling.

"That's Connie. You remember her, don't you. She's my niece." Vince dealt with the young boy with a gentleness that would have made most of the guys on the force wonder which planet the alien had come from that had replaced him.

"Yep." Jimmy nodded in the exaggerated manner so common to a child his age and then looked very confused. "But papa always said she was a little girl. That there's a lady." He pointed again at the Connie, who couldn't contain her laughter to mere giggles anymore. She was almost falling out of her chair when Joe appeared with their food.

"Jimmy, don't bother our friends." Joe smiled apologetically, but Vince smiled and put his hand on Jimmy shoulder.

"No trouble, Joe. Jimmy here was just explaining to me the differences between girls and women." Joe's eyebrows rose at this and then he grinned.

"I wish he'd tell me, then," Joe remarked. Vince chuckled again. Joe never ceased to make Vince feel happy. Sometimes he almost forgot this was the same man who had faced down an angry mob ready to torch his place during some riots a few years back. He'd cracked a few skulls before the police had arrived and cracked even more jokes before they had left.

Joe set out the food and then ushered Jimmy back to the main dining room.

"Kids." He sighed. "Two months ago he wanted to be a spaceman, now it's a sheriff.

"I don't know if the world ready for a Yamaguchi on the force. The rest of us may have to pack up and go home." It was Connie who spoke, though Vince was about ready to say the same. She had recovered from her fit of laughter and was now just smiling widely.

"I somehow doubt that. Enjoy, you two." With that Joe followed after his son.

Connie nodded to Joe as she began to pick up her chopsticks. It had taken her longer to learn to eat with those two little sticks than it had to

73

become a cop, but she now attacked her food like a professional.

"Jimmy's a great kid, isn't he?" Vince said after Joe had gone. He couldn't help envying the restaurant owner in his happiness.

"Kind of makes you want to have one doesn't it?" As soon as she had said it, Connie dropped her chopsticks, and looked over at her uncle, but it was too late.

Vince looked as if he'd just been socked in the gut by a heavyweight. The merriment he had experienced earlier was gone from his face, and had been replaced by the look of the dead.

"Oh, my God." Connie reached out to grasp her uncle's clenched fist. "Uncle Vince, I'm sorry. I didn't..."

"It's okay." He rasped, like a man drawing his dying breath. "You said yourself it was a day to speak of the dead."

The rest of the meal continued in silence. Connie couldn't help thinking how old her uncle looked as he picked at his food. She cursed herself a million times for her stupidity before she had cleared her plate.

"I'm sorry." She whispered after an eternity.

"So am I." He replied, wearily. He dropped his money on the table and looked over at her. "You ready to go?"

She nodded and the two rose and began to move like a funeral precession towards the door.

They hadn't even cleared the paper screen into the rest of the dining area when they heard a scream and the sound of breaking glass.

"Okay, folks! Nobody moves and nobody gets hurt!" A rough voice shouted from near the door. Vince froze in his tracks and peered around the screen.

Two men stood near the door. One was tall and thin with a black bandanna tied over the lower half of his face. It did the job, except for the guy's needle-like nose that poked out over the dark cloth. The other was somewhat shorter and had a bit of extra weight on him. He had his coat collar up in an even less successful attempt to obscure his features. That was okay though, because most of the customers seemed more interested in what the men were carrying in their gloved hands. The thin one was holding a cheap revolver that he was waving in the air and the other had a sawed-off twelve gauge leveled across the tables at the customers, who were statues in the face of a gun.

"Okay!" The thin one shouted. "Everybody put your money on the table." Then he swung his piece over towards Joe. "And you! Empty the register!"

For a moment Vince thought Joe was going to jump the robber, but instead he pushed Jimmy behind him and began to move slowly towards the register. As he was doing this the thin man with the revolver turned to his partner.

"Check the back." His partner nodded and looked around before heading back towards where Vince and Connie were hidden. Vince smiled slightly to himself, the kitchen entrance wasn't visible from the front, but where they were was. Sawed-off must have thought that he was heading to the back to frighten some waiters and a cook or two.

*Surprise.* The little voice in Vince's head cackled like a ghoul.

Vince heard a click behind him and turned to see Connie standing ready with her pistol out. Vince shook his head and she thumbed the hammer back into place. There were too many people to start a shoot out, and Vince wanted to avoid Joe's boy seeing anyone get shot, even lousy bastards like these.

*So what's the other option? Sit in a corner a sulk as they rob your friend blind.*

"No," he whispered in a tone so low only he could hear, "There's one other choice."

He stepped back and waited. Seconds later a masked figure rounded the corner. His eyes barely had time to grow wide before Vince grabbed his wrist. He ripped the shotgun away and followed up with a hard left hook. The hoodlum's head gave a sickening thud as a reply and he fell hard against the table.

That's one.

"What the hell's going on?" His partner shrieked. He sounded sacred, and Vince knew that made him more dangerous.

One chance, Vince. *Question is, can you do it?*

Vince stepped sideways and came out from behind the screen. Connie slipped behind him and came up to his left, aiming her pistol in a picture perfect firing stance. The customers had hit the floor when they heard the commotion in the back, and now the young cop had an unobstructed shot at the remaining perpetrators head if she decided to take it. She didn't though, she just stood motionless, waiting with everyone to see what would happen next.

Good girl, just keep me covered.

Vince could see the clown with the pistol's jaw drop from beneath his mask. For a second he was so limp with shock he almost let go of his piece, but instead leveled it shakily at Vince.

Steady. Keep calm.

"Hold it right there, mister." Vince almost smiled at the guy's attempt to sound firm and in control, but didn't. A smile was an act of superiority and aggression to this type of trash. No, if he wanted to make this work, he couldn't smile. So he didn't. Instead, he just started ed walking forward.

75

Easy, Vince. No room for screw-ups at this range.

"What's wrong with you? I said don't move." The punk was shrieking now, a high pitched wail of horror and amazement. He eyes darted nervously from the big man moving towards him to the gun barrel gaping at him from where Connie stood. It was the old dilemma, the lady or the tiger. Except this time the lady was going to blow a hole through your head, and the tiger was just going to slap you around and cart you downtown. It would have been an easy choice if the guy wasn't so rattled by the fact that he had to make the choice in the first place.

Wrong line of work, tough guy.

"No, you said hold it. I've got nothing to hold, boy. My hands are empty." He spoke in even tones devoid of respect for the gun aimed at his heart and raised his arms to show his hardened, weathered palms to its wielder. True to his word, they were barren of any tool, weapon, or adornment, and betrayed not even the slightest hint of trembling or unsteadiness. The crook began to shake almost uncontrollably.

Just a bit more.

Vince stopped when his chest brushed the barrel. The gunsel looked deep into Vince's eyes and turned white. He looked Vince not with a look of understanding, but a complete lack of it. He saw something in Vince's old cop eyes that he neither had, nor could bring himself to challenge. His arms dropped and the gun clattered to the floor.

"Take care of him." was all Vince said as he renewed his step and walked by the masked crook who slid sideways to let him pass. Connie crossed the room to cuff the young hood. She looked a little nervous and maybe a bit scared, but she mostly just looked excited. Vince smiled, she hadn't learned to truly understand all the things that could have gone wrong in the past few minutes. She was just caught up in the rush of the moment and didn't realize that whole little drama was a one-in-a-million event. Myerson had tried it and gotten himself killed. One day, it might kill Vince too. But not today.

Vince turned on his heel and walked to the back of the room as Joe attempted to calm his customers. He reached down and picked up the other crook's shotgun and walked back to the front. There was no use giving the big guy a chance to turn the whole thing rotten again before the paddywagon arrived.

He got maybe five feet before he heard Jimmy Yamaguchi shout.

"Bandit, twelve o'clock!" Apparently he'd seen his share of aviation war films as well.

Vince turned in time to see the hood he'd put down earlier come back at him with a knife. He swung the blade in a wide dangerous arc that showed deadly intent and a lack of skill. Vince slipped back out of the knife's reach and then stepped forward after his attacker was unbalanced himself with his frantic assault. He grabbed his attacker's hair, dragged his head downwards, and drove his knee up into the guy's face. His pants leg came away bloody as the robber almost oozed to the floor. This time he didn't get up.

No, not today.

He turned around and started to move towards the door. He stopped when he neared Joe and his son. He smiled at Jimmy and tussled his hair again.

"Thanks, kid." He nodded to Joe who returned the nod and mumbled something quietly to himself in Japanese.

Connie had the guy on the ground and cuffed as he neared her.

"I'll radio it in." He told her and began to walk out to his car. As he left Kyoto Joe's the little voice piped up once more.

*Feel better, Vince?*

"Yeah, I do." He had lost his focus for a while. He'd let Myerson's death and the Cooper case awaken doubts and pains in him that he'd put away long ago. He had been so worried about what he'd lost, he had ignored what he had. And what he had was a job to do, and people who depended on him. This didn't mean the past would just go away. He'd still have those times. The bad ones, where the spirits of the dead circled him like greedy vultures and waited for him to break. But he wouldn't let himself crack...he couldn't. He was a cop and a Vincent, and as long as those things still meant anything he'd wouldn't let them break him.

Inside the restaurant, little Jimmy Yamaguchi tugged at his father's sleeve.

"Papa, I want to go to bed." He said it with such firm certainty, that his father took his eyes off the friend who walked into the street and looked down at him with concern.

"Jimmy, it's only two in the afternoon. Are you okay?" The boy seemed to be in good health, but he wasn't about to take any chances.

Jimmy nodded. He was fine. It had just occurred to him that he had better get extra rest if he ever wanted to be as big as Vince Vincent.

# protector
## by fred schiller

"Are you sure you don't want a lawyer?"

"I am a lawyer. I already told you that."

"Oh, that's right. I forgot. I also forget...what was your name again?"

"Sigh...If I told you my name, Detective Sanborn..."

"Right, you'd have to kill me, because that would compromise your secret identity."

"You still think I'm joking."

"Are you kidding? A lawyer who fights crime dressed up like a black cat? I think you're serious as a heart attack."

"You have got to let me go. The city is in serious peril. It needs her protector."

"Which is you."

"Someone's got to do it."

"You are serious."

"As a heart attack, Detective."

"Tell me again how it is one of our prowl cars comes to find you in the alleyway behind the Fulton Street jewelry exchange at 11:02 this evening with the alarm screaming like a cat in heat."

"My informants had given me information that Toshiro's men were..."

"Hold on. So now the vaults inside the exchange have been cleaned out, and there you are taking a nap on the pavement with a goose egg swelling up on the back of your noggin--which just happens to be wrapped up in a mask."

"A cowl."

"I beg your pardon?"

"It's not a mask. It's a cowl."

"Okay. You were wearing a cowl."

"We've covered this ground before, Detective."

"But it's the first time on tape. Humor me and I'll get you a saucer of milk."

"...whaaa?  Hmmm...nice sucker punch.  They teach you that your first day at the academy?"

"Nobody hit you, sport.  You got all bent out of shape when I offered you a saucer of milk.  You tried to grab me, but as soon as you got on your feet you went all loose-kneed and passed out like a drunken sailor. You whacked your chin on the table. I better have a doc come in and look at that head of yours."

"I'm fine.  It's just a minor concussion.  I've had medical training."

"You told me you were a lawyer."

"I am degreed in a number of fields."

"Yeah, me too.  I knew we had something in common."

"You hold no degrees, Detective Sanborn.  You worked at your father's drugstore until he died during your senior year in high school. You were drafted shortly after graduation and did your tour overseas. You re-enlisted and spent the next four years an MP at Fort Duffy down south.  You came home five years ago and joined the academy.  You spent one year on the streets in blues while studying for the detective's exam.  For the past four years you've been wearing cheap suits and try-ing to protect the innocent.  You never turn down a free meal from a restaurant in the precinct, but other than that you're a clean good cop."

"I knew there was a reason I didn't ship you over to the loony ward when they brought you in.  I want to show you something. Look up at the ceiling.  Yeah, right there."

"Now that was the sucker punch they taught us at the academy. Playtime's over, nutcake.  You are in a world of hurt if you don't start talking to me.  Now who the hell are you, and how is it you know how many scoops of sugar I put on my cereal and how many times a week I give it to the old lady."

"You're no longer married, Detective.  You wife passed away last year."

"I swear to God...you say another word that isn't the information I'm waiting to hear, and I'm going to take you and your cowl and..."

"It's my job...to know.  I've made it my job to know.  I've made a pledge to fight crime in this city and I'm a methodical man, Detective. I thrive on information."

"And knowing how long every cop in the city was on the nipple as a kid makes you a better masked crime fighter?"

"You can't tell the players without a scorecard. You know as well as I do, Detective, there are as many good cops out there as there are bad."

<u>Interrogation Room #3  Tape #169  October 12th  1:09 a.m.</u>

"Guess where I've been."

"The pencil that was tucked behind your left ear is now behind your right. You are clearly left handed, so I'd hazard a guess that the switching of the pencil indicates that you've been on the telephone. You've also been in the men's room recently, as indicated by your fly being open and a dribbling of urine on your left pant cuff."

"Yeah, some of that, but I was also deciding your fate, Sherlock."

"Indeed?"

"Damn straight. What with you being smarter than a room full of English teachers, you probably have a good idea of what would happen to you if I turned you over to city hall, into the capable hands of Police Chief Hastings. If even a fraction of what you're saying is true, I'd be Hastings the Horrible's best friend for life."

"He's as corrupt as the night is long."

"Just this once, I'm way ahead of you, Sparky. On my way back from the men's I got flagged down. It seems the honorable Chief Hastings was on the telephone and he wanted to know if we'd unearthed any unusual or suspicious characters connected with tonight's jewel heist. You immediately sprang to mind, falling into both the unusual and suspicious categories."

"Hastings is in bed with Toshiro. He profits enormous sums from the decay that is eating away at the soul of this city."

"He put four kids though Yale on a police chief's salary. I didn't figure his wife was taking in mending. Anyway, I told him that I didn't have anything yet, but that I'd call him in a hot second if I found something."

"So you know I'm telling the truth and you're going to let me go?"

"For starters, Ace...er...what did we agree to call you?"

"I am the Ebon Cougar. Few men have heard my name, but countless have felt my sting."

"Cougars sting? I was not aware of that. Right. So, Ebon...Eb...er, Cougar, it's like this. A, even if I opened the door wide for you, I doubt you could find your way through it. Whoever gave you that crack on the head nearly split it wide open. Your eyes are looking in different directions and you're talking like you just socked away a fifth of the good stuff. Unless you got busfare tucked away in that kinky little tights number, you're not going anywhere."

"A was a delight. What about B."

"B is I'm going to need to know a whole lot more about you and the planet you come from before I start unlocking doors."

"I've committed no crime. You found no trace of the missing jewels when you searched me, did you?"

"Nope. But we did find these."

"I'd be most careful how you handled those, Detective. That's...no, you..."

"Calm down there, Cougar. Don't get your fur up. This looks like some sort of high-tech piece to me. What's it shoot--shotgun shells?"

"Magnesium. If you touch the green button we'll both need to be fitted for white canes."

"And these little glass balls?"

"Acid. Highly concentrated."

"And I like this best. A hypodermic and...dope? You don't look the type, Coug."

"Of course I don't. Those vials contain truth serum, sedatives..."

"Well now. Perhaps I can learn from some of your crime fighting techniques. Which did you say was a truth serum?"

"You don't need that, Detective. I've been telling you the truth all evening."

"Maybe I'm just getting tired of the tiny helpings. I'm not a big fan of being strung along. So what do you say you start really opening up, or do I try my hand at playing doctor?"

"The more you know, the more you'll be in danger from my sworn enemies."

"I'm leaving you no choice, and besides, I like living on the fringe. So spill."

My parents died when I was fifteen. They had been three days into a two-week ocean cruise when an unexpected summer squall sprang up and washed the two of them, along with twelve other passengers, who were no doubt equally inebriated, overboard. Their bodies were never recovered  I was both grief-stricken and annoyed by their loss.

Father had been a terribly successful lawyer. You may recall the famous Kingston Park triple homicide. Father was responsible for freeing Jackson Stonegate III of all charges stemming from the case. That Stonegate later admitted in a suicide letter penned in his own blood that he had in fact murdered his three sleeping children had no discernible effect on Father. He claimed that he was hired to defend the man, not judge him. To this day I wonder if Father knew the truth all along about Stonegate.

81

Father's law practice billed in the hundreds of thousands of dollars each year. That figure was unheard of in that day, but it was a drop in the ocean compared to Mother's fortune. Immigrating to America at the turn of the century from his native France, Grandfather Christophe had worked in his father's textile mill most of his childhood. Arriving in the land of opportunity, Grandfather Christophe borrowed five thousand dollars from his father and opened his own textile mill. Using manufacturing techniques perfected by his father in the old country, Grandfather Christophe's business struggled along until the outbreak of the great war. Opportunity knocked and he answered. Everything from ammunition belt webbing to tent fabric to boot laces were produced by Christophe Textiles. By the end of the war he had eight plants up and running, employing nearly a thousand people. Rather than diminish, his business flourished in peacetime. Grandfather Christophe died at the ripe age of eighty-two the day before Mother and Father's wedding day, leaving her a dowry worth in excess of forty million dollars.

My arrival into the world was, to say the least, unexpected. I doubt either Mother or Father ever desired progeny, with Father spending six days a week and most nights in the city to attend his practice, and Mother playing the part of the wealthy philanthropic matriarch from the luxurious confines of our upstate manor. Several hospitals were built and countless charitable institutions benefited from her fundraising teas and charity drive balls. She also contributed heavily to the arts, serving as patron to a number of young painters and sculptors. Several of these bohemian young men took up temporary residence at the manor in the servants quarters. Mother spent a great deal of time with them, going over their works.

As I say, my arrival was unexpected, and I might have left the world a short time later at the hand of a physician in some secluded Austrian clinic, if news of Mother's pregnancy hadn't been leaked to the social columnists by a household servant. Once her condition became common knowledge, Mother had no choice by to carry me to fruition, perhaps lulling herself to sleep each night with private dreams of a miscarriage.

My birth was a public affair. Well, as public as was socially acceptable. Every time I soiled my diapers it made the papers. Every birthday party for me had more members of the press than children present. The truth to be known, I wasn't actually in the room with another child my age until I turned six, and that was the chauffeur's daughter, paid to be my playmate. I didn't leave Warren Manor's confines until I was five. Everything I needed was brought to me. Our family doctor visited once a month, and a barber and personal valet took care of clothes

82

and appearance. Private tutors came to stay for months at a time, schooling me with fairly revolutionary practices, to which I credit my ease with collegiate courses later in life.

The reason for the isolation was fear. Father was convinced that I was going to be kidnapped and all the family millions drained away. He was certain it would happen, and this prompted insanely intense questioning sessions and background checks for anyone wishing to call on my parents at the Manor, or apply for work there. For the longest time we didn't even have a telephone at the manor. All mail or telephone calls for the family were directed to a secretary in the city. Father was paranoid. Not, you understand, for my safety, but for what a kidnapping would do to him.

When I was twelve I demanded to be driven to a local movie theater to see a new film playing there. Father refused and the following evening he had a projectionist arrive with a print of the film and we had our own private screening. I refused to attend. Later that week I orchestrated my own kidnapping. I never left the Manor grounds, and there was no ransom note, but for all intents and purposes I had been kidnapped.

I had hidden in the hayloft above the stables, and in the hot summer afternoon had dozed off in the hay. I awoke hours later to the sounds of aircraft. I peeked out of the barn to see several airplanes and helicopters landing on the lawns and dozens of federal marshals and FBI agents swarming over the grounds. I rolled around in mud a bit, lightly scratched my forehead with my pocketknife, and stumbled out of the barn into the arms of the federal agents. I concocted a story that began with me brushing down my favorite mare Margaret Anne. I told how she had become skittish over a mouse in the hay and had unintentionally kicked me, knocking me unconscious. Heraclio, the stablemaster, looked a bit skeptical when questioned about this. He knew that Margaret Anne was gentle as a kitten and it would've taken a freight train to scare her, but he told Father that it was possible. I found out the next day that Father had ordered Heraclio to put Margaret Anne down. I watched through tear-filled eyes as the vet loaded her dead body in the back of a pickup and hauled it away. At the time I believed that Father ordered the death to punish the animal. Today I realize that he saw through my transparent story and had my horse destroyed simply to punish me.

Interrogation Room #3  Tape #170  October 12th  1:50 a.m.

"You okay there, Warren? You passed out for a second. I'm going

83

to have to do all sorts of paperwork if you die on my watch, y'know. I got you a cup of coffee and here's a couple of sinkers. They're prewar, make sure you dunk 'em for a while."

"Thank you, Detective, and yes, my name is Warren. Peter Warren."

"If you don't mind me saying, you're not looking too good there, Cougar. Maybe you should get a little shuteye."

"Bad idea, Detective Sanborn . Judging from my behavior I'm still in shock from getting crowned in that alley. If I doze off on top of this concussion I'll probably never wake up, and as you said, that would require you to do all sorts of paperwork."

"Damned considerate of you, Cougar. I put fresh tape in the machine, so whenever you're ready."

"You keep calling me by my crime-fighting name, even though you know my secret identity. You're a tough nut, Detective. I don't know if you're mocking me or you believe me."

"Time will tell, I guess, eh?"

There was no love lost between my parents, and certainly none between myself and them. It was a peaceful coexistence, though. They had their lives and I had mine. I received an extraordinary allowance, and this permitted me to actively pursue any and all interests. I wanted for nothing but love and attention. I attended university in Europe and developed social skills and graces I'd never needed. Several potential friendships budded, but they died on the vine. It's surprisingly tough to reach out of your shell after you've been your own best friend for so many years.

Back at Warren Manor all was well until Mother convinced Father that they needed to go on a cruise. Mother's timing was impeccable. Father had just finished arguing one of the only four cases he'd lost during his career. He'd spoken to me of it during one of the few times we actually spoke, and he had predicted an open and shut case. He had been defending a colleague accused of dirty dealings in handling a multi-million dollar trust fund. The evidence was circumstantial at best and offered no threat. The lawyer in question insisted on taking the stand, even though it wasn't necessary, in order to erase any shadow of suspicion off his otherwise pristine reputation. On the stand, during the final day of testimony, Father's client suffered a full-blown nervous breakdown. Not only did he freely admit to skimming from the trust fund, but he reeled off a long list of criminal activity he'd taken part in over the past thirty years. Father felt disgraced, and getting out of the country for a few weeks sounded especially good. Claiming that there was still work to attend to, he arranged for his private secretary to join

84

them on board. She had her own luxury cabin, and Father spent several hours a day in there taking care of business. I'm certain Mother found diversions of her own to keep herself occupied in his absence.

After Mother and Father were officially announced dead my life changed dramatically. The courts decided that even with dozens of servants to care for my every need, I was too young to live by myself. I wrote a six page letter to Judge Martini complete with statements from over a dozen people willing to testify that I'd been living without parents my entire life and I was pretty normal. Martini ignored my letters and decided that I was to live under the custody of my closest living relative. I was unaware that I had any living relatives. It turns out my father had a younger brother who was a bit of disgrace to the family. He'd gotten a girl pregnant when he was a teenager and the two had run off to her hometown, down south in the sticks. My father and his brother hadn't spoken for years, but the court had tracked him down. The only choice I'd been given in the matter was where I wanted to live, Warren Manor or Hicksville, USA. A week later my newfound Aunt and Uncle arrived at Warren Manor.

Evan and Jody Warren were the polar opposites of my mother and father. They were coarse, unrefined, ignorant of the finer things in life, and prone to public displays of affection. Aside from a handful of dry pecks on the cheek, I'd never seen my parents kiss. My Aunt and Uncle kissed at the drop of a hat. There was a lot of hugging going on as well. When Peterson, the butler, showed the two of them to their new bedroom, Uncle Evan was so overcome he gave Peterson a great big bear hug. Apparently the suite of rooms were larger then their previous three houses combined. My jaw hit the floor. Peterson, always cool as a frozen cucumber, snorted out of one nostril and held his tongue. Warren Manor became a much different place with my aunt and uncle living there. Gray, drab sitting rooms at the Manor were opened up and repainted and people actually started doing things in them. Uncle Evan, a huge horse lover, spent a lot of time with me in the stables. When the trails that circled the manor got boring, we began racing up and down the immaculate lawns. Heraclio, who in his childhood had been a semi-professional jockey in his native Spain, took to racing with us. The horses seemed happier than ever.

When fall came and I was scheduled to go back to a prestigious prep school in Europe, I changed my mind and transferred in City College (The day I registered I knew my parents were spinning in their watery graves). My accomplishments were such that I qualified for college courses at an earlier age than most, and I decided that that was were I belonged.

Another addition to Warren Manor was people. After introducing them to the place through a series of parties, friends and classmates from City College became regular visitors. The house was alive for the first time ever and I was happy for the first time. I began dating, and the years of being a lonely secluded child were washing off of me. That's when the bottom fell out.

Ironically it was my father's worst fear come to life. I had taken a close circle of friends skiing up in the mountains for the weekend when a group of armed men lay siege to Warren Manor. They wanted cash and they wanted to hold me for ransom. They were unskilled thugs with guns. It had become pretty easy to get on the grounds. I wasn't home and the only cash in the house was a few hundred dollars in grocery money. They got mad. After they drank most of the liquor in the house, they started killing. The police report said they used up all their ammunition on the servants. There's an outside chance that my aunt and uncle would have survived, except the men found Father's cache of hunting rifles. They were grotesquely expensive and not a one had ever been fired at an animal, but they served well to gun down the only two people who had ever loved me.

Interrogation Room #3   Tape #170   October 12th   2:31 a.m.

"Jeeze Louise. I remember that. It happened when I was in high school. There's more to you than I thought, Coug. You're not going to start balling your eyes out on me, are you?"

"I've no more tears left, Detective. They've all been spent."

"Yeah. I know the feeling."

For years all I felt was rage. The only thing on my mind was to find those men and get even. But they were in prison--at least three of them were. The fourth had ratted out his friends to the cops and he walked. I wasn't a minor any longer. I had access to my fortune and I spent a lot of it tracking down number four. He had drifted to the west coast, but I found him. It was a Saturday. A blazing hot Saturday. I had flown out to meet him, and to make him pay. He was living in a pay-by-the-week dive motel. I sat in a rental car until he came out of the unit and I confronted him. He knew me from the trial. He laughed at me when I told him he was going to pay. He laughed and then he beat me. I had the tire iron from the trunk of the car, and all he had were his fists and he nearly beat the life out of me--laughing all the while.

I woke the next day in a state-funded hospital. I was receiving the minimum amount of medical treatment due the indigent. My wallet and all identification was gone, my hands were broken, and my jaw was wired shut. I couldn't tell them that I had hundreds of millions of dollars and that I deserved better treatment than this. I couldn't even tell them I had to go to the bathroom . I was helpless, and after a lifetime of excess I was getting only the minimum of everything.

I healed slowly, with plenty of time to examine the world around me and to think. Past my eyes there revolved a steady parade of abused wives, abused children, beaten (some even set afire) homeless people, and a stream of outcasts, hammered down by society, with no one to protect them from the bullies.

Agnes was my angel of mercy. A mountain of a woman in nurse's whites, Agnes helped me suffer through the unbearable. It was Agnes who was there on the bad days with pain killers, even though the doctor hadn't ordered them. It was Agnes who would supplement my diet once a week with a chocolate malt from the hamburger place across the street from the hospital. It was Agnes who finally made the call for me, three weeks after my time in hell had begun. The swelling inside my mouth had gone down enough that I could finally whisper words and be understood. I whispered a telephone number to Agnes, and even though it was long distance, she dialed. Two hours later I was on a private jet heading home, attended to by the best doctors my lawyers could track down on such short notice. I failed miserably at attempts to repay Agnes. She turned down houses, cars and a mountain of cash. Today she runs one of the top free clinics in the nation. That clinic is funded solely by Warren Industries.

It took me the better part of two years to heal properly. Physically, that is. There were many corrective surgeries to repair the damage that had been done, and in the end I was in pretty good shape. That's when I got serious. I brought in a total of eight personal trainers, who worked with me almost around the clock. I got strong. I got tough. I got hard. I trained and pushed my body to achieve peak performance and then I pushed harder still. I studied all the martial arts disciplines, every one that I could find a trainer for. After six months I had the body of an athlete and I could kill a man over a hundred different ways. I was ready for a rematch.

I'd had the fourth man under constant surveillance. During the time I was out of commission he'd gotten involved in an armed robbery and stayed true to form by ratting out his partners when things got hot. He only did one year in a minimum security prison and I was waiting for him when he got out.

"Don't tell me. I know what happened. He beat the hell out of you again."

"How did you kno?."

"Easy. He wasn't afraid. You don't have the goods...what it takes to hurt somebody...and he knew it. You could've held a gun to his head and he probably would've laughed it off."

"I had the skill to kill him. All the skill I needed."

"Like I said, you could've had a loaded gun, aimed and cocked, but it would mean nothing, because you don't have what it takes to pull the trigger. So, what happened? He cleaned your clock again?"

"I managed to block most of his blows. He was crossing the street to get a baseball bat from a couple of kids playing ball when a metro bus ran him over."

"We take justice where we can find it."


I returned home bruised and battered, but still convinced that there was a need for someone to protect the people who have no one to fight for them, but I was scared. I had developed my body, so I decided that I would develop my mind. Working with a slew of private tutors and members of academia I studied any and everything that I thought would help me fight the disease of crime. I hid for nearly eight years behind books and test tubes, shielding myself from all outside stimuli. I took no newspapers, listened to no radio news, rarely left the manor. I had successfully deluded myself that I was on the right path, and that things weren't so bad as I thought, when I happened upon the chauffeur's newspaper in a box of laboratory equipment fetched from the city. I read every word of it and immediately realized the lie I was living. The world outside my doorstep was decaying and it was going to take a physical force to keep it at bay.

I decided that if I were to right the wrongs of society I would have to strike at night. From the shadows. If I were unseen and mysterious I would have an edge. Fear would be a tool I could wield as a weapon. I decided to take the identity of one of the most feared animals in nature, the cougar. Dozens of people were put to work anonymously, creating costumes, specialized weapons, customized cars. I spent into the millions. I even had a base of operations constructed in the vast wings of Warren Manor, with hidden entrances and passages. I was set. I poured money into the hands of informants and built a network of information that was constantly flowing into my secret base. The criminals were identified, the location of their lairs were marked and their activities were charted.  All was in readiness.  I was ready to strike.

<u>Interrogation Room #3  Tape #170  October 12th  2:59 a.m.</u>

"And everything would be perfect, if you weren't such a big chicken.  That's what you should have picked instead of the Ebon Cougar.  You could be the Yellow Chicken."

"It's a good plan.  This city could be saved with someone like the Cougar operating in ways the police can't.  You are very aware of the corruption among law enforcement."

"If you're looking for an argument, you won't get one from me.  It would be the greatest thing in the world if you were for real.  I'd take my hat off to you.  Law enforcement in this city is the rotten tooth you say it is.  The few honest cops out there can't make a difference anymore.  With crooks like Hastings making the rules and calling the shots, it's a losing proposition."

"But there is a way to make things right."

"Yeah, but you're a wimp."

"But you're not.  I've seen your record, Detective.  You've got the goods and you can deliver them when and where they're needed.  Join me."

"You really took a good whack, Warren.  You're talking nuts."

"No I'm not and you know it, otherwise this whole thing would've ended hours ago.  I'd be locked in the loony bin and you'd be napping at your desk.  This works for you...this concept works for you.  You could be the Cougar, Detective.  You could be the Ebon Cougar that this city needs.  There are people out there who need you...need what you can do."

"And I'm supposed to run around in a costume like yours and you're going to bankroll the whole shootin' match.  Keep the money flowing in for more Cougarmobiles and Cougar CatCuffs."

"Exactly."

"You're sick, Mister Warren.  I suggest you seek professional medical help.  You've got a cracked skull, but I think the brain inside went bad a long time ago."

"You know I'm right."

"I know you're out of here.  That's all I know.  I've got nothing to hold you for on the Fulton Street heist.  Now make like a drum and beat it."

"But..."

"You heard me.  Make a like a drum."

"You've proven to be a great disappointment, Detective Sanborn."

"Yeah. Happy to oblige. For the record, this Detective Arnie Sanborn in briefing room number three. October 12th 3:15 a.m.."

"Up here. On the fire escape."

"Get the hell down from there. You're still half-cockeyed from that whack on the head."

"You came. I can't believe it. I thought you were giving me a clue, but I wasn't sure."

"Relax, before you pee in your Cougar suit. The walls in that station house have more ears than a bag of old spuds. Gahh...what am I doing here? This is a stupid idea. What was I thinking?"

"Some of the best ideas in history have started out as stupid."

"Name one."

"Fire. Think about it."

"Here. Take these. They're burning a hole in my pocket."

"The interrogation room tapes from my trip down memory lane?"

"Yup. I begin my career as a vigilante crime fighter by stealing police property."

"I appreciate the effort, but you really needn't have bothered."

"You're...not Peter Warren, are you?"

"Mmmmm...no. He's in a private sanitarium at the moment. The shock of his aunt and uncle being murdered unhinged the poor boy."

"So none of what you told me is true?"

"Some. The important parts. The bits about needing your help were certainly true. While I am quite skilled at criminal deduction, judicial logistics and I am a fairly talented strategist, I do lack, as you so eloquently put it, the goods. Oh, and I really am rich."

"I should kill you right now, you freak."

"And you could, too. I really admire that."

"You honestly think we can make a difference? Just you and me. Clear scum like Hastings out of town? Maybe even give Toshiro a bloody nose?"

"Positively. I've got it all planned out."

"Yeah, well, I'm not wearing tights or a mask. I'll tell you that up front."

"We can work around that. I'll introduce you to my tailor."

"I can't wait."

# available light

## by matthew s. mayer

The wind was cold and stiff blowing in the storms of Autumn. Dawn was breaking over the skyline of the city, and the tops of the taller buildings were half hidden in the low lying clouds. The first light pouring over the horizon, gave the city an almost fantasy quality. Closer to the ground hung the darker clouds bellowing out of the smokestacks that rose just high enough to make themselves seen above the warehouses on the dock. Wyatt watched the smoke roll forth. It stayed low and clung to the buildings, darkening the streets, casting its shadow on the city. His gaze was soon distracted by the sunlight playing across the water, and the creak of the ropes as men dragged the nets across the bay. He watched, listened, drew a deep breath, and knew he was safe.

"Going to be a beautiful day," the captain said from the rail beside him.

"Sure it is," Wyatt answered. "It's been a long time since I've been so happy to see the sunrise. I'm glad I made it out before you left this morning. Thanks for letting me come aboard."

"Think nothing of it," the captain said. He was an old man, and the sea spray had left wrinkles deep into his face. His eyes shone clearly through them, like a harbor of wit and vitality set in a storm of old age and hard work. The morning light glinted off his white beard. "It's been a long time since we've seen you out this way, Counts. Shooting more pictures for the paper?"

It didn't rattle him being called by his last name. It was common practice. He even referred to himself as "Counts," and the captain was an old friend from when Counts had spent a day aboard some years ago.

"Feature photo," he lied. "I've been too busy doing news to come out and just shoot. It's a nice change of pace to be out here." The last part was true enough anyway. He leaned against the ships rail and turned the collar of his trench coat up against the still chill morning wind. His wispy grey hair blew forward around his worn but smiling face, and his eyes looked alertly about not missing any detail. The early edition would be on the streets by now. The presses had finished their nightly roll without him. This would be the first morning in thirty years one of his photos wouldn't be on the doorsteps of the city. His amiable mood belied his bitterness.

"Cute kids and kitty-cats," he muttered under his breath. "That's all they'll consider for feature photos these days. Pretty pictures they can hang up on theirrefrigerators. Nobody's interested in real life anymore." It was all he could do to keep his thoughts private and tell the captain nothing of what had really brought him out on the bay that morning. "Damn fool vanity," he thought as he focused for a picture of the men hauling aboard a net. The camera felt small and strange in his hands. "That's what put me here. My damn fool vanity."

The morning sun came all too early for Jenny Counts, as it always seemed to lately. She had been, at one time, a morning person like her mother, but her life of late had been lived until the early hours of the morning. It had forged in her a certain conflict. She wanted to wake up and needed to stay asleep. She rubbed the sunlight a little further into her eyes as if it would remind her it was time to be up and about

She tied her robe around her and walked down the bright staircase. The windows of her father's house let the early light flood in. She filled the coffee pot and set it on the stove to boil. She had brightened considerably since her first stirrings. She didn't resent the mornings. She liked them. They were virtually her only chance to see her father. He slept as late as the dispersed sunlight through his drapes would let him, but eventually he would come down for coffee on his way to work. Like yesterday, and the picture of the little black girl skipping rope on the sidewalk. It was one of the best stand-alone photos the paper had run in months.

By the time he came down the stairs was had leafed through most of the paper. "I saw your picture," she had called when he heard him on the stairs. "The editor must have been impressed. He ran it full frame."

"How can you tell?" he wondered as he poured himself some coffee.

"You hate to crop your pictures and only a four-by-five camera has that shape. I would have know it was yours without the caption. You're the only one I know still using a Speed Graphic."

"Yeah. When that little girl found out I could only shoot one picture at a time, she told me I needed a new camera," he answered with a little laugh.

"Of course it's not surprising that it's run full frame," she continued, "The *Neighborhoods* editor was probably so happy to get a good photo he didn't know what to do."

"*Neighborhoods*," he wondered picking up the paper, "That was a feature photo. It should be on the front page or with the feature stories, not *Neighborhoods*."

It wasn't unusual for him to be slightly unhappy with the way his photos ran in the paper, and Jenny hadn't been surprised to see him upset. Only yesterday it had seemed more vehement. He had insisted that it was a personal attack toward him. Misusing his photo to push him further toward retirement.

"Creatures of habit," she thought to herself, "Both of us." She was beginning to see that something was going to have change.

The clock struck eight thirty as she was critiquing the photo on the Arts front. It was taken at the gallery open she had attended the night before. Her friend Catherine, and her boyfriend were visible in the background as the artist unveiled one of several sculptures. "I could have done better," she thought to herself. "I wish dad hadn't taken my camera yesterday, I felt strange at the party without it. Since when does he listen to eight year old anyway."

Aboard the fisher it would be a long, unpleasant day full of hard work. Unlike the men laboring on the deck Counts was unused to the job before him. Lying and pretending to take pictures offended his journalistic sensibilities. Still, however horrible, it was a welcome change from the night before.

The sun had gone down, and a soft rain had slipped through the fingers of the clouds which seemed to be holding something bigger for another time. He saw them almost immediately, though they were dressed in black, matching the background. They moved slowly at first, trying not to attract attention. Years of worrying where strange shadows might fall had taught Counts to see detail in the darks. He worked in light and was most at home in the darkness. The shadows and the quiet times of the night were his. Any light meant work to be done. He saw even in the limited light two uniformly black shapes sulking close behind him.

They approached. Increasing speed, they grew more intimidating as they came close. They grabbed at his camera ripping it from his grasp. They threw it to the ground. Counts heart shattered as he saw his camera smashed on the ground. It had been his truest friend    Instant daylight assaulted the shadows. Struck hard and fast, driving them back. Blue and red shapes attacked the men in the shadows. Blocking their vision, disorienting them. Even as the men closed their eyes in imagined pain, the shapes stayed. They converged, blended, and finally melted away. The thugs were left with no option but to watch the light show and wait for it to end. Counts was left with no option but to run.

"David Briegel, City Desk" the reporter answered the phone. After Jenny had asked about her father, the reporter replied, "No I didn't talk to him after the press conference last night, but I intend to. My piece got pulled from the front page because it didn't have a photo to run with it. I had to wait around to confirm a rumor with my source, but he didn't show up. I figured your dad had gone back to develop his picture; that is his job, after all. I guess he's not too concerned about that."

"Well, I'm sure he had a good reason," Jenny said, grudging the "Thank you" she murmured just before she hung up. She wasn't sure what to do next. She had to think. That wasn't easy with last night's party still ringing in her head. She made her way downthe stairs, crossed the kitchen, and set the coffee back on the burner to keep warm. As she turned on the stove, a light came on, and she suddenly knew her father had been home.

Counts could feel their eyes, like hot studio spotlights, on the back of his neck. His gamble had worked. "But for how long," he wondered. He was old and tired. Apparently a lot closer to retirement than he had been willing to admit. Any second the traffic would clear, and they would be after him again. He looked around, and slowed somewhat. Thankfully, the alley didn't dead end. It split at a 'T' behind the buildings. Counts came to the crossing and looked around. There were a few lights in the windows of the upper story apartments. Their lights shone down and cast muted diffuse shadows on the wet brick of the buildings, the red appearing blood-black in the low light. Fire-escapes were belied by the shining raindrops clinging to the rails and glowing in the night. Puddles collected in the middle of the alley, and here and there litter threw long shadows on the ground from the light reflected off the wet roads. A dumpster halfway down the street to the right offered some shelter. "Risky," Counts thought, and then suddenly,with hurried and resounding footsteps two men rushed into the alley. They came to the 'T' and stopped. Each looked in both directions. Shadows abounded, and the two men stood a moment, as if unsure what to do. Then they split. Each walking carefully down one way of the alley, stomping at shadows and peaking into corners. Neither could find any trace of the man they were chasing. They looked around the corners of the alley, scouring the dark distance in both directions as far as they could see. They turned and came back together in at the 'T'.

"He couldn't 'a gotten far," the bigger one said.

"Yeah, but which way did he go?" his partner replied. "By the time we look everywhere, he could be anywhere."

"This is bad. If he tells the cops I …"

"He's not gonna tell the cops. Hell, we don't even know what he saw. Maybe nothin'. But if he tells anyone, it won't be the cops."

"Who then? How are we gonna find him."

"He's a journalist. He don't give a shit about justice. If he knows anything he'll go straight to the paper. If he tells the police everyone's gonna know about it. Won't be his story no more."

These words drifted up to Counts as he crouched in the shadows of the fire-escape below a blazing window. The light cast a glare into the alley, and all around it was black in comparison. So long as he stayed in the shadow he was safe. He heard the thugs, but he wasn't really listening. What they were saying was true, but he was already several steps ahead of them. He couldn't go to the police. He would surely loose his exclusive. He needed this story. He had to show them all. He was old, but still he could still hustle news. He couldn't go to the paper either. He would just as assuredly loose his life. He needed somewhere to go. He needed help. Some one to trust with his work. With no other option, he waited for the men to leave, and started home.

Counts unlocked the door to his house. Inside it was dark and quiet. He hung his coat in the hall closet, and walked to the kitchen. He found a modest dinner waiting warm in the stove. "Jenny never forgets," he said to himself. "Whatever else she may be up to, she never forgets." Counts was used to dinners alone in his half-empty house. His wife had left them for him all the years they were married. She had always made sure dinner was waiting for him, even if she wasn't. It was a trait she had passed on to her daughter, before she died. Though she still lives with her father Jenny leads her own life, and is often away at the evening's top parties by the time he returns from work. As he ate his dinner, Counts glanced at the photos on the wall. They were all pictures of the family, photos of his wife and daughter that Counts had taken in his studio downstairs. There were some pictures of himself as well.

Just after her mother's death, Jenny had declared turnabout was fairplay. If she was to have her picture taken, then she was going to take pictures of her father as well. In the following years she had grown quite good. She was especially good at portraits. She was pretty and nice to be with, and it was easy to smile when she was around. Counts considered the scrawny child in his family pictures. A blond tomboy with a fierce smile and long limbs. How little she resembled the gentle and beautiful woman his daughter had become. He had thought that is was time for the two of them to go back into the studio. "Later," he thought, "tomorrow, next week. Sometime shortly after I retire. Now there are other things to attend to." He took out his caption book, scribbled a few instructions and ripped out the page. That was the best he could do. He turned out the lights as he left. He crept through the dark, quiet night looking for a safe place to stay.

The lights came on at her touch, and she felt a little bit better. Being in complete darkness in the middle of the day made her uneasy. She opened the door of the darkroom and looked out into her father's studio.

"Ten percent per stop, at two stops," Jenny reminded herself as she did the math. She checked her father's note again, just to make sure she had read it right. Seeing she had, she set the timer and began over-developing the film she had found. "How odd," she thought, "it's not like Dad to push his film." Of course it wasn't like her father to leave a roll of film in the oven either. None of this made much sense to her. All she knew was that her she didn't know where her father was, and this roll of film was her only clue. She watched the second hand of the timer run its way around the dial. 15, 14, 13, 12, 11, 10, agitate. She turned the tank over in her hands kept turning it until the timer said to stop. She watched carefully, though her mind wandered and wondered what pictures might appear when she finished.

Slowly and deliberately she poured the developer out of the tank and into the sink. She watched the little whirlpool disappear down the drain, and began rinsing her film. She filled the tank, agitated, poured it out, and filled the tank again. She repeated this process three times, exactly as she always did. Then added the fixer.

"Almost done," she told herself. "Soon the film will be fixed, and we can see what's so important." Soon everything will be fixed, she hoped. Four more minutes.

"Sun's going awfully slow today," Counts thought to himself. It was three or perhaps three thirty. The sun had only begun to sink, giving him that bright harsh Autumn afternoon light. The sparse colors of the-ship stood out spectacularly. The were beautiful in contrast to the drab bay, and the hard work all around. Counts almost wished he was shooting color chrome, instead of black and white. "I should count myself lucky to be shooting at all." he reminded himself.

They had almost killed him last night. They smashed his camera. They ruined his film. It was blind luck that he had escaped at all, and it was a blessing he still had his other film. He had grabbed Jenny's camera on a whim that morning on his way to work. It was a Leica, small and dependable. Expensive for a newsman's salary, but he could-n'tbegrudge her that. He had bought it for her when she began taking both her parties and her photography seriously. It took professional quality photos, and still fit in her handbag. It was light and quiet. Counts had slipped it into his breast pocket to keep it out of the rain. That decision had perhaps saved his life.The crew of the boat fell into a sort of automatic rhythm. They worked diligently, and they knew there would be no rest until it was time to head in sometime after sunset. Counts tried to stay out of their way while working his way to different parts of the ship. The roll of film in his camera was his last, but he needed to pretend to continue shooting. He had to keep up the facade. He didn't want to look like a fugitive. He hoped all the while that his other film had been found. This thought was almost a prayer as he looked out over the water.

Water beaded on the reel in her left hand, and ran down the film as she held it up to the light. At some point along the way, it fell onto the old sweatshirt she had thrown on before coming down to the darkroom. It was the oldest of her habits. Jenny had to unroll her negatives before she washed them. She had to hold them up to the light, stretched tight between her two hands. She had to make sure her images were there. It had been a long time since she had messed up a roll of film. Still, it was important that she check. If she didn't, who knows what might happen.

The negatives were mostly clear. She thought at first sight that she might have used the chemicals in the wrong order, and erased the pictures. When she looked closer, she saw a spot in the middle of each.

"Dark," she thought. "And far away. I don't know what dad was up to when he took these, but it must be hot if the photos are this bad." Of course she couldn't read the pictures. The images far were less than an inch-and-a-half across. They would have to wash and dry, and then she could look at them. Things had to be done in their proper order.

"David Briegel, City Desk" he answered exactly as he had earlier that morning.

"This is Jennifer Counts," Jenny repeated. "I talked to you earlier about my father."

"Yeah, I'm sorry about how I acted this morning. It's not easy having your piece pulled from the front."

"Tell me about it. I've seen my dad get mad when his stuff is pulled. Like yesterday. They ran his photo on page sixteen. He swore it was buried because the girl in the picture was black."

"Have you heard from him?" Briegel asked.

"Sort of," Jenny answered evasively. She wasn't sure she could trust him. There was a reason no one had heard from her father, and Jenny was going to be careful until she knew what that reason was. Besides, she needed to keep herself occupied while the film dried. Otherwise so was sure she'd go crazy.

"So what can I do for you?" David asked. It was a loaded question. All reporter's questions are. He knew she had called for a favor, but he didn't have any idea what it might be.

"You told me this morning that you were waiting to confirm a rumor. What was it you thought was happening?"

"Well, it was just a rumor. And it looks like it's going to stay a rumor. My source was found dead in his office this morning."

"You can still tell me what you thought he was going to tell you. If you didn't have some idea then you wouldn't have waited around."

"Well, one of the mayor's aides was murdered late last night. Said he had some scandal for me. It was something about city money being used to buy derelict properties from gangsters."

"Maybe you could help me find my father," she said, making a leap of faith. "I've got something you might want to look at."

"What's that?" David asked, a little less than interested. He didn't have the time or inclination to chase around an old man who didn't have the good sense to go home.

"You'll have to see for yourself. But if you want to see yourself on the front page tomorrow, you'll be at my house in two hours."

"Okay," he sighed, "where do you live?"

"You're a reporter, you should be able to find out," Jenny told him, happy with her snippy attitude. "Two hours." she finished and hung up.

"It's funny that it was all an accident," Counts thought to himself, "the lot of it." It was intentional that he had shot a good feature photo. It was coincidence that it happened to be a black girl in the photo. It was bad luck, or a subtle hint, that they had shifted the picture from the features front to the *Neighborhoods* section. It was probably just as Jenny as said. That they wanted to give *Neighborhoods* a decent photo for once. Counts had just figured they used Ashley's race as a reason to run his photo on page sixteen. That had frustrated him. He had taken Jenny's camera with him to work the next day, simply as an exercise. He hadn't intended to shoot anything important with it. He wasn't used to it. It was too light, too small, and focused strangely.

It was a lucky thing that he brought it to the press conference. The reporter, a brash young man named Briegel, had told him to look and listen for anything suspicious. Counts hadn't paid too much attention to that. It was a press conference, and he would handle it as he handled all press conferences; take a head photo of whoever was talking at the podium. Looking for a press pass he had walked down the long grand hallway toward the mayor's office suite. The floor was hard cold marble, dimly lit by lamps mounted at intervals along the wall. As the hallway emptied of people toward the offices, it seemed to grow larger, with more shadows. His footsteps began to echo, and then suddenly stopped.

There was another sound in their place, one Counts had stopped and strained to hear. Raised voices—an argument. He let the sound lead him.

The noise came from upstairs. It was hard and impatient. Jenny walked up the stairs through the kitchen and approached the front door.

"Who is it?" she asked, before opening the door.

"Briegel," a man's voice came back muted through the door. "You called me earlier. Told me to come over and look at something."

"It's only been an hour-and-a-half." Jenny said opening the door part way.

"I'm early, but we need to get to work if we want to make deadline."

"Well, I haven't finished, but you can see what I've got."

"These aren't quite dry yet," she apologized holding them away from Briegel over the sink. "They're the only two I've had time to finish."

"Does this make any sense to you?" She asked, showing him the first photo.

"Sure," he said in little more than a whisper. "That's my source, there," as he pointed to the photo. "Seems your father may have been the last one to see him alive."

"Maybe he saw more than that," Jenny said triumphantly, revealing the second photo.

David let out a low whistle.

The sound had been faint. Counts had to strain to hear it. He crept silently across the hall and stopped as a thin beam of light drew a line across the floor in front of him. The light came from an open office door. Counts crouched low and looked through the small opening.

Nothing much to see. More darkness. The only light was a small desk lamp that burned brightly in the center of the office. There was some one at the desk. Nervous. There was precious little light to see by, but there was enough.

He reached into his pocket and brought Jenny's Leica to his eye. It was small. It was silent. There was no flipping of mirrors. No loud snap when the picture was taken. No reason for anyone to know he was there. He watched and he waited.

One of the men's faces came into the light.

Click.

A look of terror on the man's face.

Click.

Voices raised. Shadows moved.

Click.

The Mayor's voice. The Mayor's face.

Click. A lead pipe, and a stifled scream. Nothing Counts can do but watch.

He's gagged. He's tied. It showed as he reeled forward from a blow from behind.

Click.

Click.

Click.

It was ending. Blood welled black in the low light and spilled othe desk. The mayor leaned down into the light to gloat a few inaudible lines over the lifeless, but bleeding body. The two shadowy men started toward the door.

"Can't be caught," Counts thought desperately. He stood up quickly, and quietly. He tracked backward until he was three doors down the hall. He called the name of the press secretary from the hallway, alerting everyone in the office. He walked forward and called as casually as he could. "James?"

The commotion was enough. The mayor seemed to accept that he had only been looking for a press pass. He had given Counts an authorization and sent him on his way. The mayor had a dead body in the next room and couldn't afford to have anyone looking around. He also couldn't afford to have papers missing staff members. It might arouse suspicion. Although he was allowed to return to the press room, Counts knew he wasn't safe.

"So this proves the Mayor was in on some scheme," Briegel said confidently, looking at the print. "Now we just need to establish a connection between the local gangs and these warehouses the city recently bought. They're all owned by dummy corporations and, almost impossible to trace back to the source."

Jenny looked at David's list. Most of the addresses and even the street names were unfamiliar scattered through the poorer boroughs of the city. A couple of company names did ring a bell however, and she knew where to find her answers.

As they sorted through the negatives in her father's archive Jenny was glad for once that he'd used a four by five camera. The huge negatives were easy to read and file. It didn't take long before they found photos of the groundbreaking ceremonies for three of the warehouses. In each one they found somewhere in the background one of Lou Dewey's lackeys. It wasn't much, but still proof enough to run the story.

The light was fading, behind him. The smell that had grown consistently stronger throughout the day was now a stench that clung to everything on the boat. They were headed back to the dock with the day's catch. There was a general quiet on the ship. Except for a few silhouettes climbing toward the skies, mending the nets, there was no motion aboard.

All he could do was hope that he wouldn't be caught, as he made his way to the paper. It was late. It was dark. He was confident that they had given up waiting for him by now. He walked into the news room and found it unchanged. Even at this late hour it was full of sound, and activity.

"Counts!" the editor said, surprised to see him. "We've been looking for you all damn day. You need to substantiate your work, if you want the front page. We can't run just any photo we find lying around. You have to claim it or it's no good to us."

"So you got my film then?"

"Sure ! We got a whole exclusive out of it. Briegel had been working on something all along. The photo made some rumors concrete. It gave us enough evidence to blow the story wide open. Come back here and see for yourself."

The editor led Counts to the back shop light tables. Jenny and David were there watching as the stories and photos were being run through the waxed and pasted on the page.

"Dad," Jenny cried throwing her arms around him.

"I'm okay," he said holding her tight. "I knew you would know what to do with my photos."

"She's her father's daughter, that's for sure," the editor added. He was standing over two versions of page one. One with a follow up on Eric Stanton's murder as the lead story. The other with Counts' final photo run three columns, and the headline -"Mayor Discovered in Murder and Bribery Scandal" in big bold type. "Which of these are we going to run?" Counts nodded to the one with his photo.

"All we need is a caption and it's out the door," the editor said smiling, "A goddamn exclusive that'll have half the city government behind bars before lunch."

"I'm sure whatever copy desk came up with is fine," Counts told him seeing that there was already a dummy caption in place. He smiled, looked at his daughter, took her by the arm and turned to leave.

"Counts," the editor called after, "See you first thing tomorrow."

Wyatt was about to explain that he was taking a day off, and couldn't work until he had a new camera at the very least, if he decided to come back at all.

He never got the chance, because before he could open his mouth, Jenny turned her head and said, "Sure thing. Bright and early."

Wyatt thought about his day on the water and said, "Yeah, I might even have a feature photo for you."

Art by Ang Lee

# wild card

## by wendi lee

It was a slippery, wet night and I was anxious to get home to my kid, Allie. But I had another three hours on my shift at The Harbor Grill in Westburg. Cars went by, their tires hissing like startled snakes on the wet asphalt, and people hurried by under umbrellas or in raincoats with old newspapers covering their heads. The damp chill seemed to seep into the Harbor Grill and wrap itself around my shoulders. Even the warm deco-style wall sconces that graced the Harbor Grill couldn't warm me up enough when I looked outside the picture window.

I stopped at a candlelit table to straighten a cloth napkin, then pushed back drooping tendrils of hair from my neck, my hair color being russet this week, and put on a smile for the lone gentleman who stepped inside. His hat was pulled low and his hands were deep in the pockets of his raincoat. I pulled a menu, looked around to see if he had a ladyfriend, then asked in my pleasant hostess voice, "Will you be alone this evening?"

"I hope not for long," he replied in a familiar growl of a voice.

I swallowed hard. It had been a long time since I'd heard that voice, and it took me back to a time before my seven-year-old daughter was born, an unpleasant time when I was just barely hanging onto life by my flame-red lacquered nails.

He removed his hat and raincoat and I numbly accepted them, pawning the outerwear off on the hatcheck girl, Sheila.

"Are you just here for dinner?" I asked cautiously, hoping that the fish was the only thing that was going to be grilled tonight.

Vince Vincent, lieutenant with the 32nd precinct, smiled in his militaristic manner. "The police commissioner will be joining me in a few minutes." He turned serious. "It's good to see you, Karla. You've reinvented yourself. You look good." His eyes strayed to my hair color. "That color suits you."

I reached out and touched a strand. "I—I just happen to be auburn this month."

Vincent smiled and nodded. "I've kept an eye on you."

"You wanted to make sure an ex-junkie wouldn't get back on the horse?"

He shook his head, a puzzled almost hurt look in his eyes. "I just

103

wanted to make sure you didn't need anything. You're doing all right, though. Got a kid, I understand."

The thought of Allie made me smile in spite of myself. I relaxed and clutched the large menu to my chest like a shield. "Yes, she's the reason I've kept straight."

"How come you're not singing anymore?"

I gave him a sardonic grin. "What do you think got me on the horse in the first place?"

He frowned and shook his head. "You think the singing did it?"

I shrugged. "The lifestyle." I didn't mention that I occasionally went to the Blue Note Lounge to belt out a few old standards, just to keep my voice in practice.

Vincent's eyes darkened as the door opened again and another man came in. Liam Coleman, Police Commissioner. I knew his face. Never missed an opportunity to get his picture in the front page. He was a handsome man, young for the job. Several older, more qualified men had been passed over in favor of Coleman. And he seemed to be doing a good job so far. At least, I thought he was. But then, I wasn't on the wrong side of the law anymore, was I?

The commissioner glanced at Vincent and nodded, then looked me up and down. I put on my most professional demeanor and led them to a table in the corner, Coleman glad-handing at tables where he was recognized. When I had seated Vincent and handed him a menu, I turned and waited for the commissioner to finish chatting with an obviously wealthy businessman and his wife. The woman kept laughing in a high and annoying manner and I wondered how her husband could stand it. He probably slapped her around at home–it was her price for the lifestyle. A few minutes later, Coleman came over to the table with apologies to Vincent, who didn't seem to care one way or the other.

"Thank you, Miss-?" He raised his eyebrows and waited for me to give him my last name.

"Karla. It's just Karla," I replied, pointing to my name tag and smiling back.

"Yes, Karla, thank you." He took a seat.

"May I get you gentlemen anything to drink?"

Coleman ordered a martini with an olive and Vincent, true to form, ordered a whiskey neat. He hadn't changed in all those years. I often wondered if anything would have happened between us if I hadn't been a junkie and someone else's girlfriend. Vince Vincent was good-looking and still unattached. I had seen him out and about at various places, and he never seemed to have a woman with him.

After the two men ordered, Coleman seemed to forget I was there, but Lieutenant Vincent would catch my eye every once in a while and wink. They must have had plenty to talk about, and there was a sudden late-night rush of customers that kept me busy. When I next looked up, The two men were standing by my station, donning their raincoats and hats. I decided it was time to put the past behind me.

"How was your meal?" I asked as I slipped some menus into the side slot of the stand where I took reservations and answered the phone.

Coleman nodded. "I haven't been here for almost a year. I'll have to remember to come back more often." He said this while looking at me thoughtfully. Just like a politician—he dodged the question while making promises.

"Please do," I replied. "My boss loves to see celebrities dining here."

Coleman began to demur that he wasn't really a celebrity when Lieutenant Vincent interrupted. "Celebrities like Lou Dewey or one of the Ghilonis?"

I wasn't very good at keeping an impassive face when I got angry. I'm sure it showed on my face. I didn't answer.

The lieutenant seemed to sense that I was angry and he softened his tone. "I apologize, Karla. That wasn't fair of me."

I took a deep breath and forced a smile. "That's all right. I know how frustrating that trial must have been for you."

"Frankly," he went on, "I'm surprised that Dewey left you alone after you became a witness for the prosecution." I kept the smile in place and shrugged. "The judge threw out the case because of lack of evidence, remember. And who was going to believe a junkie like me, anyway?" I wouldn't have believed me back then. Now I was an upstanding citizen. "I'm just sorry that I wasn't able to help you after all."

I had mixed feelings about having tried to help the police years ago. Back then, it was my only way out of a long sentence for possession of drugs, but it was a relief when Judge Reiner threw out the indictment and I wasn't called to take the stand. Lieutenant Vincent had reluctantly watched me leave the safe house, both of us believing that it would be the last time I would be able to walk the streets safely. I fully expected to turn a corner to face one of Dewey's legions of thugs with a gun or knife in his hand.

But it never happened. Instead, I got clean, got a job, fell in love, had a kid, fell out of love, and now lived in an apartment with my seven-year-old daughter, Allie. Dewey had not contacted me since I left protective custody, and neither had his righthand man, Nicky Belker, who had been my boyfriend at the time.

Of course, I hadn't been surprised that Nicky didn't call me. He liked his women between eighteen and twenty-one, and at twenty-three, I had been a little long in the tooth for him. He had been looking around even before the end. I was a little bitter about the break-up, and it tended to color my view of Nicky. Of course, Nicky wasn't all bad. He could be very generous and was proud to sit in the nightclub audience when I was performing on stage and tell people that he was going out with me.

Despite my hard early years connected to the fringes of Dewey's organizations, I still looked fairly young. The drugs hadn't taken much of a toll on my face or figure, but they had taken my soul. Bargaining for its return had cost me a few lost years, but I had repaired the damage and was beginning to feel that life was worth living–Allie had made sure of that.

The lieutenant and the commissioner seemed to be getting ready to leave when Coleman turned back to me as if it was an afterthought. I knew it was calculated. "By the way, Karla, have you heard from Nicky recently?"

The question caught me off guard. Nicky was history, in my book. I know I blinked before answering. "No, of course not. Why do you ask?"

Coleman glanced at Vincent, who nodded slightly. The lieutenant was giving the commissioner permission to believe me. If I didn't know what a stand-up guy the lieutenant was, I might have been insulted.

"I was just wondering," Coleman replied. It was clear that there was more to it than that, but he wouldn't tell me, of course. He took a card from his breast pocket and flicked it at me. "But if you do hear from him, give me a call, okay?"

I took the card and made a big show of putting it in my pocket. "Yeah, sure. He must be hard to find right now, huh?"

Coleman's expression turned impatient, but Vincent stopped him from saying something that he might regret.

"Nicky's had a little disagreement with Dewey and is laying low, Karla. The police commissioner just thought with your past connection to Nicky that you might have heard from him is all."

I nodded and smiled. They thanked me and left.

It was a half hour till closing when Lou Dewey and his thugs came in. The rain had become a downpour and if I was one who believed in omens, I would have thought that this was a sign of a night going from bad to worse. I glanced at the manager, Bill, whose face had gone from ruddy to pale in the course of several seconds. I can't say how pale my complexion was, but I hoped that I looked composed. Dewey was a dangerous man with a trigger temper. There was a rumor that he had gunned down a wine steward who had brought him the wrong wine. There were other stories as well, but I had known the wine steward and whenever I thought about him, little icy fingers crept up and down my spine. Dewey looked around the joint before settling his piggy eyes on me. Except for his eyes, Dewey was a handsome man. But the eyes were small and close-set and I swear I've seen the Arctic wind blow in them. He smiled. "Karla, you were Nicky's girlfriend a few years ago, weren't you?"

My fingers began to sweat. One of the little things I hadn't let Bill know when he hired me was that I had once been connected. I tried to find Bill, but he must have scurried back to the kitchen. Coleman's assessment of the Harbor Grill as a place of mob business had been essentially wrong. We occasionally got a crime boss or a couple of soldiers in here, but it wasn't a favorite hangout or anything. Which was one of the reasons I had chosen to work in this place.

I nodded shortly. "I used to be." I changed the subject as smoothly as I could. "Will this be all of you or will someone else be joining you later?"

"Just me and the boys here," Dewey said. "You were a good singer, as I recall."

I sat them at a table near the back. I didn't think Dewey wanted to be on display at the window. Dewey pulled out a cigarette and began to light it. Before I could stop myself, I said, "I'm sorry, this is the non-smoking section."

Dewey looked up sharply at me. One of his thugs, a giant with a handlebar mustache, began to stand up, but Dewey put him on hold with one look. "But I smoke. You should know that."

I took a deep breath and hoped I would make it back to my daughter tonight. I gestured toward the front with the picture windows. "That's the smoking section."

Dewey held my gaze for a few long seconds, then nodded shortly and ground his cigarette out on his bread plate. "Thanks." The thug, frozen in a half-sitting, half-standing position, plopped back into his chair and picked up his menu. Before I could turn away Dewey asked, "What would you recommend here?"

The hair on the back of my neck had relaxed, but I was anxious to get away. I remembered that he liked seafood. "The Caesar salad with grilled giant tiger shrimp is always very good," I replied, "and the special tonight is a combination of blackened shark and batter-fried alligator with sweet potato soufflé. I'll leave you gentlemen to decide. The waiter will be with you in a few minutes."

I had started to walk away when Dewey caught me with another question. "By the way, Karla, you seen Nicky recently?"

I froze and turned around slowly. "As a matter of fact, you're the second person in here tonight asking me that. I left that life eight years ago, and I haven't heard from Nicky in all that time. Why would he come to me now?"

Dewey, like Coleman, was the consummate politician, never answering a question straight. "You know, Karla, you probably don't make a lot working at this joint. My regular singer just quit on me. You come back to work for me at The Parisian and I'll double your salary."

All I had to do was tell Dewey where Nicky was. Except I didn't know. "Thanks, Mr. Dewey. But I haven't heard from Nicky. Honestly." I smiled and went back to my station.

I have never seen faster or better service than what Dewey and his buddies got. They ordered steaks, except Dewey, who ordered the special–I guess he figured it was better that he eat the predators before they ate him.

An hour later, Dewey came up personally to pay the tab. He flashed hundred dollar bills at me. "I meant it," he said.

"Meant what?" I asked as I gave him his change. He tucked a hundred dollar bill in my hand.

"About you coming to work for me. We could use a good torch singer at the club. Think about it. You still got my number?"

I nodded somberly. "Yeah, I've still got your number."

When Dewey was gone, I tucked the bill in my purse. I wasn't proud about accepting the money at the moment, but Allie had to have braces and every hundred would help. As tempting as going back to singing sounded, the idea of working for Lou Dewey, even in a legitimate capacity, filled me with dread.

Bill, the waiters, and the cook came bustling out of the kitchen to help me close up fast. We didn't want any more mob figures coming in here tonight.

"He sure took a shine to you, Karla," Bill said, shaking his head. "So did the police commissioner."

The cook nodded. "I saw the commissioner hand you a card. And Dewey seemed real interested. You weren't thinking of going out with him, were you?"

"Are you kidding?" I said, and gave a shrill nervous laugh. "No, Dewey offered me a job at his nightclub, The Parisian. I used to sing and he remembered me."

One of the waiters, Ricardo, piped up. "That's a real swank place, Karla. You thinking of taking the job?"

"I don't know. I don't know if I could leave this place," I said, then switched topics. "I need to get home to my little girl."

We said goodnight and everyone left except Bill and me. I was about to lock up when Bill said, "Wait a minute, Karla, and I'll walk you to your car. I gotta use the john first." I appreciated his concern for me, and even though I was sure cops and mobsters alike were watching me, I took his offer. Westburg at midnight was no place for anyone to walk alone, even to their car.

The phone rang and I almost didn't pick it up. We have an answering machine that gives the hours, but I thought it might be Allie, wondering where I was. She was known to stay up past her bedtime at my neighbor's apartment in Oldentowne, especially when I had a late night. Allie was a worrier.

I picked up the phone with the usual greeting.

"Karla." The voice on the other end of the line took me into the past as surely as seeing Lieutenant Vincent and Lou Dewey had, as surely as seeing Lou Dewey had.

"Nicky," I said sharply, then added in a whisper, "what the hell are you doing, calling me now?"

"I'm in trouble. And so is Annabelle."

"Annabelle," I repeated stupidly.

A beat went by before he replied. "A friend."

No one had mentioned an Annabelle to me. Not the commissioner, not Vincent, not Dewey. Maybe they wanted to spare my feelings. But I hadn't exactly been pining away for Nicky all these years. I had moved on, but I guess men's egos make them think that all we women want is a man, any man. And if we're dumped, we are vindictive.

I repeated my question. "Why the hell are you calling me, Nicky? I had the commissioner here, Lieutenant Vincent here, Dewey here. They all want to know where the hell you are, and they think I know."

"Karla—"

I didn't let him continue. "No. Don't tell me. I don't want to give Dewey the wrong impression."

"Karla, please. Help me. Help Annabelle. You were the only one I ever trusted." I almost hung up, but there was a tinge of desperation in his voice.

I didn't have much more time to talk. I could hear Bill opening the door to the john. "Spare me the BS. What do you want?"

"Meet me at our usual spot."

I started to say, "Are you out of your—?" but he hung up.

"Are you ready to go?" Bill asked, shrugging on his coat. I nodded. "Everything okay? I thought I heard you talking to someone out here."

I shook my head. "The phone. I picked up because I thought it was Allie. It was just a wrong number."

It had stopped raining and a fog was building up.

Bill escorted me to my new car and said good night. I'd been saving for this car for three years and was proud of it.

It symbolized my hard-won freedom and as I thought back to Nicky's desperate phone call, I got angry. I'd distanced myself from that way of life and I'd be damned if some old boyfriend would try to pull me back into the mire.

I started to head home, but somewhere along the way–I think it was at the corner of Meridian and Axis–I turned around and headed for the edge of Chinatown. I knew Nicky could take care of himself, but I wasn't so sure this Annabelle, whoever she was, should be in his company with the cops and Dewey looking for him.

There was a little park along the bay where Nicky and I used to walk, before the needles and the horse, before Nicky's complete allegiance to Lou Dewey, back when Nicky was an independent numbers runner. More fog swirled in off the bay, enveloping the park. All I could see was the iron spiked gate where people entered to saunter around. Ghostly pools of light battled the heavy mist and lost, not able to throw light more than a couple of yards from the top of the streetlight.

Despite the fog, I was able to find my way to the fountain that used to work. Now it was dry with dead leaves scattered in the concrete bottom. I didn't call out. I figured if he found me, I was meant to help him.

"Karla," the voice that called out was a strangled whisper.

I turned, not seeing him at first, then making out a shadowy form. "Nicky?"

A second figure appeared beside him, the ghostly silhouette of a young girl.

Nicky had changed quite a bit. He was thinner, sickly almost. Worry haunted his expression. His hair, which had always been his pride, was thinner on top.

The girl beside him was barely eighteen years old. She had long, curly dark hair and large eyes with thick eyelashes. She was beautiful, like one of those girls painted by artists like Renoir.

I turned to her. "You must be Annabelle."

"Yes," she said in a wispy voice that matched her appearance. "Pleased to meet you, Karla. Nicky's told me all about you."

That was hard to believe, but it might be true. I turned back to Nicky. "What's this all about? What did you drag me into? I have a little girl to think about."

Nicky smiled. "But I knew you wouldn't let me down, Karla."

110

Footsteps clicked purposefully on the cement sidewalk, coming toward us. Nicky pushed Annabelle toward me. "No time to tell you. Here, hide her. Please. I'll take care of our company."

Annabelle's childlike hand clasped my arm. "But how will I reach you?"

"No need. I'll be in touch," he said as he faded into the fog, in the direction of the footsteps.

I tried to remember where I'd put my little snubnose, but when I left that life, I'd tucked it in a shoebox and vowed be a normal citizen. Now I made a mental note to look for it when I got home. As I herded a terrified Annabelle in the direction of my car, we both heard the sounds of a scuffle breaking out, the sound of gunfire, and a shout.

I had locked my car and now my fingers were shaking as I tried to jam the key in the door lock. Annabelle crouched down by the passenger door, beating it with her fists to get in, I had a crazy thought– they weren't after Nicky, they were after Annabelle. And Nicky had been protecting her. Once the doors were unlocked, Annabelle practically tumbled in as I turned the ignition and skidded away from the park, leaving Nicky to his fate.

After a moment of whimpering, Annabelle looked up and said, "Do you think we should call the police?"

I'd been watching the rear view and didn't see anyone behind us, so I came to a jerky stop just a few blocks from the park. Diesel fumes mingled with sea air, which meant we were still close to the wharf. "How the hell should I know? No one has told me a thing. Who's after who?"

Annabelle fell silent and blinked back tears. I made myself calm down and tried a gentler tone on her. "Look, Annabelle, I don't know what this is about, so I don't know how deep to hide you."

She remained silent while I ticked off the number of places I could take Annabelle for safety: my place was out, my mother's place was a possibility, my neighbor's apartment was out.

Before we had a chance to say anything else, Annabelle's door was ripped open and she was dragged out, screaming and struggling, by a pair of dark-suited figures. I started to get out of the car, but only made it halfway out before someone hit me on the back of the head and knocked me unconscious.

I awoke in the hospital, my daughter by my side. Her face blurred for a moment, then came into focus–sweet, concerned, eyes much too old for her seven years. "Mama," Allie said, resting her hand on top of mine. "You're awake."

111

I tried to sit up, but my head felt as heavy as a bowling ball. I gasped with the effort and fell back to my original position.

A door opened and Lieutenant Vincent came in and leaned over me. "How are you feeling?" he asked.

"You need to ask?" I replied. "How did I get here? What was the last thing you remember?"

I frowned. "It was foggy. I was near Chinatown, down by the wharf."

"Was there anyone with you?" the lieutenant asked, prodding my memory.

I remembered Annabelle. "There was a girl. A young girl named Annabelle. Is she all right?"

Vincent shook his head. "You gave my people the slip."

"It was foggy," I replied. "I looked for your cars, but I didn't see anyone behind us."

"You peeled out of that park like demons were on your heels."

"You didn't see Annabelle?"

"Like you said," Vincent replied with a wry smile, "it was foggy."

"What's this all about?" I tried to sit up again, this time more gingerly. I was successful.

Vincent fluffed some pillows behind me, then called to a uniformed officer in the corner. "John, why don't you take Allie here to get some ice cream."

Allie piped up, "But Lieutenant, it's two in the morning and—"

I reached over and put my hand on her arm. "Honey, it's okay this one time. I have to talk to the lieutenant alone."

Only we weren't alone. When Allie and the officer left, Liam Coleman came in. "You should have contacted us when Nicky got in touch with you, Karla."

I waved a dismissive hand at him and turned away. "I hadn't planned on meeting him. It just happened."

Coleman raised his voice. "Just happened?" I winced.

"Coleman," Vincent said in a low, warning tone.

"No, Vince, I think the little lady ought to hear what she's being charged with."

If my ears could have pricked up, they would have. I turned sharply toward him. "Charged with what?"

"Manslaughter, at the very least. You killed Nicky."

"Killed? How—?" I sputtered.

"You hit him with your car," Coleman replied. "Perhaps it was an accident–you didn't see him?"

"He was alive when I left him," I said in a steady voice, then turned

112

to Vincent. "But you said that your people found me. Didn't they witness Annabelle's abduction?"

Vincent frowned. "This is the second time you've mentioned an Annabelle. We found your car down by the wharf with you slumped over the wheel. The treadmarks on Nicky's head match your tires."

"I didn't kill him," I protested and suddenly realized how hollow it sounded. "Wait, how do you explain the lump on the back of my head?"

Vincent came around to the head of my hospital bed and checked it out. Coleman sat there, his arms crossed tight in front of his chest as if he wouldn't believe me if I told him the sky was blue on a sunny day. "She's right, Coleman, she has a lump."

The commissioner gave me a sour look. "I suppose you'd better tell us about it from the beginning."

I spilled my guts, not leaving out one detail. After all, I'd been dragged into this mess against my will, and I was damned if I was going to jail for something I didn't do.

By the end of my report, Coleman was looking less sour and Vincent was looking downright thoughtful. "A young girl, you say?"

"Yeah. Annabelle. Don't ask me her last name." I was getting impatient. I wanted out of there and back to my nice, safe life. Which wasn't looking so safe anymore.

"You say that Dewey asked you to come to work at The Parisian?"

Now I gave him a sour look. I could see where this was leading. "No, I won't do it. You can't make me."

But they could, and they laid out exactly what I would go through if I didn't help them.

"What about my daughter?" I asked. "What about my safety as well? You're asking me to do a dangerous job."

"We have people in there," Vincent assured me. "You won't be alone."

"What about my job at the Grill?" But I knew the answer: they'd fix it with my boss. They'd fix everything.

Two nights later, I was well enough to call Dewey.

"Yeah, babe, I'm glad you called. You think about my offer?"

I closed my eyes. "Yeah, sounds good. I'd like to make a little more money."

"Maybe you can make a little more than what you get for singing, if you know what I mean." He named a weekly sum that was three times what I made at the Harbor Grill. Then there was a pause before he added, "Too bad what happened to Nicky."

I played dumb. "What happened?"

"He was a hit-and-run. No one seems to know who the driver was. By the way, can you start tonight?"

"Sure." I hung up, wondering if he was subtly telling me he knew it was my car because his men set me up, or if he really didn't know. Vincent and Coleman had suppressed the information, but there was always the possibility of a leak. In the end, I decided that Dewey never did anything subtle, so it was a safe bet that he hadn't heard that someone driving my car had killed Nicky.

I pulled out the old evening gowns that I'd worn when I was a singer, and shook the dust off them. Most of them had long sleeves to hide the track marks, and my arms didn't look much better now. But my shoulders were still nice, still inviting. I selected a black velvet number, low décolletage, tight sleeves with zippers that I'd installed so I could shoot up in the ladies room between sets. I tried it on and it still fit.

It hadn't been that long since I sang in public–I'd kept my pipes in tune by singing at the Blue Note Lounge on my nights off. The band still included a couple of fellas I knew when I first sang at The Parisian. I felt as if I'd never been away.

"Hey, Songbird," Brian, the saxophonist, said–he'd always called me that when we were playing at the same club, "long time, no see. Where've you been?"

"Straightening out."

He looked down at the zippered sleeves with a questioning look. Brian had the most incredible bedroom eyes, the kind of eyes that most musicians got after a few years of shooting junk.

"Just decoration these days," I said.

Brian was one of the few musicians who didn't need something up his nose or in his veins to feel good. He always used to tell me that the music was enough. I hoped it would be enough for me now. Just coming back here, back to The Parisian, I wondered if this was all a mistake. Would I end up hitting the junk by the end of the night?

The first set was shaky–I hadn't had time to practice with the band–but by the second set, it was going pretty well. "*Stormy Weather*" was a good number. My voice was strong and Brian's sax solo had the customers requesting more by the end of the set. By the third set, I was in full swing, and didn't even think about the junk, the zippered sleeves, or the past.

The night came to an end all too quickly and as we were breaking down the equipment, Dewey walked in and came up to me. "I heard you from the office," he said, taking my hands. "You're good."

I shrugged, wanting to withdraw my hands, but knowing it would be a shooting offense with a guy like Dewey.

"Thanks. I just hope tomorrow night will be even better."

Dewey shook his head. "You did just fine. You'll be back tomorrow night?"

I nodded and he squeezed my hands. I headed for the bathroom to wash my hands.

The rest of the week went well at The Parisian, and pretty soon, I felt comfortable enough with the bartenders, waitresses, and bouncers to ask questions without anyone getting too suspicious. I thought about Annabelle every night and wondered where she was being kept, if she were still alive.

Vincent arranged to meet me in Chinatown one day and show me where Nicky had been run over. I was able to show him where I'd pulled the car over when I tried to elicit some information from Annabelle–it was only a few blocks away. "So what was with Nicky?" I said.

Vincent shrugged. "He called Coleman one day and asked if he wanted to get the goods on Dewey. Coleman told him yeah, it's not like he hasn't been trying for years to put the SOB away. Nicky wouldn't tell the commissioner what he had, but he just said he'd been working for Dewey for years and had never had a disagreement with his boss until now–he said Dewey had gone too far."

I thought about that for a moment, trying to remember what I knew about Nicky. Most of Dewey's thugs were stupid sociopaths. They enjoyed hurting people and getting paid to do it was just a bonus. Nicky been different. He'd actually been smart and had wanted to some-day run some part of Dewey's operation. Vincent told me that Nicky had realized his dreams and had been running the city's illegal gambling operation successfully for several years.

I frowned, thinking back to Annabelle. She was young, definitely not even eighteen. Nicky liked young women, but usually not that young. She hadn't acted like he was her boyfriend, more like he was her protector. Nicky had drawn the line at eighteen. He liked children, but not in that way.

Dewey, on the other hand, was ruthless, ambitious, and greedy–a dangerous combination. What was Annabelle to him?

It was on my second week that I finally found out. After the last set, Dewey came up to me. "You want to make a little more money, Karla?"

I smiled as I counted the tips, dividing them between me and the band members. "I seem to be doing all right." I indicated the money on the table in front of me.

Dewey put his hand down on top of the money as I tried to pick it

115

up. I looked up and Dewey was smiling. A smiling Lou Dewey did not make me relax. It was the smile of an crocodile ready to drag its victim off to the muddy bottom of the river. "Come with me where we have more privacy."

I hoped he wasn't going to make a pass. I'd made a point of avoiding romance, and I didn't intend to start with this guy. He led me to his office where we were alone, except for the tall dude in the corner who was pretending to be a Doric column.

"Karla, I got a proposition for you, but if you ever say anything to anyone outside this room, you're history."

It was original, I'll give him that. It had my knees shaking. I managed a smile. "Oh, gee, thanks, Mr. Dewey, but really, I'm happy with my job right now. I don't need any more money than what you're paying me."

Dewey turned his back to me and continued as if he hadn't heard me. "I got operations all over the city. The city is mine for the taking. I'm always expanding. I want you to help me get information of a highly sensitive nature on certain politicians and law enforcement officials high up on the food chain. You know what I mean?"

Yeah, I knew what he meant–blackmail. He wanted me to seduce certain men for him so he could use the leverage for money or power. "Can I think about it, Mr. Dewey?"

"Call me Lou," he said, waving a hand. "Let's have a drink." He didn't ask, he ordered. The Doric column in the corner detached itself from the wall and walked over to a bar. I asked for a club soda with a lime twist, Dewey had a bourbon on the rocks. "So you got yourself a little girl, huh?" he said, making conversation.

"Yes."

"How old?"

"Seven," I replied.

"Does she look like you?" Dewey's eyes swept over my body like a radar detector.

"Well, she's not so old, and she doesn't have as many curves, but yes, I like to think she favors me."

"Then she'll be a beauty when she grows up."

This turn in the conversation was starting to give me the creeps. I looked at the door longingly.

"Maybe she can work for me someday when she's a little older. You know, in a year or two," Dewey said.

I frowned, trying to figure out what an eight or nine year old girl could do to make money for Dewey. Not many options came to mind, and the ones that did were too creepy to even consider.

Dewey waved a hand and stood up. "Ah, we'll discuss that at a later date. Maybe you should bring her around one night, introduce us. You better get home to her, huh?"

I stretched my face into a smile and nodded, even as revulsion crept down my spine. "Yes. She worries about me." I didn't tell him that Vincent had sent Allie and my mother on a long visit to a distant relative.

The next morning, I met with Vincent and reported the blackmail scheme. "Could that be what Nicky was going to give us?" he asked.

I shook my head. "Dewey's been extorting and blackmailing for years. Nicky never had a problem with that before. It's something else, something different." I described my conversation with Dewey. Vincent looked serious. "Maybe you should stop now, Karla. I could get you some money and you could get out of the City. This sounds too dangerous."

"I'm sure Police Commissioner Coleman would be most unhappy," I said, then shook my head. "No, I've got to see this thing through. I've got to find Annabelle."

Annabelle was still on my mind. I found it incredible that I could care about a young girl I had only met once for a few minutes, but it was hard to forget the way she had been ripped out of my car, and with Nicky dead, I wondered if she had parents who were grief-stricken about her disappearance from their lives, wondering where she was. And if she didn't have parents who cared, I might be the only one who worried about her. I was beginning to think that if she wasn't already dead, time was running out for her.

That afternoon, I got to The Parisian earlier than usual. Brian was working the sax, ironing out the kinks.

He stopped long enough to give me a wink and a smile. "Hey, Songbird. What gives me the pleasure?"

I sat down next to him and looked around. "Brian, you want to go out for some coffee before we work up a couple new numbers?"

He raised his eyebrows. "You picking me up or something? It's a good thing I'm not married."

We went down the block to a diner that served bad coffee and great doughnuts. Brian ordered three doughnuts. If I didn't know any better, I'd have said he was a junkie. I used to crave sweets back then.

"Brian, Dewey asked me about my daughter last night."

He shrugged and swallowed a bite of doughnut, leaving a trail of powdered sugar on his clean-shaven chin. "He takes a personal interest in his employees."

I leaned forward. "Brian, look. I'm not stupid. This was not just a

117

casual conversation."

Brian began to shake his head, but he could see that I was not going to buy his innocent act. "You've been at the Parisian through it all, Brian. You know what's going on. Tell me. My daughter could be in danger."

Brian looked serious for a moment, then laughed loudly. "Dewey wouldn't harm her if you didn't want to sell her."

I practically leapt out of my chair. "What?"

Brian shrank back. I forced myself to sit still. "He's running a child prostitution ring?"

Brian nodded silently, his eyes a bit wary. Sweat had beaded up on his forehead. I covered one of his hands with mine. "I'm sorry, Brian. I didn't mean to frighten you, but that's pretty scary stuff."

His eyes were wide now, his expression frightened. Brian leaned close. "Don't tell him I told you. It's a secret. Not many know about it."

I shook my head. "How do you know, Brian?"

He shrugged and had the grace to look ashamed. "I meet my connection near the place where he keeps them."

Fear gripped my heart and squeezed. "Oh, Brian. I'm sorry."

He closed his eyes as if it had been painful to tell me. It probably had been. Tears welled up hot in my eyes and I blinked them back.

"Please, Brian, tell me where. I think a friend of mine is there and I have to find her."

He shook his head, his eyes empty. I had seen that look when I stared in the mirror eight years ago. God, why hadn't I seen it with Brian before? He was a junkie like the others. It made him unreliable. He could turn on me at any moment. I hadn't seen it before because I was remembering him the way he used to be and he'd played along. Junkies are good at changing sides, at becoming whatever you wanted them to be.

I touched his face and saw the bleakness in his features that I had chosen to ignore over the past few weeks. "When?"

"When the music stopped making me high." A tear rolled down his cheek. He told me the location of the ring, then he stood up. "But don't rely on me to stay quiet, Karla. It's been fun playing with you again." He smiled shyly. "If things had turned out differently, maybe–" He touched my hair, then was gone. I knew it was over. Brian was going to tell Dewey and the crime boss would either move the kids or kill them. With Dewey, you never knew. He was a wild card.

I made a quick call to Lieutenant Vincent, who was in a meeting with his superior, his brother Harry "Tank" Vincent. No, he couldn't be disturbed. They were having a meeting with the Mayor and the Police Commissioner about strategies for cracking down on crime in the city. Yeah, good idea.

"Well, you tell them that they can start with a child prostitution ring over on San Juan and Brendan. Lou Dewey is responsible."

"If you stay on the line, ma'am, I can--" I hung up before the desk sergeant could tell me what he could do.

I was fortunate that I'd found my little snubnose buried in my bedroom closet and had cleaned and oiled it recently. I'd left it in the car glove compartment because I figured I'd need it more there than in my apartment where I kept an old baseball bat for company.

Why am I doing this, I thought as I drove over to San Juan and Brendan. I'd done my part, I'd told Vincent where the child prostitution ring was, but it was clear that he wouldn't get here in time. But Dewey would, and if I could save only one child, I would. Annabelle. This was what had been the breaking point for Nicky. Good old Nicky would do anything Dewey wanted, except this. Nicky didn't want to be associated with child prostitution, but Dewey didn't care, as long as there was a buck to be made.

The thought of it caused bile to rise to my throat and I had to take a couple of deep breaths to keep from vomiting.

I parked across the street from the brick building and noted that I was already too late. Dewey was too smart–he would make sure he wasn't connected to this place. He'd sent the clean-up crew to take care of the problem. My problem was, I wasn't sure what he would do with the children.

Moments later, my worst fears were answered as the men left empty-handed, then I saw black smoke curled up from a bottom floor window. I was certain I could hear the thin wails of children trapped inside.

I got out of my car, my ears straining for a siren's scream, but none came. I took my coat off and, carrying it, trotted across the street. The door was closed but not locked. The fire had raced its way up the front stairs, but I fought my way to the back stairs, feeling the heat singeing my hair and scorching my back. The smoke made it impossible to see, but I found my way up the stairs. The fire hadn't touched the back part of the building yet, but it was just a matter of time. The building had once been elegant, perhaps a hotel or a high-class boarding house. But it was dilapidated now, an obvious fire hazard.

I kicked in the first door and found a young boy, sobbing hopelessly. He looked up at me and screamed. "Help me, help me, help me." I looked at the handcuffs that bound him to the wooden bedframe. I touched my gun. Would it work? His face dissolved in fear when he saw the gun and he shrank away from me.

"Hold your wrists apart," I said. If there were more like him, I'd need all the bullets in my gun–if there were more than seven children here, I could only save seven. He turned away, the links taut as I steadied, aimed, and shot through the metal links. He ran out before I had a chance to ask him where Annabelle was.

Door after door, I found child after child handcuffed to bedframes. Tears streamed down my face, from the smoke or the frustration of wondering how I could help them, I didn't know. I didn't have enough bullets and I hadn't found Annabelle yet. When I fired my last one, the young girl shouted that there was a fire ax down the hall. "Get out," I yelled. She obeyed me.

I raced down the hall, finally finding a fire ax in a glass box. I broke the glass with my gun, and blood welled from my cut hand as I pulled the ax out and hefted it.

I was up on the third floor and at the end of the hall when I heard the fire trucks and the police sirens. The children were probably huddled outside now, telling their stories of being found and rescued. Maybe there was some fireman battling the blaze right now. The thought that I might get out alive was comforting.

I opened the last door. A small girl with wavy dark hair was curled in the corner, handcuffed to a bed like the others. I gasped, maybe sobbed. She looked up. Annabelle. I'd found her.

"Oh, my God," I said. "Annabelle."

She didn't respond. Her eyes were dull–had she been drugged? No time to think about it. The fire had reached this end of the hall. I closed the door. Then I broke through the bed frame with the ax, nicking Annabelle once. She didn't seem to notice. Her eyes were red-rimmed. Yes, she had been drugged.

"Try to stand," I said above the roar and heat of the fire raging around us.

She looked up at me. And she smiled.

I broke the window. There was a ledge outside wide enough for me to stand on. With a drugged child, I wasn't sure, but we had to try. I gathered her in my arms and stepped gingerly out on the ledge. It didn't crumble, which surprised me. The brick wall was hot against my back and I wondered how long we'd be safe up here.

Down below, I could see the fire trucks, the police cars with their red and flashing lights, the hoses turned on full blast, the firemen and policemen milling around down there. I didn't see the children. Annabelle was heavy against me. She was sagging and I was trying to hold her up.

Someone below pointed in our direction and brought an inflatable bag for us to jump into.

"Jump! Jump!" The voices called out from below. Out of the corner of my eye, I saw the ladder truck, but it was blocked in by other official cars, and not able to get to us in time.The window to my left blew out and an orange ball of flame spewed out, sizzling the down on my cheek. I grabbed Annabelle around the waist and jumped.

When we hit the bag, all the air in my lungs exploded out and it took a full minute to regain my breath.

Lieutenant Vincent met me as they wheeled me to the ambulance. "How is Annabelle?" I asked.

He looked troubled, then said, "She's been shot up with something. I hope we can save her."

"What about the others?"

"Others?" He looked puzzled. But I understood. The kids had run away. I would explain it to him later.

I was back in my hospital room, only Allie didn't come to visit. I was under heavy guard and would be leaving the City behind as soon as I recovered. The lieutenant came in.

"How are you feeling?"

"How do you think I feel?" was my response. "How's Annabelle?"

"She's fine," he replied. "We found her parents and she's back with them now. By the way, she corroborated your story about the night Nicky was killed, so you're in the clear."

I tried to smile, but the burn on my cheek prevented it. "Thanks. I don't suppose you ever found any of those kids."

A muscle in Vincent's face twitched. "No, we didn't. But no dead bodies turned up, either. So I can only hope the kids got away."

"Is there a higher than usual rate of runaways on the streets these days?"

Vincent looked thoughtful. "I'll see."

"I wish I could testify," I said.

"To what? A building fire? You couldn't even pick out the guys who started the fire."

I turned my face away. "How is my daughter?"

The lieutenant touched my shoulder. "She's doing fine. I don't think she wants to leave that farm."

My thought strayed back to Annabelle. "You think Annabelle will be all right? Dewey won't come after her, will he?"

He shook his head. "She never even saw Dewey. Couldn't pick him out. But she did pick out one of Dewey's flunkies. He must have been in charge."

He patted my shoulder and promised to be there when I came out of the hospital in a few days. "I'll make sure you get to your new destination without any trouble. You're a brave woman, Karla. You've got more courage than I would have had under the same circumstances."

"Thanks," I replied, "but I know you'd have done the same."

When he left, I looked out the window. There was one thing I hadn't been truthful about–that I hadn't seen the men who set the fire. I'd seen them, and I had recognized one of them. But I couldn't give him away. I knew they wouldn't let him play his sax in jail. I had asked the lieutenant about Brian, telling him that the sax player had helped me with information. Vincent reported back that Brian had disappeared. I should have been mad at him for betraying me, but I had insight into what it's like to depend on a drug so much that nothing else matters, and I could only feel sorry for Brian.

I like to think that Dewey hadn't had him killed. I like to think that he's drying out somewhere, and that he'll be finding that high in his music real soon.

# spiro, spero, sparo
## by timothy toner

The first rays of dawn weaved and dipped through the ratty curtains, at last descending on the poor man, and pummeling him into waking-ness. His body went taut, the spasm not only strangling the last vestiges of heavy sleep from his muscles, but also forcing him off the bed and onto his feet. Once again he had awoke in this place, despite his best efforts to drink himself into a pine box.

He reached under the mattress and stabbed around. His clutching hand brought back two fives and loose change. Damn. He'd have to go to work. Already on his knees, he stared at the impassive ceiling, and promised that this time, this money would last him as long as he need-ed to finally get the job done.

He dragged on some clothes that would probably give the washer-woman a fit when he finally got around to turning them in a couple of weeks from now. That was her job, though. No one had an easy job these days.

After putting on his shoes, and running a comb through his angry locks, he retrieved a five and the loose change. Almost as an after-thought, he reached back under, grabbed his breadwinner, and jammed it into a pocket. The chances of getting a job this early was slim, but maybe he could get some work on the side.

The hallway outside his door was just as he had left it, the smell of piss battling fiercely with the pungent stench slithering from under the door of the new tenants, from some godforsaken country, people too stupid to realize that America just wasn't the land of opportunity any-more. From the smell, he figured they had discovered the local rat pop-ulation just fine. He didn't want to guess at how many humans were crammed in that hole.

Next was Marcia's, a whore. Marcia had her place fixed up really nice, and she never took her johns up there. That meant a lot of alley action, which meant a lot more scraping and bruising than the average girl got. She didn't mind it so much, as long as she had a place to go when the bumping and slamming stopped.

Inside, he heard moaning, like she was in pain or something. He reached for the doorknob, then remembered that she hated it when he came in uninvited. They had a system set up, in case she needed a lit-tle help. He'd come over with the clean bandages, the iodine, and his piece, and make all the pains go away, no matter what their name was.

Sighing, he passed by her door, and went down the stairs like he couldn't stand being in there a second longer.

The street was filled with the usual noise of late Tuesday morning. It was a school day, and yet the delicious crack of stickball echoed through the canyons. He remembered, way back when, his friends would skip school to play. He wanted to go, but he knew that his father'd find out, and beat him senseless.

"School is important," he'd squeak out. Now his father was dead, and he shot people for a living. "Thanks, pop." After work, he'd track down the boys, and maybe buy them a new ball or something.

He lived ten blocks away from the hole that George, his boss, operated from. The people inside were lazy with sin, and he knew that it would take a supreme force of will to send someone out after him. This meant that when he didn't want to work, he didn't have to, and that was all right with him.

The bar was as dingy as ever. Some stain on the front stoop told him that someone either died there last night, or maybe left his opinion of the establishment's rotgut where everyone could see. Whatever it was, it stank like hell. Of course, that was roses compared to the crowd inside.

He caught the edge of the door, and pulled hard. It lurched open, noisily announcing his arrival. About three heads meandered up. When Fatso, the bartender, called his name, everybody else looked up at the door.

"Un Sparo!" Gianni. He hated this prick. "How's it goin'? Mr. Vincento's been lookin' for you. Where ya been?"

"Where's George. I need to talk to him."

"Mr. Vincento," Gianni reminded him. He ignored it. "He's in his office. He's got this job for you. I hear it's a smoothie."

Somewhere between Gianni's correction and his opinion of the job, Gianni managed to snake an arm around him. He stared deeply into Gianni's thin, white, greasy face, and imagined that the little man under him was a brown rabbit, waiting to be skinned. Gianni yanked his arm away, lucky to escape some hidden trap.

"Sorry, Un Sparo."

He walked to the back of the bar, and opened the door to the office. Joey the Razor was sitting there, carving something out of a bar of soap. He snorted when Un Sparo entered the room. That woke George up from his light nap.

"Christ, Sonny. Where ya been? I almost had to send Joey out to haul your ass in here."

"I've been around."

124

"I hope you haven't been taking some on the side, cause that'll just ruin everything, you know what I mean? It takes a lot of work to get your rep up, and to keep it up. What's the matter? You don't like the jobs?"

"I like em all right, I guess."

"Good. Good, cause I just got one fer you. It's right up your alley. It's your specialty. Lemme get the number." He got up and headed for the bar.

That left Sonny and Joey in the room, staring at one another. Sonny had this guess that Joey didn't buy this "Un Sparo" crap for a second. In fact, Joey was the number one ice man for George–that is, until Joey was sent after this guy with a bodyguard from hell. Now everyone was calling him Joey Razorface, and with good reason. When Joey got hurt, Sonny took his next job, and a legend was created.

And Sonny hated every goddamn second of it.

George blew through the door carrying a few pieces of paper and an envelope. He passed between the two, and finally broke the lethal gaze. "Here ya go, Sonny. Here's the address and some stuff." He passed the envelope.

Sonny glanced at the paper. "The Plaza? You've got to be kidding me. I'll stand out like Joey here at a beauty contest!"

"That's what the other envelope is for. There's fifty bucks in there. Get yourself a new suit over at Hiram's."

"Yeah, and take a bath." Joey probably just figured out that crack. Sonny couldn't tell how pissed his was. Every time he smiled or frowned, he ripped open his face somewhere.

"Fifty buck? Isn't this a little low?"

"Nah, Sonny," George finished. "Trust me on this. It's just the down payment. Go to the hotel, and ask for Mr. Richard. Well, it's spelled Richard, but it sounds more like Reesh Ard. Or something like that. He's the hire. He'll tell you who he wants done."

"And how much are we talking?"

"Plenty," Joey spat out. "Don't worry."

"How much?"

George stood there, mulling it over. Then, "Ten Grand."

Sonny stood there, stunned. Christ, he'd take out Cardinal MacNamara for ten thousand. "Okay, George." He stared at the paper, and George hustled out into the bar to call a cab. Sonny was so enraptured that he failed to notice Joey flicking soap chips at him. He scowled down at the freak.

"Don't screw this up, pretty boy," Joey spat, "or else it'll be you and me at that contest."

Sonny turned to go. He opened the door, and turned about for a second. "Well, when they find out what you looked like before that, I'll still win, prick." He slammed the door, and waited for the razor to fly. It never came.

Normally he went to Vesuvio Tailors, a nice place on Third, when he wanted a good set of clothes. They made pleats for no extra charge, and Mary, the old man's daughter sure was something to look at. But George told him Hiram's, so Hiram's it was. He tipped the cabbie a little extra for running two yellows and a red. He had no idea when he should show up at the Plaza, so figured sooner was better than later.

He had never been in Hiram's before, and it was a class act. Apparently he wasn't the first guy to ever come in here, needing a little prettying up. Next door was a barber shop with a shower in the back. They took his measurements, and let him get a shave and a haircut while they fixed up the suit. Two hours later, he was escorted outside to a waiting cab. All that for only forty bucks. He tried to imagine how many times he could do that with ten thousand burning a hole in his pocket.

They arrived at the Plaza, the kind of place that let rich people pretend the Depression wasn't happening. Some guy with plenty of meat on his ribs opened the door with his hand out. He had the overwhelming urge to spit in it, but he had to play nice, so he gave him the skinned rabbit look, and watched the guy hurry away.

He stood at the door, and stared thoughtfully at his reflection. Christ, he looked terrible. Not sick, or ugly, but wrong. He looked like an alley cat who'd been grabbed out of a garbage can, cleaned, trimmed, and fluffed, and dropped in the middle of some mansion. No matter how many flea dips they gave that old cat, they couldn't take the alley out of his eyes. And that's what he saw as he stared into his reflection.

"Ah hell," he muttered, "Maybe that's what they're buying."

Mr. Richard wasn't in his room, or wasn't picking up the phone, or something. He hadn't eaten all day, so he wandered over to the restaurant to check out the prices. Five minutes later, he was across the street in the park, buying a hot dog and an apple from some poor chump who needed a break. Sonny may have looked like a million bucks, and he may have been worth $10,000, but he only had seven and change in his pockets.

He watched the people enter and leave, enter and leave. In four hours, he was the only person to make the sojourn across the street from the hotel into the big, bad park. It wasn't even dark yet, and they were staying away in droves. Why? It was a beautiful day, with the sun beating down. Sonny wanted to take a stroll through the park, but thought better of it. Still, why couldn't they come down from their high horse, and walk a while in the green?

The sun was getting a little too hot, so Sonny stepped back into the shade of the trees. He turned to watch some kids chase one another in something that was a cross between blind man's bluff, football, and a bar brawl. Just as he was rolling up his sleeves to either stop a fight or join in, a blaring of car horns attracted his attention. In that second, his mind slipped, and he saw the world in a way he had only once before. The large building, half seen through the foliage seemed different, as if it didn't belong here. It was like those pulp stories he picked up from time to time. He was a brave explorer, coming upon a world that didn't rightly exist here and now. He stepped forward, almost scared of something undefinable out there.

As the cold, dead structure filled the field of his vision, he realized why no one from there came here, and why no one from here ventured across the river of black asphalt and speeding steel into the hotel. Fear.

"Un Sparo?"

The name seemed so alien in this setting that he actually jumped at the sound. The speaker was a man, with short brown hair, impeccably dressed in suit and overcoat–despite the heat of the day–wearing thick wire rimmed glasses. His accent was foreign, a bit like the people at Hiram's. Who would know him here?

"I am Mr. Richard," the man answered. He extended a hand. The hitman took it out of reflex, and blanched at the cold, soft clamminess of the touch. He wanted to squeeze it until some life asserted itself. It was apparent that Mr. Richard hadn't done a lick of work his entire life. Of course, that made him wonder just how soft his hands felt.

"I recognized you from the description Mr. Giancomo gave me. He has an excellent eye for such things, I must admit. I spotted you as I was coming out of the cab. Have you been waiting long?"

Sonny really didn't hear that. In fact, he heard very little after "Mr. Giancomo." Salvatore Giancomo was the head of one of the largest gangs in the city. Out of his stable of hitman, Mr. Giancomo had somehow picked Un Sparo for the job. Most people prayed that Salvatore wouldn't hear their name, even with good news. Sonny was pleased as all hell.

The hitman abruptly became aware of the chasm of silence.

"Huh?"

"Have you been waiting long?" The man stared at Un Sparo as if he was addressing a fool.

127

"That depends," he shot back, "What time is it now?"

"Tut, tut, tut, Mr. Un Sparo. That won't do. Timing is everything in your trade, or so I'm told." He reached into his waistcoat and retrieved a pocket watch. "Here, take mine. It hasn't lost a second in twenty years."

Sonny took it without looking. This creep was far too casual, almost as if he was playing with the hitman–which was usually a very bad mistake. "Thanks."

"You're welcome. Shall we walk? I find the hotel so stuffy, so impersonal, and the park is so vital and spontaneous, as life should be. Besides, she's in there."

"Who?"

"My wife. You're going to kill her, you know."

"Now wait a minute. There's been some mistake. Maybe you don't understand how I operate, but I don't kill anyone I don't want to. No one makes me do anything. You come to me, and you drop names, and for all I know, you're one really smart cop."

"A policeman? Oh, no, Mr. Un Sparo. I assure you I am anything but."

"Yeah, if you were, they'd thrown you off the force years ago. Whatever. You come up to me in a park, and you start talking to me, and now you're talking about killing people like we're ordering bagels on Central. I'm saying that unless I take control of this conversation right now, you're gonna see the back of me walking away from you. Understand?"

"Absolutely." He was now filled with a nervous energy, as if he was ready to burst into tears. The man seemed terrified of something. Sonny checked it off as suddenly realizing that a hitman was pissed at you, and left it at that.

Sonny glanced in all directions. As usual, no cops. He started to walk down the path, then had to stop and turn around, and motion Richard to follow. This he did in a terrible hurry, a speed he probably hadn't reached in years.

Huffing and puffing at first, Richard eventually settled into a nice, easy pace next to Sonny. His demeanor changed rapidly. Apparently he was getting comfortable, and Sonny thought that maybe it wouldn't hurt to shake the little man up from time to time. He was certainly planning something behind those thick lenses, and Sonny hated to be jerked around.

"So let's talk about her."

"Her? Oh, my wife. Yes. Well, I suppose I want her dead..."

"Mr. Richard, you seem to be under the impression that I give a damn why you want her killed. If you want to get rid of your grief, see a shrink. I really don't care."

"What do you want to hear, then?"

"Tell me about her. Tell me her habits, her mannerisms. If I could count on her being in one place at one time, where would that be?"

"Ah, I see. Stalking the prey, learning the hunting grounds."

"Sort of."

"Well, she and I are currently residing in the Plaza, behind us. When she wants to shop, she sends for designers. Her hair and nails are done in the hotel spa. She seldom travels outside, except perhaps to the opera, though I suppose that if we could fit the opera house into our suite, she wouldn't go out for that."

"Huh. Well, I guess I could take her when she was getting into an elevator, or walking in a hallway."

"Oh, no, nothing like that. When I asked for you, I wanted to buy more than your finger. I want your expertise, your God given ability."

Sonny doubted that God had much to do with his ability to kill. He looked at the man as if Richard was one of those crazy saints, who had their arm hacked off and eaten in front of them by savages, and returned the next year to show them that their faith in God was bigger than that. Richard was all passion, and little sense.

"Another way to put it, I suppose, is that my wife is an exceptional woman, and she deserves the best."

"So what?"

"So I want you to take her at a distance. Any clod can kill her at close range. I could pull some soul selling apples off the street, and do as much. She's a delicate thing. She cannot see it, or you, coming."

"So I follow her then."

"Following is good. Of course, it would have to take place outside of this hotel. As it is, I can imagine you wanting to set the scene elsewhere. After all, the establishment prides itself on the privacy and safety of its guests. The murder of one so young and lovely would attract too much attention."

"Right. Thanks for looking out for me," he spat sarcastically. Then Sonny considered, "Long range?"

"Pardon?"

"Long range. You want me to do it long range?"

"Yes. She can't see you."

"Well," he groped, then grabbed, "I don't have a rifle. Just my piece."

"No rifle. Mr. Un Sparo, I thought you were resourceful."

Sonny stiffened. "As I need to be."

129

"I'll be sure to get you one. Here's $100. Get yourself a new wardrobe. You'll be following her, and it's paramount that you blend in. I'll send a copy of her schedule through the usual channels. Take the rest of the day off, and enjoy."

Richard tipped his hat in a funny sort of way, crossed the street and entered the hotel without looking back. With every step, he seemed to exude confidence that all would go as he desired.

Sonny was glad somebody felt that way.

After a quick stop at Vasari's, he returned home, arriving by cab. The local kids were home from school, and half of them stopped in their games to yell out cat-calls. "Hey, Sonny, Mr. Big Shot!" one brave soul screamed. "Lend me a five, and I'll let you date my sister."

Another shot back, "Sonny, he's robbing you. She does guys on the back porch for a buck."

Sonny smiled and ignored the prattle of a vicious fight just beginning. He'd seen the kid's sister, and they'd have to pay him ten bucks to come near her. Maybe later he'd come out with the iodine and bandages, and see if he could save some lives.

No mail. Good news. His momma always told him stories about getting mail, and the news was always bad. He tried to point out that she only remembered the bad stuff that happened in general, but she stuck to her stories. She wouldn't let a phone in the house, because she was convinced it was just another way to let bad news travel faster, and what was the point in indulging it?

He passed Marcia's door, and noticed it was opened a crack. Marcia had three bolts put on the door after a customer she turned down after hours decided to follow her home. He didn't get any, but cleaning up the blood in the hallway was a pain, and she wanted to discourage the wrong kind of people. It wasn't like her to be so...open.

He pushed lightly on the kickplate with his foot, and the door groaned open. Marcia was lying on the floor, her face resting peacefully in a puddle of vomit. "Crap," Sonny muttered. She probably hit it big last night, and didn't know when to stop.

The first thing he did was to get out of his clothes. Marcia was a friend, but not that good of a friend. He picked up some dirty towels and an undershirt that came back from the cleaners with holes in it, and cleaned up Marcia and the mess. Random bits of ham–looked like she had a couple of bowls of split pea– matted into her hair. She was still breathing, so he thanked God for small favors, and dropped her on her bed. He put a pan next to her mouth, and a tall glass of water on the table nest to her bed. Later, he'd bring around some aspirin and maybe dinner.

He dropped all three bolts, and stepped out onto her fire escape, closing her window as he went. With a deft move, he jumped onto his, and entered his own place. Sighing, he put another notch on the sill. The way he figured it, he still owed her ten or twelve "rescues." Then again, she never bothered counting.

He let he rest for four hours, and brought in some bread and a bowl of soup. When he came in through the window, she tensed momentarily. "What do you want?" she snapped.

"You need some food...well some food that'll stay down."

Perhaps for the first time, she looked down at the mess on the floor. "Crap."

"Yeah. I'll get the bucket and everything."

She sighed heavily. "Don't bother. I didn't clean the rags from the last time." She got awfully quiet.

"What happened?"

"I thought you didn't want to hear about this kind of crap."

Sonny shrugged. "It not like you, I guess."

"Well, yesterday I get a call to meet Janice and two of her friends at a club. At first I think it's nothing fancy, but Jesus you should have seen the spread. It must have been a party for some out of towner, or something. Anyway, they tell us to dig in, help ourselves. The johns want to get a good look before they make their picks.

"I got lucky. There's this old fart there, he walks up three sheets, and tells me he wants to talk. So I go to a table in the corner, and he just sits there, watching me eat. He buys booze by the gallon, and doesn't say a damn thing. Just watches.

"So I ask him what he wants. He gets off on being generous, and wanted to make sure I had plenty of food in me. To keep my strength up,' he says. What a laugh! We go up to a room, and he falls asleep in the middle of a blow job. So I go outside to get back to the party, only there's this goon standing there, and he tells me to "stay with him," and hands me a fifty. There's booze in the room, so I decide to have my own little party.

"When I wake up, I'm in a car with the kind of hangover I had when I was a kid. They drive me home, and the gorilla in the back seat shoves me out with a kick in the ass."

"You don't look bruised."

"Yeah?" She looked at Sonny with a mischievous look in her eyes. "I barely made it in before I blacked out. I'm lucky you came along when you did. Oh, hey, hand me my purse!"

131

Sonny reached over, and grabbed the pocketbook. Marcia rifled through it, counting a fistful of bills haphazardly. "Whaddaya know..."

"What?"

"I thought they swiped some cash. There's over a hundred in here. They gave me extra."

"What's the matter? You look spooked. Shouldn't you be happy?"

"It's just no one's done that before. People don't usually tip, y'know." She tried to absorb it all, then blurted out, "What does it mean?"

"Relax. I think you're someone's alibi. Think about it. There's this old guy from out of town. They throw him a really public party, then basically lock you in a room with him. Someone's probably gonna stop by in a couple of days, to check the story out. I'll ask around, see who's dead."

She looked at the money again, afraid it might burst into flames. "Thanks." Staring at the food, she added, "Maybe I should pay you back."

"Don't worry about it."

"I made you pay me back."

"Yeah, and sometimes I think it was you doing that that pulled me from the edge. But you're not me. And I just got a job."

"Oh." She liked talking about his job even less. "How much?"

"Too much."

"Is that a bad thing? You used to say that you preferred the big money. The more you made, the longer you could stay away, right?"

"I guess. But what would happen if someone walked up to you, and offered you..." He stopped. He had no idea how much she charged. Sure, he knew how much the average prostitute charged, but I didn't know her rates, and he sure didn't want to insult her.

"$400."

"For what?"

"You don't know, but he seems a pretty normal guy. Wouldn't you get suspicious?"

"How much are we talking about, Sonny?"

Sonny looked deeply at her, like she was his mother.

"$10,000."

"Holy shit!" she breathed, "Who?"

"Some bird, lives in the Plaza."

In the silence, mental wheels turned. She was asking the same questions that he was, but he couldn't ask them. He needed her now more than ever to mouth the concern, the worry that was ripping at him. She wasn't going to let him off that easy.

"I remember some drunk idiot, coming in here, telling me all he wanted was the big score, so he never had to kill again. Looks like you got it. What's the problem?"

Sonny just sat there. He brooded over a thousand responses but none cut deeply enough. Finally, he stood up like a shot.

"Look, I just don't know. It's so much money. Maybe, maybe if I knew what she did."

"Bullshit. You're a goddamn professional, just like me. I can't care what the john looks like. If he treats me good, that's just icing on the cake. It doesn't make a difference if she's Ma Barker or the Virgin Mother. Dead is dead. That's the only thing you have to think about."

"Christ, that's cold."

She had never talked like this before, so bluntly. It was like she was a different person. Something new was in the air. He shivered involuntarily.

"I'm sorry, Sonny. I guess I'm a little jealous, is all. You know what I'd do with ten grand."

"Yeah, sure." He was still pissed.

"Look at us. A whore who doesn't like to fuck, and a hit-man who doesn't like to kill. All we need is the scarecrow and Dorothy and we're on our way."

Somewhere in the building, far away, a baby began screaming for its mother. Sonny wanted to be anywhere but in this room right now, in this building. "I'm going out," he announced. "I've got some things to look into."

Marcia tried to smile. "Thanks for the food. Do you think you could pick me up some Luckies?"

He nodded. "Here." He handed her an unopened pack that had just been weighing down in his pocket. He was too nervous to smoke. If he had to hold something in his hand for too long, someone might see it shaking.

"Thanks." She held out a bill, and looked at it, then at Sonny. For his part, Sonny stared at it like it was a coiled adder, waiting to bite. He smiled back and took it. He really didn't need the money, not now. But this was normal business practice between them, and that's what he needed right now.

As he walked back out the door, he glanced back at Marcia, who was looking out the window. Maybe she needed it, too.

The next morning, he stopped by the bar. The atmosphere was just as he left it: stale and muggy, with the usual whiff of urine and vomit, and a tinge of rank sweat that gave the illusion that working people, legitimate people, came to this bar for a good time. Sonny glanced at Fatso, and wondered when was the last time he sweat for a buck a day. Then he stared deeply into the dirty glass behind the bar, and asked the same question about the wretch looking right back at him.

"Fatso, where's George."

"Oh, hey, Un Sparo. I didn't see you come in. Do you want something to drink?"

"Where's George," he repeated, with no change in intonation.

"Uh, I think he's in his office, unless he went out the back door–"

Sonny shot past him, ignoring all the greetings he got. News traveled fast, apparently, and everyone wanted to catch his good eye. They figured he was on the rise, and they didn't want to be forgotten in the gutters. Sonny had an odd feeling that by the time this was done, they'd be using him to step over the bigger puddles.

He knocked on the door. Decorum was decorum, and George deserved respect. "Come on in, Sonny." Sonny turned the dirty brass knob, and pushed the door open. The light that flowed from the room's onlywindow seemed stale, and George's normally pasty skin took on a deathly pallor.

"You don't look well."

"I didn't get much sleep. I woke up at five this morning. Two gorillas were on my stoop, trying to wake the whole goddamn neighborhood. They had a package to deliver. This."

Resting next to Sonny was a large flat package, covered in brown paper. "It belongs to you. I was informed by the two that I was less than diligent in getting the first message delivered. I was told not to leave my bar until you arrived to pick up the package. If I did–"

"Christ, George," he interrupted, "You should have sent someone over. I would have come."

"I would have. But I got no one to send. Those lushes out there couldn't remember an address if it was printed on the bottom of a bottle of rotgut. The regular guys...they don't come in until noon. The phone...the two took the phone with them."

"I don't know what to say. I'm sorry. I just didn't know."

"It's all right, Sonny." George sighed heavily, and propped his head on the desk with his forearm. "It's not about you. It's a message. They're telling me I run a sloppy ship. I get in here at 10, the boys get in whenever they feel like it, and to them, that's bad business. I've been doing it for the last ten years, bringing in steady numbers, and now it's no goddamn good? Fuck 'em!" George's rage seemed to teeter on the edge of a vast chasm of fear. Someone had scared him this morning, and Sonny guessed that George wouldn't be taking this heat if it wasn't

134

for this job.

"Well, you can do me a favor, and take the damn package off my hands. It's addressed to you, so I didn't even think about opening it up. No telling what kind of breech of loyalty' that would be." He grabbed one end, and slid the long, crinkling parcel at the hitman. "Damn, I need a drink. I'll be back." George stood and walked out the door.

The paper was the normal delivery wrap, used by butchers and art houses alike. Anything could be in it, but the twine that wrapped it wasn't frayed in the least. In fact, Sonny noticed that someone had taken the time to wax it, to prevent the normal fraying which seemed to be an essential characteristic of twine.

He removed a knife from his pocket, and sliced off the cords. The paper had a stamp on it, but the ink had smudged. Some kind of sporting' store...but near the park? With an address like that, Sonny would be surprised if whatever inside didn't have mother of pearl inlaid screws.

He wasn't far off. Under the paper was a hand tooled leather case, a supple, pliant yet firm bag. He had seen pictures of hunters carrying such guns on trips. Popping the three clasps, he opened it up on the desk, and looked inside.

It was a rifle, though calling it just a rifle was a bit of an understatement. Its grip was exquisitely polished wood, its metal surfaces bearing no hint of vulgar machining. This was virtually hand-tooled, from the case all the way down to the trigger guard.

Sonny noticed that his hand was trembling as he reached out to touch its surface, and he quickly pulled it away. Despite its intense beauty, it was a frightening gun. It somehow reminded Sonny of a knife he had picked up at a carnival when he was twelve. It was sharp and beautiful, and Sonny had to have it. It cost him four weeks worth of errands, but the mere motion of swishing it through the air erased all doubts from his mind. Then the gems dropped off, and the blade took on a nasty greening color. Finally, when he needed it most, the blade had snapped off. He never trusted anything so beautiful again. The door opened, and George came around to look at the piece.

"Hey, nice! You order this special or something?"

"The client offered to pick something up for me. I figured some war surplus. Definitely not this."

"Can I take a look?" His eyes were on the piece, slowly bulging with intensity. He would have reached for it, no matter what Sonny had said. "Sure."

There was something else—a folder, hidden in the leather case. Sonny grabbed this while George hoisted the rifle and aimed it at an imaginary target in the next room.

"Christ, this butt has to be rosewood! It feels like it's a part of me. Y'know," he added, aiming the weapon out the window, into the alley, "I was in the war."

"Yeah, I heard."

"Ah, I woulda killed for something this sweet. Those bastards woulda lined up to get shot by something like this. It's even got slots for a...hey, a scope!"

Sonny slid open the folder. It was, of course, from Richard. His wife's schedule was detailed in a meticulous handwriting that caused the hairs on his neck to stand on end. It went for pages and pages. There was only one way he could have gotten this kind of information–he had asked his wife directly. Christ, he thought, how can I trust this? Maybe she fed him a line?'

By this time, George had mounted the scope and was beginning to look fondly at the cartridge of bullets that came with the rifle. Sonny snapped the folder closed, and tried to figure out where he stood. "So how is it?"

"When I heard the payout, I figured it was a set-up. Honest. The word came from so far up, though, that you would probably been better off being caught by the cops right off, rather than sitting in a greasy little hole, waiting for someone else to rat you out. If you went down, I figured, you'd go in good company.

Then I see this morning how important Mr. Giancomo thinks this is. He's no fool. Hell, he'll ice people if he even gets a bad vibe about em. Even people like Giancomo can be wrong, right?

Then...then I see this. Christ, I can't even put a price on this. It's handmade! This ain't a rifle. It's a work of art."

"Damn shame," Sonny tossed in.

"Eh?"

"Damn shame it's gonna be at the bottom of the river in about a week."

George blanched at the thought. He gripped the rifle more tightly, as if he was making a stand against Sonny.

"C'mon, George. I'm not going to pop some woman, and put the damn thing on my wall. If Richard wants to pay me to kill his wife with the president's tea set, then it's ending up at the bottom of the river, with all the other crap we put there. It's his fault his taste is so good."

George stared intently at Sonny. "I've got some good pieces in a warehouse by the river..."

Sonny rolled his eyes. "George, correct me if I'm wrong, but didn't Mr. Giancomo offer to break your legs for showing up to work late? If

Mr. Richard spent cash to get this piece, I think I'll use it."

"Yeah, you're right. Fuck. Okay, here's the problem. It's bolt action, no cartridge loading."

"Huh?"

"You get one shot, and you have to reload. I know you, Sonny. You like your revolvers, six shots and all. Well, he's making you live up to your name. You got one shot before you have to reload, and since I think you haven't been this close to a rifle before, reloading ain't going to be a choice."

He slammed a bullet into the chamber. "Action's good. Nice and smooth."

"Any problems?"

"None from this end." He hesitatingly put down the rifle, and scratched something on a piece of paper. "Here's the address of a gallery. You can work on getting used to the rifle there. Just show him..." George stared at a second piece of paper that he was scratching on, and finally crumpled it up. "Just show the rifle. They'll know you're for real."

"Thanks. I really appreciate the help, and all. This is the weirdest job I ever took."

"Y'know what they say about the weird ones."

"Yeah, I know. They always get you killed."

Sonny didn't have time to check out the range. The schedule said that she was eating lunch crosstown today. It was one of the few times she would be out for the rest of the week. If he wanted to get a good look at her, now was the time.

He slung the leather case over his shoulder, and held the folder in one fist, reading it as he walked to the streetcar. Occasionally he'd glance about, and once or twice, he'd notice his reflection in a storefront window. He was neatly groomed, wearing a nice blue suit and shiny shoes that looked good but pinched a bit. Even the case he was carrying didn't seem out of place for the places he was going. Sonny thought for a moment about maybe renting a room near the Plaza, to cut down on travel time. Like this, maybe he could fit in.

Some moron came out of a deli too fast, and almost spilled beer on his lapel. Sonny shoved the man out of the way, and issued a string of words that would have cracked the beads on his mother's rosary. The man blanched, and ran back to whatever rock he climbed under.

Sonny stopped, and looked at his reflection, and then beyond that, at the scared faces peering out, hoping he wouldn't come in. He sniffed, and started walking. Foxes could steal the occasional chicken from the hen house, but it wasn't in their nature to move in.

The restaurant was just as classy has he had anticipated. Even the doorman had manners enough not to sniff when he walked in. He was fifteen minutes ahead of the schedule, which somehow translated into an hour and fifteen minutes ahead of Mrs. Richard. Taking a seat at the bar, he read a paper as an endless line of the rich and powerful were herded to their troughs for their afternoon feed. Not once did anyone come up to him and ask his business, or wonder if he might like to eat something. It was like he was being allowed to observe another way of living, a kind he could smell and hear, but never truly know. More than the food, something about this place made him hungry, and knowing that he could never feed turned that growling into a quiet anger.

Finally, she showed. The paper said that she was a blonde woman wearing a green dress and a green rose. He had never seen a green rose before, but that didn't bother him very much–until he saw it. It was a delicate thing, perched on her left breast. It hovered between being a pin and a brooch in size, and it was formed of a mass of emerald shards. Glass? Glass never caught such light. Somehow they were real.

The rest of her seemed less so. She was thin, tight, and drawn. She wore her smile the way she wore the rose, telling the world just how much it cost her to own it, and how risky it was to put on each day. She seemed neither happy nor sad, just tired.

She came with a flock of admirers, it seemed. The women who came to lunch with her were just as rich, though by no means as beautiful. Some were younger, but most were older, the bloom at last beginning to fade. They marched past the maitre'd without even acknowledging him, and he rushed behind them, awkwardly trying to get past them, to make sure all was ready.

They sat at a circular table in the center of it all. Stalks of fresh cut flowers sprang upward from a breathtaking centerpiece. She sat down first, and all followed, fanning away from her. Menus, all different from those passed out to the regular patrons, were passed around, but the ladies only glanced. Sonny was certain that they hadn't come to eat as much as to be seen.

Who was she? Rich, yes, but so were all these other women. He had never seen her before, or heard of her. She wasn't a film star, as far as he could tell. Why did she stand out in this crowd, like the single lily which rose above the rest of the flowers in the middle of the table. He didn't realize that he had been staring at her until he became aware of someone standing next to him at the bar. Sonny turned to face the waiter, who seemed just as content to wait until he was done looking.

"What do you want?" he snapped.

138

"I've prepared your table." He turned, walked a few paces to a table set for one. It provided an excellent, unobstructed view of her. Food was already on the plate, a steaming mass of meat and sauce.

"What is this?"

"Your lunch, sir. Seared medallions of beef in a dried plum sauce, with cubed vegetables."

"Who ordered this?"

"Mr. Richard, sir. He informed us that you would be sitting at the bar, and that you might be hungry."

"Huh." He sat down, and barely remembered to lay his napkin across his lap. Sniffing the food, he turned to the waiter. "Uh, do you think you've got a steak back there?"

"Yes sir. It's already cooking. Mr. Richard would like you to try this first, however."

Sonny raised an eyebrow. He picked up the knife and fork, and sliced off a piece. Gingerly, he laid it on his tongue, and slowly chewed on it. "Good," he spoke to no one in particular. When he noticed that the waiter had not yet moved, he turned and said,

"This is fine. I'll have this."

"Very good." He walked away briskly to attend to another table. Sonny noted that the bastard had never asked him how he wanted his steak cooked.

She ate very little, that was for certain. Some of the women were wolfing down their food in mouthfuls, while others lightly nibbled at greens. She simply stared at the food, as if wondering which leaf was poisonous. Occasionally she would take a bite, but a pained expression would lash across her face with each swallow. He sensed she didn't want to be here, but she had to. Why?

She saw him. Her eyes momentarily flashed across the room, and their gaze locked. Something pulled tight in his groin, and his grip around the fork intensified. Just as quickly, she looked away, but the sense of wonder was destroyed. Sonny had seen that look in her eyes once before. He wanted to get this business over with as soon as possible.

He got up and stormed out without even attempting to pay. He knew, of course, that all this would be paid for. Everything. Too bad that foreign bastard hadn't thought to buy him a bottle of rotgut. Sonny bought one just to spite him, crawled on top of his bed, and let it all just float away.

He remembers this street corner. He was in a bar, and some loudmouth told everyone in earshot that The Man would be here. So here he is. The gun feels heavy. Soon, in a few months, it will sink so deep in his pocket that it will create its own home in there, but for now, it burns against his thigh.

Someone walks right up to him, and looks deeply into his eyes. The stranger says something, but Sonny can't make it out. It's like they're underwater. Sonny just shrugs, and the man pushes him against the wall, and walks past him.

Sonny is mad. He wants to fight back, but that will ruin everything. He needs to wait, to be patient. Soon, soon.

There's a noise from a doorway, and people begin rushing outside, some toward an idling car. Strong voices cry out from down the street, coming closer. The runners are scared of those voices. They draw their guns, and turn away from Sonny. There are others. Sonny is not alone.

He grips the gun and his fingers go cold as it drinks hiswarmth.

Shots ring out, pop, pop, pop. Sonny waits, a stupid bastard too dumb to duck. More pops come from the building, and at last, He comes out.

Sonny doesn't remember him glowing, but he is. He's beautiful. Looking at that light, Sonny can't kill. He can't do his job. He raises the gun, but his finger rebels. The Man is too powerful. Sonny needs to say his name.

Sangallo.

The Man turns. Only he hears. His face is grim and angry, and he will kill Sonny very very soon. Then, for a second, their eyes lock. Sonny sees within them the same liquid that pulsed out of the rat's eyes when he put them out at twelve years.

The aura fades. The Man's death becomes tangible.

Sonny is aware that the strong voices are gone. The running men are turning toward him. he has one shot. One shot.

Un Sparo.

Christ. He hated that dream. Sonny slid out of the wet bed, and got out the rags he used to soak up the mixture. Tomorrow he'd buy a new mattress, and maybe rubber sheets. He knew the dream wasn't going away, because the memories never would.

She had no appointments over the next two days. Sonny still went to see George bright and early, and spent the balance of the day at the range. Fortunately, no one knew who he was. Fortunately, because he was the worst shot ever. The old men who probably fought in the War (and then again probably not) laughed at his feeble attempts to "get it right," and his anger just made it worse. Twice he felt like leveling the rifle at one of them, but then he remembered that he would only have one shot, and they were all toting guns.

On second day, Sonny learned how to drown out their voices. It didn't make him a better shot by any means, but it did curb his homicidal impulses. He also patiently watched them. He never asked for help, because he knew (rightly) that it would have been thrown right back in his face.

Near the end of the second day, someone Sonny had never seen before entered the range and picked a spot next to Sonny. He had an odd smell to him, a bit like the incense they used in Church. Great gouts of it had blown into Sonny's face when he had been an altar boy, and these memories touched off a bit of queasiness.

The stranger set down a case, but instead of unpacking, he simply turned and watched Sonny slowly take aim and squeeze off a shot. He never spoke a word. Instead, he would occasionally touch his mustache. Sonny soon realized that the stranger would touch only if he did something wrong, perhaps holding too tightly, or sighting before aiming.

Despite this silent assistance, Sonny was becoming extremely self-conscious. He settled on a quick scowl to throw at his patron, when he heard a chorus of chuckles coming from the corner of the room. The stranger silently turned and walked over to the regulars. He heard quiet whispers issue from the man, and they seemed to hang in the air like his scent. The group suddenly blanched, and even the manager of the gallery hastened out the door.

Now alone, Sonny broke into an impromptu smile. "Thanks."

The stranger ignored Sonny's politeness. Instead, he closed the distance, and hovered perhaps a foot away. He seemed intent on studying Sonny's face, specifically his eyes. At last he spoke.

"Do you want to kill someone?"

Sonny had never met this man before, and yet he trusted him. "Yes."

"Want to, or have to?"

Silence, then, "I don't know how to answer that."

"People kill for two reasons. Because they want to." He held up his right trigger finger. "Because they have to." He held up the left. "Why do you kill?"

Sonny opened his mouth to speak, but nothing came out. This man had managed to rattle him, something no one had been able to do in years. Finally, he closed his mouth and stood there.

The stranger nodded. "You really don't know, do you? That is why you cannot make this shot. That is why you cannot kill this woman. You pretend it is your job, but it is not. It is something more. Before

141

you can kill, you must make that decision. Until you do this, you will never come close. You do not need to practice. You have the hunter's eye. Now you must develop the hunter's resolve. Go home."

The stranger picked up the case he carried, and walked right out the door. With trembling hands, Sonny raised the rifle to his shoulder, and concentrated on the target. Rivulets of sweat dripped into his eyes, and stung them. Despite this, despite the sound of his heart pounding in his chest, he aimed and squeezed.

He quickly stripped the gun and packed it into his leather pouch, and walked out the door. There was no need to check the target. He knew how bad the shot was.

Bullseye.

Sonny intentionally avoided the bar on the way home. He sensed that word had got back to George about his performance at the range, and that George had arranged for a "tutor." Right now he had a lot to think about, and he didn't need yet another lecture.

Unfortunately for him, one was waiting for him on his front stoop.

"Richard?"

With his head bent down, he almost ran into the squat man as he rose from his seat of the stairs.

"Hello, Un Sparo."

Richard didn't belong here. In every way, his presence was absurd. He was clean, his clothes were sharp and pressed, and he was alone. A trim of blood gathered around a cut above his eye, which Richard daubed with a white linen handkerchief. Sonny couldn't imagine Richard getting into a fight. "What happened?"

"Nothing. I perhaps was a bit rash in coming here, but I needed to reach you. Besides, it only cost me a wallet. Nothing irreplaceable. Here." He handed Sonny an envelope.

"Uh..." Sonny glanced around. "Do you want to come in?"

"Of course."

Sonny bustled him through the foyer, up the stairs, and through the door of the apartment. It slammed behind them, and Sonny managed to secure the three locks before Richard could react. Sonny turned on the small man, and let it out, both barrels.

"What the FUCK were you thinking!"

Richard stared impassively into his face. "I admit it's been quite a bit of time since my bohemian days, but..."

Sonny raised his hand to silence him. "No more. NO. MORE. You don't own' me. You don't control' me. I don't know what sort of sick thrill you're getting out of killing your wife, but you can't do this.

Maybe the occasional hit man will take a request, but nothing's worth $10,000!"

The small man stared at Sonny like he was speaking Greek. "What? You mean $20,000."

"What?"

"The fee. It's $20,000."

"Whatever. I–"

"Don't tell me they've...lied to you. Well, I'm sure there's some misunderstanding."

"It isn't the money, you bastard! I don't care how muchyou're paying me! You can't treat me like this!"

"Like–how? Have I been unkind? Have I robbed you, insulted you, stole the clothes from your back, the food from your mouth? Quite the opposite. I ask you to do a simple thing, a thing I cannot do myself, for reasons I cannot say. I only ask for the time and place to be prearranged, to prepare her, and myself. I do this neither frivolously, nor through a desire to see her in pain. Quite the opposite. Quite the opposite, you see.

In the envelope are two tickets for tomorrow's performance of the opera. She decided at the last moment to attend. I had to move heaven and earth to obtain these. Please attend."

Sonny stared at the unopened envelope. "I can't do this thing."

"Alia iacta est. It is too late to turn back now. You know as well as I do that you must see this thing to the end. If, however, I have read you wrong, then I must beg your forgiveness. Simply attend the opera, with my blessings, and I shall absolve you of this contract. Is that acceptable?"

Sonny looked up suddenly. "Why two tickets?"

"Hm. A single man at the opera, of your age, and...appearance, would stand out rather badly. You'll need to bring someone with you. Treat your girlfriend, or a female friend."

"I don't know, Richard..."

"Merde, take an escort for all I care! Bill me for whatever costs you enjoin! Just be there."

He turned his back on Sonny, and stormed out of the apartment into one of the most dangerous neighborhoods in the city with no wallet. Sonny was learning a whole new respect for this strange little man.

It wasn't hard to convince Marcia to go. Sonny's tongue stumbled over whether this would be business or personal. How much should he offer? Did she ever take a day off? Marcia allayed his fears eventually by insisting that he buy her a dress appropriate for the occasion. He had no stomach for shopping, but she dragged him to a place where he could get something to wear. Apparently Marcia had a stash of glamor magazines waiting for just such an occasion. When he came to pick her up, he felt like mentioning how good she looked, but, tonight at least, he couldn't deal with any of the fifty ways she'd respond to that. It might have been a night out for her, but he was working, and she'd have to understand.

On the cab ride over, Marcia filled him in about her uncle who worked in the theater, and would take her to see shows from time to time. She stopped going when he tried to get under her dress for the third time, but she'd always scrimp and save to go once, maybe twice, a year. "But never like this," she added.

Marcia didn't seem too disappointed when they hopped out of the cab a block away. Sonny knew that arriving at these things were sometimes a big deal, and he wanted to be as small as possible tonight. He showed his tickets to the man, and walked into the softest, plushest building Sonny had ever been in.

"Where are we sitting?" She was holding gently onto his elbow, but so was every other woman. Richard was right. Without Marcia by his side, Sonny looked like an idiot.

"Uh, over here. He watched her out of the corner of his eyes as her face slowly, secretly caught fire. If Richard wanted to impress him, it had failed. Marcia on the other hand could probably have been knocked out by a feather. They sat, and Marcia ate up the program while Sonny looked for her. Late, as usual.

Near as he could tell, the show wouldn't start without her. It was already ten after, and the orchestra up front were still showing no sign of getting seriously ready. In the amount of time it took Sonny to figure out what the hell the guy was doing with his oversized violin, she had arrived. He knew, because a murmur passed through the crowd. It was a quiet thing, like a fish breaking the surface of a pool at midnight, its presence felt only by ducks and dead leaves floating. He looked about, and saw her. Stunning.

"Is that her?" There was something different about Marcia's tone. He had not known her long enough to hear her full range of emotions, but it was either jealousy...or pity. Either way, it aggravated him.

"Yeah," he sighed.

"Ten thousand," she whispered back. "Worth every cent, if you ask me."

His reply was lost in the rush of chords which erupted from a dozen violins screaming as one. She settled into her seat, and was thankfully silent. Sonny–he couldn't take his eyes off of her. In a quiet place, he wished that she would turn, see him, see the malevolent intent, and call off her husband. Where was he anyway?

At intermission, Marcia pressed past him, and headed for the ladies' room. Sonny tried to sit right where he was, but she had disappeared sometime before the curtain descended. With nothing better to do, he decided to stretch his legs.

The cream of society packed themselves into the lobby, most hanging together, and from the snippets of conversation he caught, not much was being said all around. He tried to pick up a pack of smokes, but the girl didn't sell Luckies, and the guy she was currently talking to didn't give a damn about the monkey on his back.

"Sonny."

The voice came from the throng. It wasn't Richard, but the voice sure sounded familiar. Who would know him here? He moved closer to the wall, where the voice came from, and without intending it, he slammed into Don Montorsi. His boss.

From what Sonny heard, the way the food chain in this city worked, Giancomo was everybody's boss. And Sonny, in his own little way, had helped him get there.

"Mr. Giancomo. How are you?"

"Good. How are you enjoying the night?"

Sonny shrugged. It wasn't proper, but it was honest.

"This music. It comes from within. It has such power over us. Don't you agree?"

"I guess. I've never heard it before."

"Ah, the lyrics, the music, the singers, they're nothing, you see. It's only when they come together that they come alive. It doesn't matter if you've never heard a note of opera before. The moment you hear it, you're born again."

Sonny had no idea Giancomo was such a fanatic. Then again, he intentionally kept his distance from the man.

Giancomo glanced about, waved politely at someone, and looked again at Sonny, as if appraising him. "Walk with me. We must discuss the future."

Sonny noticed that the rich and wealthy knew when a wolf roamed in their midst. They parted and nodded, showing proper deference, but Giancomo must have been deaf not to hear the murmurs that rose in their wake.

"So how is this thing going?"

The hitman almost missed it. "The thing? Oh. Well."

"Not from what I hear."

145

"I would have had it done earlier, but Richard's such an odd—"

"Odd? No, not odd. Never say odd. He sees what you cannot. He's lived more lives than you've destroyed."

"Sir, I don't know. He's made these demands of me. Frankly, I've considered walking away. I don't even know why I was fingered for this."

"I did."

"What?" Sonny heard him just fine, but needed this confirmation.

"I did, you ungrateful bastard. Look at you. Almost thirty, and you're in a damn rut, with no intention of climbing out. Richard came to me, asking for someone very special, very good, and your name just came out. I almost changed my mind, but after hearing about you, Richard was hooked.

"What's the matter with you? There are ten men, killing one another to be where you are right now, and you throw it back in my face. I don't care what Richard wants. I want it done! Am I clear?"

"Yes."

"AM I CLEAR?" Heads turned.

"Yes, Mr. Giancomo."

"Good. Is George treating you well?"

Sonny was pissed, and felt like taking it out on someone. He had twenty-thousand reasons to be pissed at George, but he shook them out of his mind. "He's the best."

"Excellent." He placed his broad right hand on Sonny's shoulder. It seemed a sign of affection to all who watched, but under the grip, Sonny's shoulder trembled.

"I have plans for you," Giancomo finished. "Grand plans. Don't fuck it up."

The boss walked away, disappearing into the crowd.

Sonny made his way back to his seat with time to spare. At this moment, he wanted his rifle. Screw that, he wanted his gun. He would take the bitch out where she sat, and this would all be over. He wasn't a lick-boy, like the rest of them at that bar.

Through his fury, he didn't notice that Marcia was already seated. She remained silent for a time, and finally leaned over. "I saw you talking to him."

"You know him?"

"He was at the party. I thought he was the pope, with all that ring kissing. What happened?"

"Fuck, I dunno. He's got this thing against me. I don't know what the hell I could have done."

146

Marcia snorted. "You're a hit-man, and you don't even know fear when you see it?"

"Fear?" Sonny looked at her as if she was crazy.

"Sonny, you're a giant-killer, for Christ's sake. How many people living today can say they killed the head of a gang, and walked away to get a cup of coffee? You're probably the only person in this whole god-damn city he's afraid of, since you know he's just flesh and blood. It's no wonder he wants you under his thumb."

He knew she was looking up into his face, but he was too scared to look back. "Marcia," he said, "What if I told you that it was a fluke, that I should be dead right now, if not for blind, stupid luck?"

She didn't reply. The music started, the curtain rose, and not another word was spoken. Sonny caught sight of her up there in her balcony, and soon lost track of what they were discussing. At some point, however, he did a half turn to stretch his neck, and found her sitting there in the dark, trembling.

Marcia had recovered for the ride home. She tried to explain the opera to him, but he could sense that she was trying a tad too hard to make him open up, to throw off this gloom. He enjoyed it too much, and so he shut her out totally. He didn't care if her face took on a color given more to rage than frustration. There was a monster living inside of him right now. He had let it out, and now he had to put it back to sleep.

The taxi stopped at their apartment, but he didn't climb out. "Thanks for coming," he told her, almost as an afterthought. Sonny thought he heard her ask him to come in, to call it a night, but he didn't know if he could trust her. He certainly didn't trust himself.

He slammed the door shut, and the taxi roared off into the night.

It was Friday, and it was almost noon. Sonny woke up in George's place, lying on two tables, and using his jacket as a blanket. The bar was empty, the door closed. Fatso was behind the bar, cleaning glasses, but the place was apparently closed just for him.

Sonny rolled off the table, and barely managed to catch himself before he found a new bed on the floor. Standing very still, he waited for the aching to stop (or at least lessen to the point where he could breathe), and then stumbled out the door. All the while, Fatso was hovering around him, trying to tell him something, but Sonny just didn't care.

Maybe he took a cab home, maybe he walked the whole damn way. The result was the same: he was standing in front of his apartment building, and his stomach was now very empty. The only reason why he paused here was an odd stillness. The street should have been bustling with kids. with women hanging out of windows and men standing in doorways. Save for a few souls who seemed to be rooted to their spot, there was no one out and about. The quiet only intensified with each step upward. He could hear no argument from the newlyweds on the first floor. The radio was silent on the second landing. Even the new tenants' children were silent as he passed their door, though he could swear that he heard faint sobbing.

He never made it to his door. He never got past Marcia's. Fragments of wood were liberally sprinkled on the floor, and the door swung open freely with a touch. The room was utterly destroyed, with huge holes pounded into the wall, knocking out chunks of plaster. In the center of it all was a lump, covered in a bloody sheet.

He caught the edge with the tip of his shoe, and dragged. With each heartbeat, he told himself that he had to be sure that it was her. First came rich black locks, matted with blood, then a pale tint to her forehead that only suggested blue. He stopped at her nose when he realized that she had been kicked to death, particularly around the mouth.

Reaching down gently, he touched the stained sheet and covered her. For a moment, his eyes fell on the bucket and some rags that she had apparently got around to cleaning. In his fevered mind, he knew it would only take a second, but the need to know who did this thing and do something about it drove him out of the room.

He first went next door and retrieved his pistol and the leather case. As far as he could tell, everything was in working order, so he washed off his face and changed into something fresh. Tucking the revolver into its convenient hole, he slung the case over his shoulder and marched out without shutting the door. He wasn't coming back.

Checking the floor carefully, he now noticed bloody footprints. There were two, maybe three. They stopped at the immigrants door after they killed her. He needed to know what they looked like.

He knocked pointedly. They was a quiet, hysterical sob from the other side of the door. The mother, he guessed. He knocked again. The door rattled, and she began to scream. With all his hate, he kicked it in.

Sonny had never been in here before, and frankly, he didn't care that it looked as if eight people were living in a place designed for one. The mother sat on a bed, crying, clutching her baby.

"Who did this?"

They had never talked, but Sonny was pretty sure she knew what he did, or, at the least, that he was a Bad Man. No matter where she came from, there must have been Bad Men. It was probably why she left.

And now Sonny was convinced that he'd be the baddest Man she ever met.

"Who did this?" he repeated quietly, through his teeth. She sobbed violently into the child.

He took a step toward her, and she snapped. She let out a string of half finished words, probably in whatever language she spoke. At last, she focused on one word, and kept repeating it, over and over. "po-LICE! po-LICE! po-LICE."

Sonny glanced down. No blood in here. They either wiped their feet, or else didn't bother coming through the door. Chances are, she hadn't seen who it was, but she had the fear. Something scared the crap out of her, and he didn't have time to get a translator.

"I'll figure out later," he muttered to himself. He pulled out two twenties, and threw them on the floor. Sonny turned and marched out into the cold light of day.

He stayed away from George's as long as he could, but the need to know grew stronger than the dread of knowing. Fatso had been trying to tell him something. What?

He pushed in through the door. The place was as empty as before. Fatso was behind the bar, and it looked like someone had roughed him up. All the bartender could do was point at George's office. Sonny took the hint.

He didn't know this time. Inside, George was smoking with an almost content look on his face, the shadow of the wreck he was a few days before. "So you came back. Good. Wanna drink?"

"No. What happened?"

"I was going to ask you the same question. I got a call from our dear friend—"

"Richard?"

"Naw! Giancomo. He saw you at the opera, and congratulated me on making sure you looked presentable. I don't know if you knew that, but there were several people who had their eye on you last night. Oh, hey, and sorry about your girl." He said that as an afterthought.

He unslung the rifle case. "What about Marcia?"

George's cheeks took on a flush of grey. "You mean...you didn't go home."

"Yeah. I did."

"Oh. Well, we're sorry it happened. That is, he is, and I am—"

"Who? Who did it?"

George set down the cigarette, and appeared to think deeply.

"The police, of course."

149

"The...police."

"Sure. A coupla yahoos wanted to see if they could shake her alibi, or, rather, Mr. Cereo's alibi. There was some nasty business the other night, and the girl, well, she was keeping an eye on our man. Just in case.

"Only it turns out that these two want to nail Cereo real bad, and they need to break her alibi, so...so maybe they broke her a little too hard."

That came out a little too flippant, and George knew it instantly. "Hey, she was a talker. That's why they put her in that room."

"She talked too much, huh?"

"Sure. They needed someone to spill the beans, and that's what she did. Only she came up against a coupla hard cases. I'm sorry. I didn't know she was close to you or nothin'. The worst thing that was supposed to happen was maybe she got her caged rattled a bit."

"Names. Names and badge numbers." He reslung the rifle case.

"Oh, fuck Christ! C'mon, Sonny. You're fucking better than this! She's a whore! If it wasn't them, it'd be some john in an alley. You can't dust two cops! You've got too much ahead of you!"

"I'm finishing this job, George. I won't be back until I do. And at that time, I want the names and badge numbers. I also want the whole $20,000, and I don't give two shits if you don't get a piece. Otherwise I'm going after every bastard with tin on his chest, and hope I pick a winner."

He walked up to the front desk of the Plaza, and asked for a room. Just like that. The clerk looked up and down at Sonny, and tried to sniff him away, when his eyes fell on the rifle case. A moment later, he was signing the book, and had a key pressed into his hand. Oddly, the bell-hop didn't offer to take his bag.

As he was walking away, something momentarily rattle through Sonny's thoughts. He turned to the desk clerk. "What room is Mrs. Richard in?"

For a moment, the desk clerk looked like he wasn't going to answer, then took a step back, and glanced at the room assignments. It took a solid minute of searching, but at last he reported, "I'm sorry. There's no one by that name here."

"You're mistaken. I'm looking for Richard's wife." The look on the clerk's face told him that Sonny had got the pronunciation just right.

"Sir, Mr. Richard is not married. In fact, he is not even at this hotel. Occasionally he dines in our restaurant, or sits in our lounge, talking with friends, but I assure you that he does not live here." He punctuated that statement by turning to help another guest.

Sonny turned and scanned the lounge. He wasn't here now, but he'd come eventually, and Sonny would be waiting. He found a nice, comfortable seat, and prepared to wait it out.

Richard was about as punctual as his "wife." He came in the door, and failed to notice Sonny camped out in the corner. Taking a seat, he opened up the evening paper. A waiter approached, and Richard ordered a coffee.

Sonny stood, leaving the case sitting next to the chair. He wouldn't be long. He approached Richard from behind. He leaned in low, and whispered in his ear.

"She's not your wife."

Richard half stood and turned, poised now at the edge of his seat. He had all the looks of a sewer rat at the bottom of a garbage can, found by a persistent alley cat. "Hello, Un Sparo," he managed.

"Can we go somewhere to talk, or would you prefer I raised the volume?"

"No. We'll find a corner, all right?" In some small way, Richard was sensing what it was like to have his private place violated. Sonny smiled at that realization, but it was a struggle to tense those muscles.

When they were in a more secluded area, Richard glanced about once, then asked, "So what is it you came to tell me?"

"She's going to a play Monday afternoon."

"A matinee, yes."

"I'm doing her then."

Richard seemed disappointed. "If you're sure?"

"Yes, I am."

"May I ask where?"

"As she returns here. I'll be waiting."

"I take it you have a good spot selected."

"I think so." Every syllable seemed a challenge, but Richard wasn't biting.

"Well, that's excellent. I'm pleased. Now I have friends I'm meeting—"

"One more question. Do you even know her? Is this some sick sort of game you're playing? Why did you say you were married to her? Who is she?"

"I am married to her in all but name. I imagine that books will be written about our love affair after both of us have perished. I know her, yes, and I care for her deeply. So deeply, that I made sure that you were the very best. Some answers will not come to you now. They will have to wait until this is over."

151

"Why? I'm calling the shots. I've given my word that I'm doing it, and goddamn, I want to know!"

Richard was at a loss for words. "Michelangelo touched the stone, and felt the form within, and yet he knew not what drove him to carve out David, or Moses. Da Vinci saw a homely noble's daughter, and transformed an enigmatic smile into brush strokes, but he could not understand what caused his muscles to twitch in that fashion. We stand at a grand threshold, Un Sparo, and I am convinced that knowing the why will somehow taint the act. Give me a stay of three days, then all will be explained–that is, if you need explanations at that point.

"Good night."

Sonny went up to his room on the ninth floor. It was on the north side, with its window facing away from the park. No matter, he thought. He was only four doors away from the room that he needed.

At first, Sonny had decided to climb one of the trees that formed the wall of green which hid the park's dark corners from the city's bright lights. He would be the hunter, waiting his prey out at her watering hole, and he would lash out from the wild. No matter how poetic it would be, however, it was terribly impractical.

Instead, he decided to let the hotel and gravity do all the work for him. He knew the Plaza would be pretty well filled on the weekend, but as Monday rolled around, the place would empty. As it was, he knew that the stiff at the desk wouldn't stick him near anyone important. Looking at the dingy corridor, unlike the lavish decor on other floors, he guessed that this area would be assigned last. On Sunday, he would prove this theory.

Over the next two days, he spent a great deal of time in the park. He only looked at the paper once, and that was to scan for news of Marcia. Nothing. With no small measure of disgust, he realized that the cops would be in no hurry to arrive there. For all he knew, she was still there, beneath the sheet. His fingers twitched at the thought.

Mercifully, Sunday night came. A few well placed calls confirmed that the most likely rooms would be vacant. With no small bit of diffi-culty, he learned to jimmy the lock. He only needed to be there for an hour, tops, so subtlety was not important.

All night long, he sat up with the rifle. He didn't know how to clean it, so he took out a towel from the bathroom and tried to make the wood shine. He noticed, somewhere around three in the morning, that the city never truly slept. It was like a restless sleeper, shifting in an uneasy slumber. Somewhere in the distance, he heard a sound that could have been a pistol-shot or just a truck backfiring. It didn't matter which it was; it was out there, and he was in here.

Morning came. He hung the Do Not Disturb sign on the door, and waited to make his appointed rounds. His stomach growled, but he refused to break his stride. For the past two days, he had isolated himself into the present, collapsing his perceptions into a tight, focused cone. The only thing that mattered was that which he could see with his own two eyes. Soon, it would be thinned down to a single eye, the one that sighted through the scope.

Two o'clock. The matinee ended now, and she would be expected back at 2:30. He straightened his tie, ran a comb through his hair, tied his shoes, and walked out the door. The hallway was empty. He darted back, grabbed the case, and let the door close softly behind him. He grabbed the knife from his pocket, and jammed it into the seam of the door jamb. It struck metal and clicked. The door fell open.

His first act was in clearing the window. Sonny placed the butt of the rifle on the top edge of the window, and pushed up. It caught at first, but inevitably gave. The window slid open.

Outside, the gloom had cleared. The afternoon heat began to soak into everything. Tonight, he knew, would be the perfect night for taking off his shoes, and feeling the sun's heat stored in cracked and dirty sidewalks.

He crouched in a corner, positioning himself in such a fashion so as to give him a clear shot at anyone entering or exiting a car. He even lines up a few targets, but was careful not to take his finger off the trigger guard. His hand wasn't shaking, but it wouldn't be the first time a fear spasm got him into something he couldn't get out of.

"Merciful Mary, where is that bitch?" Twice footsteps walking down the corridor had paused in front of this door. The jamb had been loosened by the knife, and anyone who knew what to look for would know he was in here. She was now an hour late, and his legs were in agony from squatting in this position.

He closed his eyes, but all he could imagine was seeing her there, in the balcony. He wanted to think of Marcia, sitting there, but he couldn't remember looking at her once. Instead, he watched as Mrs. Richard, or whatever the hell her name was, sat on the edge of her seat, and seemed to gently clutch at her throat, massaging her frail neck.

He opened his eyes. Her car was there. He shifted his weight, and suddenly fought the urge to run to the water closet, and relieve his bladder. Sonny purposefully avoided even water, but this was borne of something deeper. He sighted on the opening door, and aimed.

There was movement, and she emerged. He called for a nice head shot, and squeezed. His finger was still on the trigger guard. "Fuck."

The shot should have been spoiled. By now, she should have been moving under the overhang, but here she paused. He aimed again, careful to stroke the trigger. The cross hairs seemed to shift in his field of vision from heart to neck to face. Again he hesitated.

Unconsciously, he was playing with her, and somehow she was letting him. The scope allowed him to pry into her aura of beauty. With the cross hairs, he caressed the delicate folds of her dress, played along the curves of her neck, touched the lines of age or worry that spread from her thin red lips. He couldn't pull thetrigger. Why?

He was paid too much. No. She hadn't done anything wrong. No. He felt he was being used. No. He would spare her, because Marcia was not spared. No. All the clever lies dissolved under that one inescapable truth: did he want to kill her, or did he need to kill her?

He stared deeply into her eyes for that answer. They glinted momentarily, reminding him of Marcia when he first met her, before he knew what she did, and she knew what he did. He stared more intensely, erasing that first impression from his mind. Her eyes were a certain color, a shade he knew before. He saw that shade each morning in the mirror, and to put it out would be to put his out. He knew he couldn't do this...

The scope caught black. Something in her eye opened in his gaze, and he concentrated on that aspect, that all consuming darkness. He saw it in the rat's eye, with a needle in his hand.

He saw it in The Man's eyes, with his lucky pistol, ready to fire.

He saw it here, and suddenly she wasn't wholly human.

He breathed.

Sonny was convinced that the rifle's crack could be heard for miles about. Any second, thousands of cops would pour out of hiding, and pounce on him. Still, he was ready. He pulled the bolt back and ejected the cartridge. It was still hot when he stuffed it in his pocket. He placed the gun back in its case, and sealed it tight. In two seconds, he could be out the door.

Only then did he allow himself the luxury of looking out that window. As he expected, there was a crowd, but unlike any crowd he had seen before, they did not look up, trying to determine where the shot came from. Instead, they looked down, at her, at her blood, pouring out on the sidewalks. He recognized a few—they were her friends—and even those whom he did not recognize were impeccably dressed, as if they were going to see a performance. They paused there for several moments, then one nodded. Like Moses parting the Red Sea, they disbursed, all turning their backs, entering limos, taxis, the hotel and the park. All walked away after watching a woman die.

A sound, heard in the first few seconds after the act, finally registered in his brain.  He was listening for sirens and screams and police whistles, and so he failed to attach significance to it.  Only now, as he closed the door on this part of his life, did hetruly understand what it was.

Clapping.  Polite, quiet appreciation.  They had clapped.

Art by Roger Robinson

# firecracker kill
## by max allan collins

From Greektown to New Harlem, countless windows, walls and telephone poles were plastered with posters and handbills advertising the
upcoming Independence Day Festival. The festival was a nighttime
affair, which was good, because the nights were cooler. Right now the
days hung heavy with a humid heat that made walking down the street
a stroll through a blast furnace.

And police detective Stan Rasher was running.

Running down an alley after the son of a bitch who, as informants
had indicated, was hanging around Westburg Elementary offering little
girls rides home—lap rides. Rasher—twenty-eight, slim, dark, as snappy a dresser as his pay would allow—hadn't even shown the guy his
badge yet, was just approaching him coolly and casually and conversa-
tionally, but the pervert had finely honed instincts, and made Rasher as
a cop and threw the detective against the chain wire of the school yard
fence. Now, four blocks later, in the rundown business district of the
old downtown, Rasher was right behind the bastard, who was running
toward another chain link fence at the alley s end.

Only this time it was the pervert who got thrown against the fence,
bouncing off it into some nearby garbage cans, causing a clatter, sending a stray cat screeching and scurrying.

"Don't hurt me !" the guy was saying, in near tears. He looked harm-
less—about twenty-two, clean-shaven, neatly dressed, his persona reek-
ing of trustworthiness; he might be Uncle Bob or even Daddy. But he
wasn't. He was human garbage, right at home sprawled amid those
trash cans.

A few minutes later, Rasher was turning the perp over to Lt. Vincent
from the 32nd precinct.

"I thought you were working Homicide," Vincent said, shoving
Rasher's prisoner into the back of a black-and-white. Like Rasher,
Vincent came from a long line of cops—including Vincent's brother, the
chief. The husky ex-infantry sergeant had a reputation for the rough and
tumble.

"Yeah, well they got me out on loan to Vice," Rasher said, trying to
smooth out his suitcoat. He was soaked with sweat.

"Not pretty duty," Vincent said.

"I hate it," Rasher said cheerfully.

And he did.

Vincent shook his head. "The worst is these young girls, kids, run-aways, caught up in this slimy scene."

The perp was looking blankly out the rear window at them as Vincent rapped the window, and the guy reared back as if the blow had hit him.

"Enough to make you ashamed of packing a pistol," Vincent said.

"Men are the worst," Rasher agreed.

A crowd had gathered, a mixture that included merchants, some white-collar workers and a sprinkling of homeless. Lost among them was a seemingly innocuous figure of average height, pudgy, not fat, balding not bald, a man of around forty in a red bow tie, sweat-circled white shirt and baggy navy blue pants, wireframe glasses riding the pug nose of a strangely child-like face. He watched with bland interest, apparently in no hurry to get anywhere.

Finally, the observer strolled down the block and stepped into the reception area of his nearby storefront business, announced on the window as ROSE PHOTOGRAPHY, locking the door, the closed sign turned out, and headed back to his studio, where a beautiful teenage girl, arcs of brunette hair brushing her bare shoulders, sat nude, tied to a kitchen chair, a slash of electrical tape over her mouth, her eyes wide with fear. Her halter top, short shorts and panties were torn discarded fragments scattered about the room.

"Nothing to worry about," he said. "That commotion outside doesn't concern us ..."

And he began taking photos of the woman, telling her to "Smile," despite the electrical tape.

The next morning just before eleven, at Central City Headquarters, Rasher arrived at the desk of the commander of the detective division, Inspector Dan Fitch, who had summoned him by phone.

Fitch, his flesh nearly as gray as his hair, his face almost as rumpled as his suit, handed Rasher a photo in a clear plastic evidence bag.

Rasher found himself looking at a close-up of an attractive girl of perhaps sixteen; it was difficult to know just how attractive she was, because her features were distorted by the fat unlighted firecracker that had been stuffed in her mouth, like a sick phallic joke.

Her eyes were wide with terror.

"What's this?" Rasher asked.

"It came with these," Fitch said wearily, and handed him a half dozen more bagged photos of the girl, nude, electrical taped-tied to a chair.

"God, I hate Vice," Rasher sighed, pulling up a chair. "You figure this girl's under age right? We're talking child porn—"

158

"No. I m taking you off Vice. This is Homicide."

"Murder?"

"Those photos came in the morning mail. These photos a police photographer took, last night, on the banks of Long River, near John Henry Tunnel."

A wave of sickness coursed through Rasher as he looked at the photos of the girl, the same girl, fat firecracker in her mouth, sprawled on the grass, hands bound behind her, ankles–dead, now.

"This has all the earmarks of a serial killing," Fitch said. "But one corpse–however kinky–does not a serial killer make."

"Raped?" Rasher asked.

"No." Fitch said, "But there was semen in a Kleenex found near the body."

"Well, that gives us a blood type, at least."

"It's your case if you want it," Fitch said. "With your Homicide background, and your recent stint on Vice, you're the ideal man for the job."

"Dirty job."

"Which somebody has to do." Fitch shrugged. "Gets you off Vice."

"I'd pay the department for a shot at nailing this son of a bitch."

A smile joined the creases of Fitch s face. "You know, I can hear your father saying that."

In his six years on the department, Rasher had waited to hear Fitch say something akin to that;

Fitch had been Rasher's father's best friend and, at the time of Pop's in-the-line-of-duty death, his partner. It had been Fitch who encouraged both Stan and his sister Melissa, who worked in Records and Identification in this very building, to "join the family business."

This casual validation should have sent Rasher's spirits soaring; but that was impossible, with those grotesque photos spread out on the desk before him.

"You want me to partner up ?" Rasher asked.

"You already are," Fitch said. "Now don t start growling, but this is going to be an inter-agency operation."

"Shit–not the FBI—"

"Yes, the FBI. The Feds are disturbed over the serial killer-like aspects of this killing, and they're sending in an agent to work with you. I have orders that go all the way up to Chief Vincent that we're to keep a lid on this thing. We don't want to panic the public needlessly..."

Rasher nodded.

"You'll report directly to me," Fitch said. "The FBI involvement in this case is not to be public–or even departmental knowledge. Anybody

159

asks, Agent Vint is in town doing statistical research on our improved crime rate. Violent crime was down in the city. Tell that to your dead girl.

If anybody asks," Fitch continued, " you're merely Vint's p.d. liaison."

"You mean, I'm not even officially investigating this murder..."

"No. Homicide already has a team on it, looking into the girl herself, her family, friends, the usual. The official investigators won't even know you're exploring the serial-killer aspects of this case."

"This seems a little odd, Dan–"

"I'm counting on you, Stan. On your discretion."

Rasher shrugged. "Sure. Why not? Beats Vice. So what dark doorway do I meet my new partner in ?"

"Meet him early for lunch at Papa's."

"You're kidding..."

Fitch tapped one of the photos of the dead girl. "You think I'm in the mood to kid?"


Papa's Ristorante, a quaint hole-in-wall in Little Italy, was a legendary local fixture. Much the same could be said for the restaurant's owner, Giacomo "Papa" Ghiloni. The Ghiloni family, whose fortune had been forged in booze, gambling, and prostitution in the twenties, thirties and forties, claimed to be strictly legitimate, now. The Organized Crime task force, however, considered white-haired, genial Papa the reigning hereditary and administrative head of a crime family still very much enmeshed in illegal activities, save narcotics, which Papa reputedly forbade.

The maitre'd led Rasher to Mr. Vint's booth, where Vint sat meticulously eating a plate of pasta. The FBI man wore a conservative but tailored gray suit, and his every graying hair was in place—late forties or early fifties, Rasher made him, though for a guy his age, Vint's face was oddly smooth, uncreased, as if it hadn't been used much for smiling or frowning. His manner verged on prissiness; not a speck of red tomato sauce would get on this guy s shirt or suitcoat, and he'd eaten a half loaf of bread without getting a crumb on the red-and-white checkered tablecloth.

After a handshake and brief introduction, Rasher cut to the chase. "So–what's prompted the FBI to get involved in a lone murder case, in such a hurry? The corpse is still warm."

Vint speared some linguini and twirled his fork. "Ever hear of Taurus?"

"The bull?"

160

Vint twitched a smile; his gray eyes were calm and cold. "The maniac."

Rasher lowered the menu he was examining. "You mean that freak in California, twenty years ago or so, who was giving Jack the Ripper a run for his money?"

"Right. Know much about him?"

"I know they never caught the bastard," Rasher said with a shrug. "I know they estimate he killed at least twenty young women. He left them nude bound, no sexual molestation, but he masterbated near the corpses. An arrogant asshole, who taunted the cops..."

But Rasher found himself trailing off as his own words began registering on him in a shock of recognition : their potential serial killer indeed did resemble the Taurus killer, in style and flavor if not exact M.O. No wonder Fitch was worried about panicking the public...

A waitress came over and Rasher ordered the cheese ravioli. Then he turned back to the impassive Vint.

"He wrote screwy letters to the press didn't he?" Rasher asked. "Detailing his visions? Wasn't there some really crazed reason why he always killed young women..."

"Taurus believes that those he kills in this life," Vint said, "will be his slaves in the next."

"So, naturally, he kills beautiful young babes," Rasher said wryly. "The Errol Flynn of serial killers."

"You've been working Vice, I understand. Taurus victims, like that girl near the culvert last night, indicate our man is into bondage. Any ideas?"

"I know a few likely rocks to turn over."

After lunch, the two detectives drove to Irishtown and entered Pleasure World, one of the biggest smut shops in town; males, white- and blue-collar alike, studied the stapled shut magazines displayed along the side walls. Behind a display case boxed 8mm loops and "marital aides" (including whips and chains) slumped Merle, a heavy-set, hood-eyed hardcase, with Joe McCarthy shadowed jowls and a stub of a cigar rolling in thick lips. Sitting on a stool, a wall of dildos behind him, his heavy arms folded, Merle word a black T-shirt beneath which he seemed to be smuggling a Volkswagen beetle. Vint whispered, "Doesn't look like the cooperative type."

"Merle's pretty tough," Rasher allowed. "But let's reason with him."

Merle's eyes were bored as Rasher requested a list of the smut merchant's clients that were heavily into bondage photos, particularly any clients who were into taking such photos themselves. And Rasher wanted to know who, locally, might provide models to a private individual interested in private bondage photo shoots, and the names of local photographers who might provide their services for bondage shoots.

"I gotta protect my clients' confidentiality," Merle said in a voice that seemed to ooze.

"You're not a lawyer," Rasher reminded him,"and you aren't a doctor."

"No," Merle said, and the cigar shifted as the thick lips smiled, "but my patrons trust me. And if we don't got trust in this world, what do we got?"

Rasher leaned against the glass counter. "Hear about that guy I busted yesterday? At the grade school?"

Merle shrugged.

"He had a shitload of kiddie porn in his apartment. Says he bought it here."

"That's a damn lie!" Merle said, rising off his stool.

"Well, I admit I don't think it's strong enough to go to the D.A. with. Say you know where we had lunch today?"

"I don't give a rat's ass."

"Papa's over in Little Italy. Some people say you work for the Ghiloni family. Funny those people those Ghilonis; selective about the sin they sell. Drugs for example, Papa won't go near that I hear. Wonder how he'd feel if sombody told him you were sellin' kiddie porn out the back door?"

"That's a load of bullshit!"

"Yeah, well, Merle, you tell that to Papa's people when they come around."

"You're an asshole, Rasher."

"Maybe." Rasher glanced around the shop at the garish obscene magazine covers. "I'd guess that's just one of the body parts you're an expert on."

Merle sneered; it was like a bad Brando impression. "Come back in and hour and I'll have a list for you."

They did, and Merle did, and the rest of the day Rasher and Vint spent thinning the list out, deciding who to interview.

Down in Records and Identification, Rasher introduced Vint to Melissa.

"You're pretty," Vint said.

"Why so surprised?" Melissa said, leaning across the counter. Her gold-highlighted brown curls brushed the shoulders of her white blouse; she was a shapely, green-eyed woman with a ready smile.

"You're his sister," Vint said, deadpan.

"Hey," Rasher said, "I'm not the worst lookin' guy on the planet."

"But you're not pretty," Vint said.

"You got me there." Rasher handed her a list. "Got a few names for you to run, Sis. How long?"

"Forty-five minutes."

"I'm getting back to my phone," Rasher said. "I got perverts to call...don't want to keep 'em hanging–Some of 'em are upstanding citizens."

"Everybody needs a hobby," Vint said. "I'll wait."

And Rasher left Vint there with Melissa, who was finding her yen for older guys kicking in with this smooth-faced FBI man.

"You guys gonna knock off at a reasonable hour?" she asked him.

"Actually, we're going to stay at it."

"Double shift?"

Vint nodded. "Maniacs don't take much time off. They're sort of over-achievers."

"Oh."

"Why do you ask?"

She shrugged. "I get off at six. Thought maybe you'd like to have a drink."

Vint's smile was small but it was enormously winning, to Melissa anyway. "America's a great country."

"Why's that?"

"Women asking men out."

"I wasn't asking you out. We're colleagues. Just thought you might like—"

"A drink? Sure."

They met at a little bar on a side street not far from headquarters, a police hangout, and Melissa had expected her brother to be along, but when Vint came over and settled himself across from her in the booth, he was alone.

"I thought you and Stan were going to stay at it—"

"We are," he said. "But we divided up a few names. We can cover more ground working solo."

"Ah. Jeez, I guess I kind of screwed up."

"How's that?"

"I was counting on Stan for a ride over to the country club. See, I'm involved with the Miss Independence Day pageant, comin' up."

"Contestant?"

"No." She smiled, flattered. "I'm a little old for that."

163

"What are you, twenty-five?"

She was thirty-one. Twice divorced, childless, and thirty-one, damn it.

"Twenty-eight," she said.

"Hard to believe," he said.

"I am a former Miss Independence Day winner myself—never mind what year. I'm official chaperone for one of the girls."

"I'd be glad to give you a ride."

"Okay. Let's enjoy our drink and I'll take you up on that..."

When he walked her to his parked silver roadster, she was suitably impressed.

"Pretty snappy wheels for a cop," she said.

"I don't have a family to sap my income," he said.

He drove her to her pageant meeting at Eastwood Country Club; they parked in the shadow of the Starview Observatory, a domed structure on the edge of the country club gold course. The car windows were down, a blessedly cool breeze whispering in, respite from another hot humid day.

"You're nice," she said.

He looked handsome in the moonlight, and very young, despite the grey hair.

"No, I'm not," he said. And he kissed her.

A tender little kiss that got hot suddenly, and Melissa pulled away, laughing, saying, "Thanks for the ride," and she slipped out of the car, into the night.

Vint watched her go, waited till he'd seen her enter the side door of the country club's stucco clubhouse, then drove to The Highball Club on the edge of the warehouse district. The joint was run by a lounge lizard named Vernon Venall; Rasher's pal Merle had listed Venall as a likely provider of models for would-be bondage photographers.

Vint hadn't mentioned to Rasher that he knew Venall already.

Vint moved across the chrome and mirrored club, settled in at the bar and the proprietor sidled up and took the stool next to him. Venall wore in a sharkskin suit and skinny tie, apparel that hadn't been in style in the memory of any of the glittery-topped slit-skirted B-girls scattered around the joint. Forty-five, his short hair dyed an obvious black, his narrow blade of a pockmarked face distinguished by black little eyes as dead as a doll's. Venall said in his lacquered voice, "Buy you a drink, Vint?"

"Long as I don't have to drink it with you, Vernon."

"That's unkind."

"Read the paper today, Vernon?"

"I don't keep up with the news. Depresses me. World's gone to hell in a handbasket, you ask me."

"I was thinking more along the line of local news."

"If you're thinkin' what I think you're thinkin'..."

"Some artwork doesn't need a signature for it's artist to be obvious."

Venall swallowed, and it wasn't any of his drink. "I don't think it's him..."

"Bull."

The double meaning of that made Vernon wince. "I can't tell you where he is without Mr. Roselli's say-so."

Vint sipped his Scotch. Nodded.

"Anything else?" Venall asked. "We through?"

"For now," Vint said.

And Vint quietly sat and finished his drink, and thought private thoughts. Just as he was about to leave, he noticed a slim young blonde in a blue spangle top and painted-on Capri pants who was being hit on by two burly guys in business suits.

Not "hit on" in the usual bar sense: hit on. Slapping and shoving her around, and nobody was doing a damn thing about it–including Venall himself, who was pacing off to one side adjusting his tie nervously. Vint sighed and went over and tapped the nearest of the two guys on the shoulder. When the guy turned snarlingly toward him, Vint smiled blandly, saying, "Don't," waving a finger as though scolding a child. Then Vint opened his coat and revealed the silenced nine millimeter in the speed rig under his shoulder. The two men backed off, patting the air, smiling uneasily and the blonde, in tears, clutched Vint's arm.

"Thank you, mister," she said. "They thought I was holding out on them. I wasn't, I swear to God I wasn't!"

"I believe you."

"Can I buy you a drink? Is there any way I can make it up to you?"

"No. I had selfish motives."

Her big blue eyes fluttered. "What?"

"I hate noise."

Shortly, when Vint approached his roadster in the parking lot, a vice-like hand gripped him by either arm, from behind. One of the burly boys from inside was standing in front of Vint, grinning as he yanked the automatic from the shoulder rig, sticking it in his waistband. The guy had a bucket head, a lump of a nose and lamb-dropping eyes; he flashed Vint a badge.

"You shouldn't obstruct officers of the law," he said.

"In the line of duty," the one holding him said in Vint's ear.

165

Then Vint was hurled to the pavement, and they were standing over him, nightsticks in hand, poised to work him over.

Vint kicked the nearest one—the one who'd been holding him, a blond round-faced dope—in the groin, sprang to his feet like an acrobat and flipped the bucket-headed bastard to the pavement, where the guy did a belly flop in the empty pool of the parking lot. Both men were whimpering, but their suffering had just begun.

Vint turned the belly flopper over and retrieved his weapon from the guy's waistband, then kicked the nightstick from his hand, sending it clattering under a parked Buick. Then Vint plucked the other nightstick from the pavement, where the guy who had rolled himself in a groaning ball, clutching his groin, had dropped it.

And Vint used the nightstick on the pair, beating them senseless, breaking at least a few bones, their cries echoing in the warm but breezy night.

They were barely conscious as Vint tossed the nightstick like a spent cigarette, straightened his tie, said, "Didn't you hear me? I said 'don't,'" got into his car and roared off.

The next morning of a brand-new sweltering day, Rasher was waiting at the counter of a cop hang-out coffee shop near headquarters, as he and Vint had prearranged.

Rasher, sipping coffee, felt a tap on his shoulder; he turned, but it wasn't Vint.Cornelison, a lanky, seasoned detective held been working Vice with, leaned in, tickled about something. "Hear about Bates and Peterson?"

"No. Tell me it's good news, like a bus made pavement stains out of 'em or something."

Bates and Peterson were two bent Vice cops that every moderately honest copper in vice wished only the worst.

Cornelison chuckled. "Scuttlebutt is they were putting the arm on some hooker, at the Highball Club when they made the mistake of going tangle-ass with that FBI guy you're running with."

"No shit?"

"None. They're both in the hospital. They got their clocks cleaned—worked over with their own nightsticks."

Cornelison chuckled again, patted Rasher on the back and moved on. Vint was coming in out of the heat, wearing a perfect tan suit and looking like he'd never sweat a drop in his life.

"Got another one," he said.

The homicide scene was a rural ditch northwest of town, in the back country. Fitch was there with a mobile crime unit, the whole nine yards.

As Rasher and Vint approached, the older cop nodded, and jerked a thumb toward the ditch.

"I think we officially got ourselves a serial killer, boys," he said. "And he left his business card."

Rasher didn't get it. "What?"

Fitch held up an evidence bag with a crumpled Kleenex in it; another semen deposit.

She was brunette, probably fifteen, maybe sixteen, kind of plump, almost pretty, wrists electrical-taped, ankles electrical-taped, with a fat phallic firecracker stuffed in her mouth.

"Jesus," Rasher said, and he dropped to one knee, as if he were about to get knighted; instead, he lost his breakfast.

Doing this kept him too busy to notice Vint wandering the periphery, using a pencil to pick up a small empty Kodak 35 mm box, wordlessly pocketing it.

Later, in the Porsche, as they headed back to the City, Rasher said, "Sorry about back there."

"What?"

"Not very professional."

"What are you talking about?"

"Puking. I mean, I worked Homicide all last year. I saw worse things than that."

"It's the heat."

And the heat must have gotten even to Vint, because Rasher noticed the FBI agent's coat was unbuttoned, allowing a peek at the weapon in the fancy rig under his shoulder.

"Is that a silencer?"

Vint seemed embarrassed; with one hand, he buttoned his coat, as if held been caught with his fly down. "Yeah."

"Since when is that government issue?"

"Since never," Vint admitted. "What can I say? I hate noise."

Rasher was on the phone arranging interviews with perverts when Vint went down to Records and Identification, where Melissa came to the counter to greet him with a smile.

"How was rehearsal?" he asked her.

"Swell. Does my ego a lot of good, hanging around with a couple dozen beautiful eighteen and nineteen year-old goddesses."

"They're kids. You're a woman."

That made her beam. "I have a reception tonight, for the contestants. But it'll be over by ten -"

"First things first," Vint said. "I need you to run a fingerprint check for me."

He handed her a strip of tape with a print he had lifted from the Kodak box.

"Sure," she said. "But since you're not officially department, I need one of those inter-agency forms, you know—the 714JW?"

"I don't have it," he said, gesturing with open hands. "I wasn't anticipating doing any investigating...this was supposed to be strictly statistical research..."

She made a click in her cheek. "Yeah, and I can't just call over there either. Verbal approvals aren't acceptable, by policy."

"I guess I can run over to the Bureau office, in Westburg..."

"Hell," she said, "give it here—you can lay the paperwork on me, later."

"Thanks," Vint said.

Rasher and Vint spent the rest of the morning on three interviews with convicted sex-crimes offenders, one an out-of-work school teacher in Greek Town, another a broker in the financial district off Axis Avenue, another a mechanic in El Barrio, where they were at an outdoor stand having tacos with sauce as hot as the day when Vint's police radio alerted him to a call from Melissa.

"You two sure are hitting it off," Rasher said with a grin.

"I won't get too friendly," Vint said. "I hear her brother packs heat."

Vint found his way to a pay phone.

"I have a name for you," Melissa said. "Michael Rose. Mean anything?"

"No," Vint lied.

"No criminal record, just military service. But here's an interesting wrinkle..."

"He was discharged on a Section 8."

"How did you know?"

"Lucky guess."

"...Maybe I'll see you later?"

"Yes, thanks," he said, more curtly than he meant, hanging up, too distracted to think of romance.

He sat back down at the picnic-style bench by the taco stand, next to Rasher.

"I checked in with my superior," Vint said. "We're going to have to split up this afternoon. Something from another case came up."

"No problem," Rasher said.

"Why don't we reconnoiter at Papa's around five?"

"Done."

That afternoon, alone, Vint entered the Rose Photography Studio in the old business district in Westburg. In the reception area, a beaming, pretty teen-age girl was greeting her mother. Vint quickly got the drift that the girl had just had her photo taken for the Miss Independence Day pageant at the Fourth of July festival.

After mother and daughter exited, Vint turned the CLOSED sign around in the door, withdrew his noise-suppressed nine millimeter and hit the little bell marked "Ring for Service."

And the pudgy, balding, baby-faced photographer himself came out to greet his newest customer, smiling. His smile faded when he saw the gun in Vint's hand, but then it almost immediately brightened again.

The photographer sat on a swivel seat at the customer counter and said to Vint, with a nervous chuckle, "Well...it's been a long time."

"Don't," Vint said, scolding him with a wagging finger.

"What do you mean, Vint?"

"You've started again. Stop."

The baby-faced photographer pushed his wireframes up on his pug nose. Mild indignation colored his tone as he said: "I'm sure I don't know what you're referring to."

Vint gestured with the long-snouted silenced automatic, like a teacher with a pointer. "This is a courtesy call ... courtesy to your father, not to you. I'd rather kill you than look at you."

A pudgy hand splayed against a pudgy chest. "I've been good, I have been good..."

"End it or die. Those are your options. And that, Taurus, is no bull." Vint tapped the air with the long-nosed gun.

"Don't," he repeated.

Then Vint turned the sign around so that OPEN faced the street, and he left.

At headquarters, Rasher was checking in with his sister at Records and Identification when she casually dropped a bombshell.

"Remind Vint, will you," she said, "about getting me that inter-agency form, on that fingerprint?"

"What fingerprint?"

Soon Rasher was at his phone, calling over to the FBI office in Westburg, asking for Agent Vint. He went through several desks trying, but kept coming up empty.

"I'm sorry, Detective Rasher, no agent of that name works out of this office," said a division head, who was pretty high up the Bureau food chain. "And I don't come up with any agent of that name, at all, in our records..."

Rasher stood before Fitch's desk ticking off the items.

"He drives a Porsche, he packs a noise-suppressed weapon, he ran a fingerprint check without telling me, he worked a couple crooked cops over with a nightstick, an activity I might approve of but which seems a tad out of character for the FBI, who incidentally have never the hell heard of an agent Vint..."

Fitch, looking weary, held up a hand. "You were to report strictly to me on this."

"What do you think I'm doin' right now?"

"You were told this was a covert operation, no one in the department was to know the true nature of your—"

"What the hell are you saying?"

Fitch's expression was pained. "A word to the wise, detective, investigate these killings, not your partner." The inspector tossed an evidence-bagged photo across the desk at Rasher. "That came in the morning mail."

The girl who'd been dead in the ditch was alive in the photo–but with a fat firecracker stuffed in the mouth of her terrified face.

"You know I want the son of a bitch doing this," Rasher said. "But how can you expect me to work with a partner I can't trust?"

"You want off the case, Stan? You want back on Vice?"

Rasher flipped the bagged photo back onto the desk. "You wouldn't pull this crap on my old man."

"You want off the case?"

"No, I don't want off the goddamn case!"

Just after five, at Papa's Ristorante, Rasher slid into the booth next to Vint, who was meticulously working on a plate of veal parmigiana. Slipping his hand beneath the table, Rasher cocked his revolver. The click was tiny, and tremendous.

The normally unresponsive Vint flinched.

"Thought you might recognize that sound," Rasher said. "The next sound will be louder, but just as familiar–and I know how you hate noise..."

"What do you want, Stan?"

"I want you to spill your guts, or I'll spill 'em for you–right onto your napkin. Like some veal that slid off your plate. Talk to me, Vint— now." A hand settled on Rasher's shoulder and he glanced up to see the gently smiling face of Papa Ghiloni.

"You know, Stanley, your father never pulled a gun on a brother officer."

Papa pulled up a chair and sat across from them.

Astonished, Rasher watched the kindly looking man in the unassuming black suit and black tie as he began to speak, softly, slowly but surely, gesturing with both hands, like he was sculpting the air.

"There are those," Papa said, "who call me the local "kingpin"–what a silly thing, a Hollywood thing. I own a restaurant, Stanley, but I suppose I do have a certain...standing. A respect. Most people would respect me enough not pull a weapon, even under a table."

Rasher eased his revolver back into its hip holster. "I mean you no disrespect, Mr. Ghiloni. But while this may be your place of business, this business between Mr. Vint and myself has nothing to do with you."

Papa laughed gently; his eyes seemed to twinkle. "Ah, but as a community leader, so much 'personal business' is also my business. You see, I'm something of a...coordinator, Stanley. Sorting out, sometimes, the conflicting desires of the so-called straight world and the underworld... and that twilight world of police and politicians that lies between."

"I fail to see how serial killings relate to any of what you're saying."

Papa shrugged. "We each have our place in the City. We're all swimming in the same waters. Our crime rate is relatively low...thanks to the help of boys like you, Stanley, God bless you. We all have our place, we all have our role, and in a way we all work together. More closely, sometimes, than others. That's why we're workin' together on this Taurus thing."

"Together?"

Papa nodded.

Rasher glanced at Vint, then back to Papa. "You say that like you're sure it's this bastard Taurus who's killing these girls."

"Stanley," Papa said, patting the air, "please. Watch your language. This is a family restaurant."

Rasher turned back to Vint and glared. "How the hell do you fit in? And just who the hell are you?"

"I'm a cop," Vint said. "I just don't work for the FBI."

"He's a trouble-shooter," Papa said, genially. "A private eye with one client."

"And I know who that client is," Rasher said, standing, throwing down his napkin like a gauntlet. "You're a fucking mob button man, and I'm having none of it."

"Please, Stanley!" Papa said. "The f-word!"

And Rasher stormed out.

Papa looked at Vint and shrugged with frustration.

"I'll handle it," Vint said.

"Don't kill Stanley," the old man said. "He's a nice boy."

Vint wiped his hands on the napkin.

"Try not," he said.

At headquarters, Vint leaned across the counter at Records and Identification: no sign of Melissa, her chair empty, though it wasn't yet

171

six.

"Melissa around?" Vint asked one of her co-workers, a pleasant heavy-set woman in her twenties.

"She took off early," was the perky response. "She's got that pageant reception, at the country club tonight?"

The Rasher family home was in a blue-collar neighborhood in Irish Town, a clapboard bungalow with a well-tended lawn and a screened-in porch; from conversation with Melissa, Vint knew she and her brother shared the place. He knocked at the screen door, got no answer, went onto the porch, knocked on the front door, which was ajar; his knock opened it enough to reveal Rasher sitting on a couch in the living room.

The detective was slowly, methodically, loading his handgun.

Vint planted himself before the man he considered to be his partner and stated his case: "I am a cop–just like you. The world needs us both. People step outside the rules, we make 'em step back inside. One way or the other."

Rasher put another bullet in the gun; his hands were unsteady, but he was getting it done.

Making speeches made Vint uncomfortable, but this was a speech that needed making.

He said, "Michael Rose–Taurus–is the son of Francesco Roselli— West Coast capo. Twenty years back, we got to the sick bastard before the cops. I should've buried him in the ground. Instead I gave him to his papa and they buried him out here. In the anonymity of your great big city. Gave him a new life. Made him clean up his act."

Rasher looked up.

"He kept his pecker in his pants for a long, long time," Vint said. "The first firecracker kill made some alarm bells go off. That's when the Commission rushed me in to check up on sleeping beauty. To see if he woke up. Which he obviously has. Well, it's time to put him to sleep again—permanently. You want to help or not?"

Speaking with some difficulty, Rasher said, "The bastard has Melissa."

"What?"

"See for yourself." Rasher holstered the loaded gun, stood and strode up the stairs to Melissa's room, Vint following. The nightstand lamp was on the floor, in pieces; perfume bottles and jewelry had been knocked from her mirrored dresser. But this wasn't the aftermath of a robbery: the drawers of the bureau were shut tight. These were the signs of a struggle.

And the artist had left a variation of his distinctive signature: in the middle of the floor were a pair of Melissa's panties, wrapped in a firecracker.

"We can call this in," Vint said, "and get a mobile crime lab in here..."

"Or we can save my sister," Rasher said.

The protective gate was down, at the front of the Rose Photography Studio, but Rasher kicked a door in, the alley door in back, and found the place empty. The same was true of the apartment above, where Michael Rose lived. The place was tidy, furnishings cold and modern.

But under the false bottom of a dresser drawer, Rasher turned up a hidden cache of photos—more photos of the two dead girls.

Carrying them in a handkerchief, Rasher took them down to the studio, which Vint was searching.

"Before and after photos," Rasher said, displaying the bondage-style shots.

"Alive and dead, you mean. Take a look at this."

Vint opened an album of photos; within were the candidates for the Miss Independence Day competition, to be held the next day at the Mardi Gras-like Fourth of July Festivities on the waterfront.

"I'll be damned," Rasher said numbly. "He's the official photographer for the pageant..."

"Keep going."

In back of the album were two more photos, studio portraits of two attractive teenage girls who looked disturbingly familiar.

The two firecracker kills.

"This," Vint said emotionlessly, "is a photo album of his victims... the ones he's already killed, and the ones he's going to kill..."

As if confirming this theory, Vint turned the pages of the book Rasher held to its final page, a photo of Melissa, mouth taped shut, eyes taped open.

"Print's still damp," Vint pointed out.

Rasher was trembling with rage and fear. "He killed one girl on the first of July, another on the second, and now it's the third and he's got Melissa."

"Obviously, tomorrow he plans to hit the rest of these girls," Vint said. "A sniperscope aimed at the stage, perhaps."

Rasher was reeling. "Why, after all these years, is Taurus launching such an orgy of slaughter?"

"There's one last photo you need to see," Vint said. "Actually, it's a negative..."

Vint nodded to a light box where he had already displayed a large chest X-ray.

Rasher, as confused as he was worried, stumbled over and said,

173

"What the hell's this about?"

"You don't have to have a medical degree to see the spots on those lungs. Of all the pictures in this studio, this one–the only one here that Michael Rose didn't take himself–tells us the most."

"Cancer?"

Vint nodded. "Taurus is dying."

And the meaning, the intent behind, the orgy of slaughter was suddenly all too clear in Rasher's mind.

"Oh God," Rasher said, feeling like held been struck a blow in the pit of his stomach. "Taurus believes that each of his victims will be his slave in the next world..."

Vint nodded. "So he's collecting as many pretty young souls as he can before he cashes in."

"We have to find him tonight," Rasher said, intensely. "Not just Melissa's life is at stake, but think of those girls on that festival stage tomorrow, and all the people in the audience who could get caught in a crossfire between that madman and the cops."

Vint shook his head, no. "He won't hit the festival tomorrow."

"But everything points to that..."

"Taurus is a madman, but he's no fool. By now, he knows we'd be on top of him, at the festival. He'll change his plans ... but not his goal."

Rasher snapped his fingers.

"The reception for the beauty pageant contestants," the detective said, "is going on right now..."

"Not a bad guess," Vint said. "Let's drop by the country club...."

"I'll take time for one call, first," Rasher said.

He caught Lt. Vincent at the 32nd.

"We were checking up on a suspect in the firecracker killings, Lieutenant," Rasher said, after giving Vincent the location. "And we found the rear door kicked in. Apparently a break-in..."

"Ah," Vincent said, not fooled, but happy to go along. "We're seeking the suspect elsewhere–there's a time factor involved–so get a car over here. There's a counter in the photo studio where we'll be leaving some key evidence you'll need to bag and inventory."

"Evidence?"

"Items we discovered in plain sight, when we were checking up on that robbery."

"Ah," Vincent said again. "My people will be on it. Go do what you gotta do."

Vint parked his Porsche along the roadside, in the shadow of a rolling hill, and soon he and Rasher were moving under the clear starry sky across the country club's golf course, shadows slipping quietly along, guns in hand. As they approached the dome of Starview Observatory, they came across a delivery van parked up off the graveled lot, by the bushes; the lettering on the van said ROSE PHOTOGRA-PHY. The van was locked, but on tip toes, looking up through the windshield, they could see the vehicle was empty.

Cautiously they approached the observatory. In an open window high in the domed structure, something glinted.

The metal of a gun?

A sniper's scope?

Vint clutched Rasher's arm. "You got to get those people out of that country club—out the front way. He has a view of the verandah from up there, but not of the front of the place."

"No, you go," Rasher whispered harshly. "I want to take him ... he may have Melissa in there..."

"That country club is packed with prominent locals," Vint said. "They know you. They'll do what you tell 'em." Rasher sighed, nodding his reluctant agreement. He bounded across the golf course, toward the country club, staying low, staying along the bushes and trees of the rough.

Vint entered the observatory through the main door, walking across the echo chamber of the marbled lobby as quiet as a whisper. He moved through the dark building slowly, past exhibits, skirting a large model of the moon, heading into the cavern of the planetarium, circling around the massive telescope's base, listening to every sound, every creak.

Then he spotted the dark shape up on the observatory platform.

Carefully, silenced automatic in hand, Vint began to climb the stairs...

Inside the country club, various city fathers were honoring the lovely young women with their presence, as the potential Miss Independence Day's in their beaming smiles and prom gowns circulated among the crowd at this well-attended reception. Rasher quickly tried to ascertain who was in charge.

"Detective Rasher, isn't it?"

Rasher turned and was facing Hiram Goldman, smiling above the rim of a martini glass. Slender, handsome, looking like he stepped off the top of a wedding cake, Goldman was the city's latest financial golden boy, a society page favorite and a pillar of this country club which, only a few decades ago, wouldn't have allowed in a member of his "persuasion."

The self-confident Goldman seemed perpetually amused. "Don't tell me my wife's jewelry has finally turned up?"

"I've been off robbery detail for two years, Mr. Goldman, but I am

175

glad to see a familiar face."

The darkly handsome financier lost his smirky smile, obviously sensing Rasher's urgency. "Why?"

"Mr. Goldman," Rasher said sotto voce, "we've got a bad situation... I want you to help me get all of these people out of here and away from the building, right now."

"Don't be silly," Goldman said. "We have a fireworks display in half an hour.

"Everyone's looking forward to it..."

"Mr. Goldman, the man who's behind the firecracker kills is out back with a sniperscope, looking for more pretty girls to murder. What do you suppose will happen, when the pageant contestants go out on the verandah to watch the fireworks?"

"Understood," Goldman said, and moving casually through the crowd, revealing no sense of urgency whatever, the financier found his way to where a small combo was playing and calmly commandeered a microphone.

"Thank you for coming tonight," he told a crowd that had quieted immediately, seeing who it was that was speaking to them. "All of us on the pageant committee are grateful for your support, but it's my unhappy duty to call a temporary halt to these festive proceedings. There's a minor gas leak and the building has to be evacuated."

Murmurs of disappointment moved across the room in a wave.

"But I will call ahead and arrange a banquet room at Le Figaro, where we can continue this party at my expense."

Now the murmur turned into approval, and then applause.

As the guests, pageant contestants among them, began filing out, with no trace of panic thanks to Goldman's efforts, the financier turned to Rasher and said, "Would you go out back, and tell the technicians mounting the fireworks show that their performance should be temporarily postponed?"

"I'll take care of it," Rasher said. "Just point me in the right direction..."


In the observatory, on the platform, Vint approached the stocky figure, who was dressed entirely in black, a chubby cat burglar, aiming a sniperscoped rifle out a window.

"Planning to gather a few slaves, Michael?"

And Michael Rose turned, revealing a big boyish smile and a shirt front bearing a home-made rendering in glitter paint of the astrological symbol of Taurus the Bull.

"Vint! I'd hoped you come." He chuckled, eyes glittering behind the wire frames. "Miss Independence Day is going to miss her indepen-dence, when she and her court serve me for eternity. Maybe you'd like to my servant in the next world, too."

"Maybe you'd like to kiss my ass in this one."

Michael laughed, a childish giddy laugh that echoed through the observatory. "Maybe you'd like to kiss yours goodbye, Vint. You should know that Taurus always triumphs."

"You were born under the sign of Taurus," Vint said, taking a step forward. "But you're dying under the sign of Cancer."

Michael frowned, and said, "Where's your policeman friend?"

"Stealing your slaves away. All your victims have been warned, by now. They're gone. Now, put the rifle down, slow."

Michael seemed to be considering that, then he shrugged and bent at the knees to lower the rifle to the platform floor. "Okay, Vint—you win. As usual." Then he straightened and smirked and said, "Of course, one slave's still available to me...your friend's sister. The love of your sad life? I saw you two, together, you know."

Vint raised the gun and pointed its silenced snout directly at Michael's forehead and said, "You're going to be my slave in the next world, asshole."

Michael opened his palm and revealed a small device, a push-button remote control. "Then say good-bye to Melissa...asshole."

Vint, finger poised on the trigger, paused.

"Where is she, Michael?"

"And if I tell you, you'll let me live?"

"Maybe."

"But Vint, you said it yourself...I'm dying already. I'd rather have one more slave and die right now then be hauled off to jail or the nut-house and never claim any more loyal subjects..."

Out on the golf course, outside the supply shed that had been appro-priated for the fireworks show, Rasher had stumbled upon the two tech-nicians who were supposed to set off the country club fireworks show. They were lying down on the job—their throats slashed. The detective stood staring at the door of the shed, wondering if his sister was in there, hoping the damn thing wasn't booby-trapped...

In the observatory, on the platform, Vint trained his nine millimeter on the seemingly amused Michael Rose.

"She's tied up in the fireworks shed," Michael said, giggling, "wired to some real big firecrackers. And if I press this little button, she'll go all to pieces."

"Then press the button," Vint said, calmly. "Only if you do, Michael, I'm going to kill you slow...I'll put one in your fat gut and let you wallow in pain; then, just to keep you alert, I'll shoot your kneecaps off, and shatter your elbows. It'll be hours of agony before you go to your well-deserved hell."

"I don't think you'll do that," Michael said.

"Try me."

"When my daddy learns you didn't put me out of my 'misery' quickly, he'll be very mad. I think you'd be the one learning how slow a man can die."

The pudgy bastard had a point.

"Then here's what we're going to do," Vint said. "We're going to walk down the steps and out of here, slowly. You're going to lead me to where you have Melissa. And you're going to let her go."

Michael frowned and laughed. "Why should I?"

The gun was still trained on Michael's forehead, but Vint's voice was almost soothing as he said, "Because if you do...and if you behave...I'll keep you away from the cops. I'll turn you over to your daddy, the don, alive. He can find some new rock to hide you under, until God kills you."

Childishly, Michael repeated, "Why should I?"

"Because if you don't, I'll take my chances with trying a head shot. You won't have time to press that button. A head shot kills all reflexes, Michael."

"What if I fall on this thing?" Michael said, holding the detonator in front of him.

"You might," Vint conceded. "That's why I'm offering you an option."

Michael thought about it; then, grinning like the goofy kid he was, he nodded, saying, "Okey dokey."

But even as Vint and his hostage were abandoning the observatory and heading toward the fireworks shed, Rasher was inside the little structure, untying Melissa, who he found in bra and panties, bound in a seated bondage position, mouth taped shut, eyes open wide. She sat in the midst of fireworks of all kinds–roman candles, rockets, piles of pyrotechnics waiting to paint the night. She seemed to be trying to convey something with her expression to Rasher, but he picked her up as gently as he could and carried her over to a practice putting green and eased her to the grass.

He removed the taped gag and she said, "I was afraid you might set that thing off!"

"What thing?"

"He's got that shed loaded up with dynamite and wired to blow... we've got to get away from here!"

Rasher finished removing her electrical-tape bonds, draped her in his suitcoat, and walked her around to the front of the evacuated country club.

"Can you do me a favor?" he asked his sister.

The brutalized young woman managed a nod.

"Call for some back-up. Then stay inside that building and don't come out till you hear help come."

She nodded, and he guided her inside, and headed back onto the golf course.

Vint and Michael Rose had arrived at the fireworks shed, having walked side-by-side from the observatory, in a Mexican stand-off, Vint's gun trained on Taurus, who continued to hold the detonator, thumb poised to press.

"Where is she?" Vint demanded, as both men looked in the open door of the shed that was filled with fireworks but empty of Melissa.

"I've got her, Vint!" Rasher called out, from behind him, seeing Vint with a gun trained on Taurus, assuming the latter was Vint's prisoner. "She's safe!"

When Vint half-turned toward the sound of Rasher's voice, Michael Rose struck out, ramming a fist into the side of Vint's face. Vint went down, his gun tumbling from his fingers and Taurus scurried into the night.

Rashe–knowing nothing about the dangerous detonator in Taurus' grasp–took off after the man, and threw a flying tackle into him, taking him down, hard, sending the detonator flying, Rose rolling out of Rasher's grip on the slope.

Michael lumbered to his feet. So did Rasher. And in the moonlight, under the starry sky, in the cool air that had followed the hellish hot day, Taurus the Bull threw a punch into Rasher the bull, whose return blow broke his opponent's jaw.

But the bloody-mouthed Taurus, eyes glittering (the wire frames had been lost in the tackle), moved in with flailing yet powerful blows that sent Rasher backward, reeling. The detectives more skillful, more measured blows caused Taurus to stagger, and as the insane slugfest careened across the course, the two men were soon back where they started, trading blows near the open door of the fireworks-filled shed.

Vint was on his feet now, and while the brutal hand-to-hand combat continued between cop and killer, the private detective who worked for the mob calmly recovered both his gun and the detonator.

"Enough of this shit," Vint said to nobody in particular, and he went over to the two men who were struggling on the ground now, Taurus on top, his heavier weight giving him the momentary advantage.

Vint hauled Michael Rose off Rasher as easily as if he were picking a flower and hurled the son of a bitch into the fireworks shed, slamming the door, latching it, snapping the Yale lock shut. Taurus, within the shed, was pounding the walls, the structure shaking with his indignation.

Vint dragged Rasher up off the ground and away from the shed, back into the night, across the golf course, toward the observatory, well away from the little structure that shook with Taurus' rage.

"What the hell are you doing?" Rasher demanded, groggily. "I wanted take that bastard in, personally!"

Vint smiled gently, put his hand on Rasher's shoulder and said, "It's after midnight. Do you know what that means?"

"What...?"

"Happy Fourth of July, Stan."

And Vint pressed the detonator.

A yellow ball of flame rose heavenward, followed by the millisecond afterthought of the roar of the explosion, and fireworks begin to fill the sky, sparkling bursts, skyrocketing streaks, in glorious celebration.

Rasher stared with wide eyes into the patriotic sky, stunned at first, and then he began to smile.

"I thought you didn't like noise," Rasher said, turning.

But Vint was gone.

And Rasher stared into the darkness of the rough, wondering if he should go into the bushes and trees after Vint, who was, after all, nothing but a mob hit man. And wasn't Rasher a cop?

Then, slowly, Rasher began to smile again. Shrugging, laughing, he looked up at a heaven filled with fireworks, a night alive with whistles and pops and bangs, and put his hands in his pockets, and walked toward the clubhouse, under an exploding sky.

The bottom line was, Vint had made a hell of a partner.

And that was no bull.

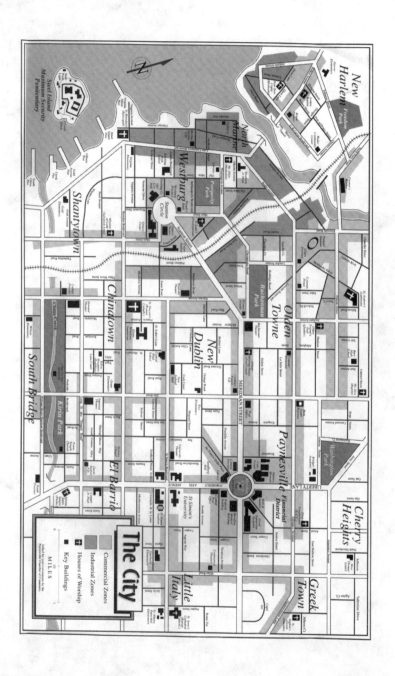

Something or someone is out there...looking for you. You've got the goods. But there's no safety in the shadows. They could be anywhere. If you can just make this score, you'll be set...if you can just stay alive...

ASHLEY WOOD 1996

Seven exciting adventures packaged together for Noir—the Film Noir Role Playing Game. You won't want to miss it.

# Adventures in the Shadows

# shades of

# noir

## book two

shades of
noir
book four
max allan collins • mal coney • wendi lee • eric luke• james robert smith • fred schiller and more.
on sale now!

# citysource

the definitive guide to
the city. for use in noir-
the film noir role-playing
game. on sale now!